SEVEN DEVILS ROAD

HELLBENDERS TWO

RICHARD PROSCH

**WOLFPACK
PUBLISHING**
— EST 2013 —

Seven Devils Road
Paperback Edition
© Copyright 2021 Richard Prosch

Wolfpack Publishing
5130 S. Fort Apache Rd. 215-380
Las Vegas, NV 89148

wolfpackpublishing.com

Paperback ISBN 978-1-64734-762-8
eBook ISBN 978-1-64734-761-1

SEVEN DEVILS ROAD

For Gina at 33

CHAPTER 1

STRINGTOWN, MISSOURI—SPRING, 1860

TOM BALDWIN'S CARD TABLE WAS NOTHING, BUT rough-hewn planks of weathered pine wood nailed together, and it balanced on two wobbly saw-horse legs. In the center, a pot of fifty double-eagles, a silver pocket watch, and a German meerschaum pipe waited for a winner.

But the winner wouldn't be Baldy. Baldy was out. "You boys play too rich for my blood."

It wouldn't be Lin Jarret either. Lin had opted not to play. "I've never had any luck at cards."

The game was down to a British dandy with a clipped goatee calling himself Griffin Kale and a black-smith who wore an unbuttoned flannel shirt, torn britches, and a floppy campaign hat.

The smith's name was Dale, and he was an unlikely card sharp.

"You're sitting there like the cat who swallowed all the cream, English," he said.

Dale's sooty hands cupped five cards in a tight, squared packet. He let a low growl creep in around the edges of his dirty black whiskers. "Show me what'cha got."

Griff held his cards and his tongue equally still.

A midday Missouri breeze rolled down Stringtown's main road and through gaps in the siding of Baldwin's Barn, stirring up smells of dirty hay and spilled beer. Stripes of sunlight cut across Griff's countenance, caught on the embellished silver tips of his braided string tie, and reflected into Lin Jarret's eyes like miniature suns.

Seated perpendicular between the two men on a twine-knotted bale of straw, boots flat on the sawdust covered earth, Lin leaned forward and ran a hand through his sandy brown hair. It was parted on one side, combed into a frontal wave, and his beard was a three-day growth of rough stubble.

He wore trail-dusted corduroy pants, a blue cotton shirt, and a sun-bleached wide-brimmed hat. "No, sir. Never had any luck at cards," he said, sipping Baldy's warm beer from a crock with one hand, pinching a cigarette with the other.

Lin enjoyed watching the game, and his money was on the Brit.

But the big smith, Dale, was a remarkable cheat.

Lin figured Griff was cheating too, but damned if he knew how. From his vantage point seated behind the action, it was hard to see every move of the dandy's hands. But wearing a single-breasted paisley vest, black hammer claw jacket, and slacks, Griff was every inch a dandy.

If the clothes hadn't convinced Lin, the single shot brass boxlock pistol positioned up Griff's sleeve surely did.

"Dammit, Lin," said Baldy from his perch across the card table, his own retired hand of tens and twos sprawled faceup on the surface in front of him. "I told you to put your cigarette out before you light this place a'fire."

"Mmm-hmmm," said Lin, amused by short Baldy.

He brought the twist to his lips and inhaled.

"If'n you ain't gonna play cards, you oughtn't smoke," said the short man.

Lin cocked his head toward the curvy blonde loitering behind the haybarn saloon's long plank counter. "I got a dispensation from the owner," he said.

Baldy's buxom wife, Verna, offered Lin a wink.

Her husband cursed. "Like hell you did."

Lin heard the jealousy behind the oath, but the man oughtn't to have worried. As candid as she was flirtatious, Verna confided in Lin before the game she regularly bathed in cow's milk. She told him the daily practice helped nourish the skin.

She didn't need to say it. The sour smell lingered in the mid-morning heat, and it certainly didn't nourish Lin Jarret's nose.

Lin returned the matron's wink anyway and scratched at the ruffle of dark hair growing down over his collar.

"Come on, English, let's see the cards," said Dale.

Lin's attention moved to the Maynard .28 caliber six shot pistol tucked between Dale's leather belt and slick belly fat. It was an awkward little gun, prone to misfires, but any firearm was deadly in the right hands.

And even more so in the wrong ones.

Considering Dale's mood, the weight of Lin's own sidearm, a Colt Walker .44, felt good in the tied-down leather holster on his hip.

"The cards?" said Dale. The tone of his voice said he wouldn't ask again.

Lin wondered what the Englishman was thinking. Griff's brows were downcast and like his clipped, well-kempt head of dun-colored hair showed flecks of fiery red.

The Brit finally cleared his throat, and even his phlegm carried an accent.

Abruptly, and without a word, Griff snapped his cards to the table.

Ten, Jack, Queen, King, Ace—all diamonds. A royal straight flush.

Griff's hazel eyes rolled up across the center pile of loot to meet Dale's gaze. "I believe the game goes to me," he said.

Dale sat frozen in place, meat hooks cradling his cards. When he spoke, it was through a sputtering rage, tightly contained. "It c-can't be possible."

Griff arched his left eyebrow and the corners of his lips climbed up both cheeks. "I'm afraid it's quite possible," he said. "Now, let's see what you've got."

Dale tossed his hand down, a quartet of eights. Four of a kind.

"As I stated," said Griff, reaching for his reward.

The big smith kicked back from the table with a roar, rearing up from his straw bale on floppy leather boots.

He floundered for the gun in his waistband.

Lin sprang into action, clamping an iron grip over Dale's forearm, blowing a cloud of smoke into his face. Dale jerked back, tried to twist away, but Lin's lightning-fast right cross to the mouth sent him over backwards, rolling off the bale to the barn's floor.

Baldy slid from his seat. "I told you when you started the game: none of your goddamn rough-house. I won't condone it in my place."

But Dale wasn't listening. Regaining his stance faster than Lin reckoned, he squared his shoulders and dragged a hairy arm across his bleeding lip. "You little piss-ant. Just who do you think you are, raising a hand to me?"

Lin flashed a warning glance to Baldy and his wife.

Naturally, Baldy babbled like a brook in spring. "He calls himself Lin Jarret," he said. "Claims to be a *Texas Ranger*."

The smith's bushy eyebrows shot up his forehead like puppets on a string. "Lin Jarret? Hey, I heard of you."

Lin cursed himself for using his real name.

"Tex-asss...rraaanger," said Verna.

"Missouri's a long way from Texas, Ranger-boy," said Dale.

He pronounced it *Missour-ah*.

"What'chu doing so far from home?"

Dale wasn't a good nor patient man.

Then again, neither were Baldy and his wife.

But Lin wasn't here for them. Lin was here for Griffin Kale.

Dale demanded an answer. "I said, what'chu want here?"

As the question hung in the air, Griff paused from brushing the gold coins and other treasures into an open valise.

His eyes met Lin's, held them for an instant, then looked away and hurried to finish his business.

Dale took a step forward, swinging his fist like an iron mace. "Well, boy—I'm the law in Stringtown. I ain't got much use for nobody else."

Lin tossed up an arm to meet the crashing blow, only to catch Dale's opposite fist on the chin. Sparks popped inside Lin's head, and he reeled away, slamming to a stop against the serving counter. The smell of sour milk wafted near, and Verna quickly whispered into his ear. "He's blind in one eye. Take him from the left."

There wasn't time to thank her.

Ducking a wide hammer blow, Lin launched himself straight ahead, coming in with a sharp jab. Dale caught the blow with ease, his whale of a hand swallowing Lin's fist like a goldfish.

Daggers of pain shot up Lin's arm as Dale squeezed. "I meant *his* left," called Verna.

Dale laughed loud and his tub gut shook like a basket of walnuts. "The devil's always in the details, ain't it?" Lin gasped as the bones of his hand ground into each other, felt knees buckle under him.

Dale towered above, judge and jury.

If Lin wanted to hold a gun—or anything else—ever again, he needed to free his pulverized appendage.

Malicious glee shined from Dale's eyes. Blood gleamed on his lips and dripped to the floor, leaving red buttons in the sawdust and streaks down his knock-kneed trouser legs.

Sinking in agony, Lin stared at Dale's knees.

Bearing down on Lin's arm, Dale barely kept his balance.

Knock-knees. Vulnerable, weak.

Lashing out with an accurate boot, Lin moved fast, smashing the smith's kneecap with his heel. The bone gave up a sharp crack, like a dry sapling split for firewood, and Dale fell sideways.

Down, but still holding fast to Lin's fist.

The bigger man's momentum carried them both around in a dancer's flourish to crash against a flimsy sidewall. Lin took the brunt of it, gasping to catch his breath as waves of dull anguish washed through his back and shoulders.

At least he was still upright.

Before Dale could climb to his feet, Lin broke free and pushed away, careening back toward the card table in time to see Griff snap shut his leather case and hot-foot it toward the barn's rickety door.

"Hold it," said Lin, drawing his Colt.

In response, the little brass gun jumped from the gambler's sleeve, landing flat in his palm.

"I don't think so, Jarret."

Lin froze in his tracks.

His plan had been to apprehend Griffin Kale and carry him the ten miles to Syracuse in the afternoon.

In Syracuse it was vital they meet the St. Louis train.

If the gambler ended up dead or injured, Lin's plan literally went up in powder smoke.

Then came the metallic click of a third firearm, followed by a voice. A hammer pulled back, catching, and Baldy. "Both of you boys need to put up your hands and lose your guns."

"Hard to do both at the same time," said Lin, turning around.

Baldy held an octagonal barreled pistol in his right hand, ready to fire. With his left, he motioned for Dale to join him at the barn's beer counter.

"All of you need to understand we don't like cheaters at our lunchtime card games," said Baldy.

"I resent the implication," said Griff, snooty-like.

"I didn't even play," said Lin. "Besides, your friend Dale was cheating too."

"Mister Dale plays for the house."

"I thought you and Verna were the house," said Lin.

"Mister Dale is my brother-in-law," said Baldy.

Lin hadn't noticed it, but now had to admit the resemblance to Verna was uncanny.

"Well, like I say—I wasn't even playing cards."

"And I wasn't cheating," said Griff.

"Both of you men are strangers around here," said

Baldy. "And you showed up more or less the same time. A traveling Britain. A wandering Texas Ranger. How convenient for two men so far away from their native lands to arrive in my barn on the same day. The way I figure it, you're in cahoots."

"Cahoots?" said Lin.

"I've never even heard such a word," said Griff. "Let alone be in...what was it again?"

"Cahoots," said Lin.

Verna agreed with her husband. "I think those two were passing signals between each other during the game."

Lin offered Verna a frown. "Looks like our romance is over."

Verna made an obscene gesture with her finger.

"You're a real peach, gal."

Verna puckered his lips and sent him a mock kiss.

When Lin arrived earlier in the morning, she had welcomed a potential new mark for Stringtown's daily poker game. Now she was pairing Lin up with the very man he was in town to collect.

Lin looked at Griff and shrugged.

Baldy strolled toward them, keeping his gun pointed at waist level. There was no way to outrun at bullet at such close range.

A flick of his wrist would ventilate Lin or Griff either one.

"Jarret, you lay your gun on the table next to Kale's piece," said Baldy. "Nice and slow."

Lin did as he was instructed. He didn't have much choice.

What a day it was turning out to be.

"Now what?" he said.

"I think Mister Dale can best answer your question," said Baldy.

Dale grinned and reached into the pocket of his flannel shirt. He removed a tarnished tin star and pinned it crooked to his shirt.

"You really are the law around here," said Lin.

The man could hardly contain his glee.

"I really am," said Dale.

"I says we hang the both of 'em," said Baldy.

Verna clapped her hands. "Oh, goody."

Lin shook his head. Yup, she really was a peach of a gal.

CHAPTER 2

"I REALLY DON'T UNDERSTAND ANY OF THIS," SAID Griffin Kale. "The Stringtown game was recommended to me by an honest bloke in Jeff City. A harmless diversion, he suggested. Gads, what I've gotten myself into. Why, I just don't—"

"Shut up," said Lin.

Griff nattered on like he hadn't heard him. "I mean, they say you're a law man. Well are you, or aren't you? You lawman gents band together don't you? Can't you talk some sense into this character? Common cause, common enemies, one for all, all for one?"

"Just keep quiet. Let me sort it out."

"I can't see as there's much to sort out."

Lin assessed the situation and, unfortunately, he was inclined to agree.

He was outside Baldy's dilapidated old barn, a rope around his neck. The opposite end was tied above to the heavy bough of an old oak tree. A bay gelding twitched under his rump.

Paradise beckoned.

In one sense, it wasn't overly complicated at all.

Griffin Kale, similarly trussed, sat next to him on a black mare.

Wrists bound together with twists of flannel cloth, the two men had only to wait for the horses to step out from under them.

The hemp pulling tight around their throats would do the rest.

A silver green forest marred the blue horizon in every direction, and the smell of lilacs was thick in the springtime air. Lin was used to the wide-open vistas of Texas, the vast flat land free of hills or an excess of woods. Missouri was a rolling, curvy land hemming him in on all sides.

The heavy loop of new spun hemp around his neck didn't help.

"I'm feeling a little claustrophobic, here," he said.

Standing in the shade of two walnut trees, Dale, Baldy, and Sour-milk Verna, laughed. The three executioners.

In the grassy pasture behind Baldwin's barn, a small crowd of onlookers had gathering to witness the festivities. A fat old woman, helped along by a prim bespectacled young man. A pair of toothless old rummies. An African man with a shaved head and arms like split cord wood. A snot-nosed kid in short pants.

Baldy held up a Colt Walker .44, and Lin recognized it as the firearm confiscated from his own hip —*his own gun*! The Colt was the Ranger's preferred six-shooter, because of its dependability. Never in his life had he wished his weapon to malfunction.

Until now.

Lin watched the short man pull back the gun's hammer. The audience gasped with giddy anticipation.

When the gun went off, the horses would jump. The end would come not fast enough.

The fat old woman nearly fainted.

"Thanks for this," said Baldy, meaning the sidearm. "I'll sleep with it under my pillow and dream of you."

"With a wife like yours, I don't blame you," said Lin. "I'd dream of me, too."

"Hang the sonuvabitch," said Verna.

"You keep that piece spit-shined, Baldy." Lin grinned. "I s'pect Verna's fairly good at polishing a piece."

"I'll polish it on your dead hide," she said.

"You're welcome to do so."

Baldy smirked. "You're full of sass sittin' up there high. After I pull this trigger and them horses pound off hell for leather, you won't have so much to say."

Griff was tired of the banter. "Dash it all, let's have some reason here. I can't imagine we've done anything to warrant a capital punishment. I certainly have no objection to you keeping your pile of money."

"How about the pipe and the pocket watch?" said Dale, feigning interest. "You got any objection to me keeping them?"

Eagerly, Griff took the bait. "Of course not. Certainly, you may keep the entire pile."

Dale waved him off. "Forget it. I was just funnin' with you. We're gonna kill ya for a cheat anyhow."

"But to do such violence over a single game of cards?"

One of the old men commented on Kale's accent. "Never heard talk quite like it before. Damned easterner of some breed, ain't he?"

"New Yorker," said the proper young man with the spectacles, "as I live and breathe, he's a New Yorker."

"Bloody hell," said Griff.

"It's not about the cards," Lin told him. "I imagine there's been plenty of cheating at Baldy's daily game, and I don't think they hang everybody. Not when a good solid beating would do just as well."

"Why hang us, then?" said Griff.

Lin addressed Baldy, Verna, and Dale. "This isn't about cards at all, is it?"

The trio kept quiet, and Lin continued. "It's about the three horses out behind your barn."

Baldy's eyes shuttered toward the old corral, then back to Lin. His finger tightened on the Colt's trigger.

"What about the horses?" said the old lady in the crowd. "I don't know anything about horses."

"They're stolen," said Lin. "I had my suspicions when I dropped rein this morning. But when you led us out here, I got another good look at the brands. Three of 'em are Butterfield Overland stock. Lifted from the stage line in Syracuse." He twisted his chin up and around. The rope was increasingly chafing his neck. "I see why you're so eager to get rid of us. Especially eager to get rid of me. Hell of a thing if wind of your horse-thieving ring got back to the division superintendent."

"Is this true, Mister Baldwin?" said the old woman. "Are those animals stolen from the Overland mail?"

"Don't listen to him, Esther," said Verna. "A rat like him would say anything to save his sorry skin."

"It breaks my heart to see what's becoming of our young men," said Esther.

"Mine too," said Verna.

When the fat woman spoke, the African next to her moved, and Lin watched close.

First, the big man took two surreptitious steps back. Then he skirted along through the crowd, closing on his objective. The black man was fixated on Baldy—specifically the Colt in Baldy's right hand.

Through pouting lips, Sheriff Dale said, "I'd like to suggest justice be done. Go ahead and pull the trigger."

But Baldy couldn't help himself. Since Lin had brought up the topic of stolen horses, he had to clear his name in front of the crowd.

"This man walks into my card game and tells me he's a Texas lawdog looking for a known fugitive from justice. Then he picks a fight with our sheriff." Baldy waved the Colt around in a loose circle. "Now the bastard's accusing me of horse thieving." He lifted his chin. "I think it's just like I said inside: lawman or not, these two men are in some sort of scheme together."

Each time Baldy jerked the gun, Lin felt the horse under him flinch. He clenched his jaw tight against the waves of nausea churning up his guts. A sideways glance at Griff told him the Brit was feeling the same way.

They only had one chance.

The black man continued to shift his position, making his way unobtrusively to Baldy's side.

Relishing his time on stage, Baldy continued his spiel for the Stringtown citizenry assembled around him.

"As this here skunk mentioned, some of those horses over there have stage line brands. Folks, it just so happens I have a contract with the Butterfield Overland to acquire some of their older steeds. I defy anybody here to say otherwise."

"I'll say otherwise," said Lin.

"Not you," said Baldy.

"I won't say anything agin ya," said one of the old timers.

"A shame what's become of young people," said the fat lady again.

Now the black man stood right next to Baldy.

After a long silence, Baldy nodded. Satisfied, he turned his face up and showed four blackened teeth. "Any last words, boys?"

"Tell me your connection on the stage line?" said Lin. "Who gave you those horses? What's the man's name?"

"I got friends in places so high, you'll never see them," said Baldy. "I got friends high as heaven, and right about now I imagine you're going the other way."

Just as Baldy's finger pressed the trigger, the big black man clubbed him from behind.

Baldy sagged to the ground.

The Colt's explosive percussion echoed against the trees.

The horses jerked their heads around and reared up in terror.

Lin tensed his neck muscles as the gelding dove out from under him.

Then there was more thunder, and Lin hit the ground hard enough to lose his breath.

Griffin Kale piled in beside him, kicking and sputtering in the dust, and Lin had a view of the big African holding a shotgun with two smoking barrels. Above them all, two buckshot-severed ropes swayed in the noontime breeze.

Micah LeMay was nothing if not a good man with a scattergun.

"But you had to wait until the last second?" Lin complained, tugging on the noose at his throat. "Dammit, Micah, you couldn't have hit him earlier? For the love'a Pete, I thought you were gonna let him hang us!"

But Micah was too busy to listen to Lin's tirade. Dale had both of his fat arms wrapped around the black man's waist, trying to bring him to the ground.

His mistake was letting Micah's arms remain free.

And Micah still held the shotgun.

He slammed the sheriff with the walnut stock, and Dale went over backwards, his face mashed like a sticky red biscuit.

At the sight of such rough and tumble, the old lady finally passed out, and her knobby kneed escort, unable to support the weight, let her slide to the grass.

Lin scrambled to his feet, then helped Griff regain his height.

"What...goes on?" said Griff. "You...know this African man?"

Lin couldn't deny it. "We're traveling together."

Directly in front of them, Verna knelt beside Baldy's prone form, caressing his skinned pate as if he were a whipped dog. "You killed him," she whimpered. "You killed him, you bastard."

"Ya killed me," whispered Baldy. "Killed me...ya bastards."

Lin picked up his Colt and kicked the soles of Baldy's shoes. Grunting, the little man's eyelids fluttered open.

"It ain't like you don't deserve killing, Baldy," said Lin. He finally succeeded in freeing his head from the confines of the noose and tossed the rope at Verna. "Good thing for you, we're on a tight schedule, or I'd finish the job myself."

Micah slung the shotgun over his shoulder and nodded in agreement. "I believe we're a bit crunched for time already." He was an impressive figure, standing several inches taller than Lin or Griff, wearing a ten-button bib-front navy-blue shirt and dark canvas duckings. His knee-high boots were polished leather, and he wore a pair of black bumper spurs with small silver rowels.

His head was clean shaven under his round, felt hat, but a sprout of whiskers grew on his chin.

Lin rubbed his neck and turned his face side to side.

Dale was curled up on the ground holding his nose, and Baldy and Verna seemed content where they were. The rest of the crowd had gathered around the old woman. The old rummies had her seated in an upright position, and the young kid was fanning her with a pair of oak leaves.

Griff looked from Lin to Micah, then back. Again, he said, "You know each other." This time it wasn't a question.

He tugged at the rope, still tight under his chin.

"You need some help with getting shy of your rope?"

"If you could, I'd be obliged."

Lin worked the noose free from around Griff's neck and made the introductions. "We owe our freedom to Mister Micah LeMay. He's a friend of mine from Texas. Micah, this is Mister Griffin Kale. At least it's what he's calling himself today. He's the man we're looking for."

Micah nodded.

"*The man you're looking for?*" said Griff. "So it's true what Baldy said? You're a lawman?"

"On unofficial business."

"You'd better explain yourself, sir."

Lin held his tongue while Griff's patience wore thin.

"Spit it out, man...what *unofficial business* might two gentlemen from Texas have in Missouri?"

"You'd be surprised," said Micah.

"Try me," said Griff.

"Not here. Not now."

"Yes. Here and now. You two are definitely in cheroots...or caboots..."

"Cahoots."

"I shan't take another step."

Lin sighed. He thought he had this part all worked out. It was supposed to be so easy. Now when the time was at hand, he was at a loss for words.

In the end, there was no other way to say it.

"It's like this, my friend. Your real name is Clem Stackpole. You're wanted in Texas and Arkansas for a variety of crimes, none of which—taken alone—amount to beans. But together, well, there's something else again."

"You've gone to all this trouble to arrest me?"

"Not really, no. Nobody cares too much about you, Griff, ol' friend. I just wanted you to know we've got a little leverage in case you decided not to help us."

"Help you do what?"

Lin clapped Griff on the shoulder and smiled. "Micah and I, we want you to help us rob a train."

CHAPTER 3

"You gonna end it like this, Brock? Or are you gonna man up?"

Flood Tyner wiped the sweat away from his thinning, white hair and clutched the heavy wheel gun in a slick palm. Held it up high in the late evening sun where Ned Brock could see it.

And he waited.

Not fifteen feet away, Ned Brock, dressed in a cow puncher's leather shotgun-style chaps, leather vest, and slouch hat flinched at Tyner's taunt. He wiped his calloused palms on the seat of his pants and chewed his lip. His scurvy trail-hand cronies backed off to either side.

But not before the inebriated gent with no teeth and flat-topped kepi hat nudged Brock in the ribs. "You gonna take such talk, Ned? You gonna take it off an old man like him?"

Built for hard labor, with steam-driven arms and an oak barrel chest, Brock was reputed to have a temper and be fast on the draw.

His fingers hung close to a holstered Colt pistol, but he didn't go for it.

On Brock's right, a wind-burned sodbuster turned his head to launch a stream of amber tobacco juice into the dust of the downtown Syracuse, Missouri street. "Now or never, Ned."

"I'm studying on it, boys," Brock's voice was a low rumble under a cake of hard flab. "I'm studying on it."

The sodbuster stepped away with a wag of his head. "I'm gonna go get me a beer at the saloon. Train'll be along before long. Might as well beat the rush."

"Pour one for me, and I'll join you in a minute," said Toothless.

Tyner felt the tension in his arm, felt the sweat trickle down the back of his white cotton shirt under his gray checked jacket. There were heavier guns than the Walch Navy 12-shot revolver, but Tyner wasn't accustomed to one-arming them.

At 60 years-old, he'd lost quite a bit of his youthly strength.

Now he was even more rapidly losing his patience.

"What's it going to be, Brock? Will you let some slip of a barmaid do this to you?"

Tyner risked a glance over the gathered crowd of bidders, stopped on the curvy brunette, her long black hair pulled tight into a single braid, her linsey-woolsey shirt unbuttoned at the collar, a faded red bandana knotted around her neck. She wore corduroy pants—like a man. But they fit unlike any man Tyner ever saw. "You'll forgive me, ma'am."

The brunette's eyes flashed pure jade green against the colors of the evening horizon. When she spoke, her voice as hard and clean as windswept bedrock. "One hundred dollars."

Toothless slapped Brock on the shoulder. "Hunnert-bucks, boy. A hunnert's a lots'a bunch-grass."

Brock hunched his thick shoulders to shove the man sideways. "I told ya, I'm a studying on it."

"Studying? I honestly didn't take you for the book-learning kind," said Tyner. "Here we have a Walch Navy .36-caliber cap and ball pistol. Six chambers, but the oblong cylinder allows the pistol to be triggered twelve times. A dozen shots gives a man twice as much firepower as his rival. How much more do you need to study?"

Tyner prayed he hadn't misjudged the big mutton head. Hoped the barmaid remark hadn't pushed him too far? Brock's expression *seemed* easy enough to read under the brick red blush, but you never could tell with an Irishman.

Brock despised being called out. Hated Tyner for chiding him. But would he rise to the occasion? Flood Tyner made his living judging the folks who bid at his auctions. A drummer of guns and ammunition, he knew Ned Brock's sort especially well.

Ten seconds.

Five.

Brock's shoulders sagged.

Dammit. The gunslinger was played out.

Tyner brought the pistol to waist level. Pulled the trigger.

Click.

"Sold for $100 to Miss..."

"Reece Sinclair," said the gal.

"Reece Sinclair," said Tyner with a grateful smile. "I'll take your payment in gold, silver, or paper currency."

"Gold it is," she said, hooking a finger into the canvas warbag between her feet.

"Hold on one damn minute," said Brock, bulling

forward. "I ain't never been outbid at auction by a female, and I ain't gonna start today."

Tyner stepped back in awe.

Maybe he hadn't misjudged Ned Brock after all?

"Bidding on the item is over," said Reece.

Tyner patted the girl's arm and addressed Brock. "Unless Mister Brock has a...er, *substantially* higher bid?"

"One-hunnert and twenty," said Brock. "My final offer."

Tyner put the barrel of the gun under his bulbous pink nose and scratched his bushy white mustache. "I see, I see..."

It was well worth considering.

"One-fifty," said Reece.

"You little vixen," said Brock.

Tyner's lips stretched across his face. "Bidding is closed, folks."

"I oughta take you over my knee," said Brock, looking Reece Sinclair up and down.

Tyner swallowed hard. He'd been a gun drummer for twenty years and never once succumbed to lead or fisticuffs. He couldn't say the same about the men who had challenged him.

The Walch was fully charged with powder and packed twelve lead balls. Tyner certainly didn't want to foster a row on the event of today's mail train arrival from St. Louis.

There were too many people on hand. Too many innocents who might be hurt.

"I'm sure we can work something out," said Tyner.

"Maybe the lady would like a different gun," said Brock.

"I'm happy with the Navy 12-shot," said Reece. "The gun I just won for $100."

Brock's growing rancor was almost palpable. His right hand went to his belt, his left poked a dirty finger in Reece Sinclair's face. "I'll bet you can't even lift the gun you bid on."

Reece snatched the big iron away from Tyner and spun it around her fingers like a child's toy, flipping it up to Brock's eye level before cracking open the twin cylinders. Staring down the iron sites, she slapped the wheels shut and stepped sideways. She used her left hand to pull an old Number Five revolver with an octagonal barrel and collapsible trigger from the small of her back.

Before he knew what was happening, Brock met the muzzles of both guns with his nose.

"Bang, bang," said Reece.

"Horse shit," said Brock, batting the barrels away with a heavy hand.

Before he could say another word, Reece brought around a quick right with the Walch Navy gripped tight between her fingers. Blistering fast, she slashed Brock across the forehead, knocked him backwards, then followed up by spinning the gun in her hand and cracking the side of his skull with the Number Five's flared walnut grip.

Tyner intervened to catch the bigger man before he hit the ground.

Reece waited until Tyner stood up, then said, "Were we at one hundred and twenty, or only the one?"

Tyner swallowed hard at the woman's tough demeanor. "No, no," he said, struggling to keep Ned Brock upright, "You're correct, ma'am, the winning bid was for one. I'm more than happy to honor it."

He watched as Reece pushed the older of her two pistols into the waistline of her pants, then crouched low next to her canvas bag. She carefully unbuckled the belt, opened the case, and dropped the big twelve-shooter inside. Then she used both hands to remove a bulky string-tied canvas sack.

From here she withdrew the proper number of glimmering gold coins and handed them over. "Naturally, I'd appreciate a receipt," she said.

"Right away."

"I ain't never seen a woman like you," said the toothless man in the kepi hat. "You wouldn't by chance be lookin' for a good man to take home with you?"

"As a matter of fact, no, I wouldn't," said Reece.

"Pity," said Toothless. "M' name's Dalton if'n you ever change your mind."

"Thank you, Mister Dalton, but I don't think it's likely."

"If you would be so kind," said Tyner, nodding at Ned Brock, "you'd best carry your man from the street."

"He ain't my man. I was just watchin' the auction," said Dalton. Setting his kepi cap square onto his head, he said, "I'm s'posed to be somewhere, anyhoo."

"Very well, very well." Tyner watched the old man wander a crooked path toward the saloon, then helped Brock stand on wobbly ankles, easing him to a nearby bench.

Then he took a pad of paper from his suit jacket and scribbled on it with a stubby lead pencil. Out of Brock's earshot, he addressed Reece with a paternal tone. "You've got some kind of grit, young missy. Ned Brock's a known gunnie. He's worked for some mighty big people."

"None are so big they can't be felled...like a rotten tree, Mister Tyner."

"Still and all, you won't do yourself any favors picking a fight with the likes of him."

"I appreciate the advice."

As he finished her ticket, Tyner took in the girl's beauty. The lilt of her voice told him she was Spanish, but her eyes were Irish. Her casual demeanor reminded him more of Texas, of the vaqueros he'd known when he was young. He couldn't say why it was, but if Reece Sinclair belonged anywhere, she belonged on a horse with a vast open range in front of her.

"Are you here to meet the train?" said Tyner. "Or maybe you're leaving on the Overland stage?"

"I could ask you the same thing," said Reece.

Tyner handed her the receipt for her purchase.

"Neither," said Tyner. "I'm just here to work the crowd." He cocked his head at a red cargo van near the long, whitewashed train station. The wagon was fixed with iron rimmed wheels and two black horses. On the sidewall, gleaming gold-leaf letters spelled out: *Tyner's Gun Service and Sales*.

"I'm something of a firearm enthusiast, myself," said Reece. "How's business?"

"Between you and me and the fence post, it could be a lot better."

"It's hard times for a lot of people."

"Used to do well here with the train coming in. A roaring, soot covered monstrosity used to draw quite a crowd. A few months in, and it's already old hat."

Tyner realized then he'd broken one of his cardinal rules. He'd gone and dropped his professional facade. He'd let a customer see the chinks in his armor. "My apologies, Miss," he said, pressing back a loose shock of snow-white hair with the flat of his hand. "I don't know what got into me."

Then Miss Reece Sinclair said something to melt an old man's heart. "Maybe next time, you'll show me the inside of your wagon?"

Tyner's breath caught in the back of his throat, and he decided he was in love.

"My, oh my," he said. "Why...next time, I believe I will," he chortled.

CHAPTER 4

THE THREE MEN RODE OUT OF STRINGTOWN AND loped down the Missouri hills on buckskin geldings, powerful horses traded under duress behind Baldy's Barn. Lin's horse carried a Butterfield Overland brand, and it was his intent to share the Stringtown story with Matt Price, the stage line's division superintendent as soon as they got to Syracuse.

It would give him and Micah something to do while Griff knocked off the Prescott-Missouri-Pacific.

"You understand, it's simply being taken-for-granted I'd accompany you in any kind of felonious action. I've certainly never been involved with a train robbery," said Griffin Kale, squinting into the sun, "and to be quite frank, I'm trying to decide what offends me more."

"Offends you more than what?" said Lin. "And you ought to wear a hat to keep the sun from your eyes."

Bare-headed Griff had been rattling on ever since they left the denizens of Stringtown behind. Lin had trouble keeping track of the conversation. He was busy making sure they weren't being followed.

It would be just like that phony sheriff or stinky Verna to hold a grudge and come after them.

Lin didn't trust anybody to let things go, least of all them. Their acquaintanceship had been short but quite meaningful. Lin ran his finger around his neck, remembering the pressure of the noose.

"What the hell are you talking about, Kale?" said Micah, his felt hat pulled down to his eyebrows.

Lin realized the big man was even more irritated than him.

Under the best of conditions, a man like Micah couldn't be sure who to trust. As a former runaway slave, he was extra prickly in the best of situations, even though he had his freedom. The long road out of Texas was wearing on his already cranky nature.

Micah furrowed his brow. "You got something to say, speak plain or button it."

"Well, first of all," said Griff, "it's offensive you would even ask me to join in such a scandalous adventure. Especially since I'm missing an entire afternoon's work. They'll miss me back in the office at Jefferson City."

Lin held his tongue at the disingenuous nature of Griff's high moral ground. Before riding into Stringtown, he and Micah had done a good deal of due diligence on one Mister Clem Stackpole, aka Griffin Kale. He might judge a train robbery as slightly higher than his own petty criminal ambitions, but he'd never consider it scandalous.

The bottom line was Griff was intrigued enough by the idea of a big payoff to tag along, but wary enough to pretend the moral high ground.

"First of all, you're scandalized. What about second of all?" said Micah.

"Second of all, you haven't told me what I might expect as a percentage of the take."

Micah couldn't hide his cynical smile. "Ah-ha! Here's the truth of the matter."

And the real sore spot, thought Lin.

Griff wasn't going to like the answer he got.

"Zero percentage," said Lin.

"Excuse me?" said Griff.

"Zero. None of us are pocketing any of the take."

"As in...nothing?"

"As in nothing. The payoff isn't for us."

Griff pulled his gelding to a stop. They were crossing a wide prairie filled with spring wildflowers, and he sat in his saddle and sneezed while Lin and Micah kept going.

The entire plan hinged on meeting the train from St. Louis at Syracuse, and they'd lost valuable time dallying with Baldy and his cohorts.

The trip to Jefferson City had gone well enough. At Hart Prescott's office in the capital city, they'd learned Griff liked to take his lunch hour at any one of several local card games. Lin was grateful they'd found him at their first stop, just a few miles out from the city at Stringtown.

Even so, he and Micah faced a time crunch.

They'd made good time starting out the week before, coming up from Texas two days behind Reece Sinclair. Lin and Micah, traveling back roads and Indian trails, stopping at Ranger way stations, trusting to old friends Lin knew along the way for an occasional meal.

Their job was to pick up Griffin Kale in Jefferson City and get him to the train station in Syracuse.

No later than tonight.

Reece would be waiting...and depending on them.

"Not good to lollygag," said Micah, indicating Griff's status behind them.

"No, it's not," said Lin. "The more miles we put behind us, the better."

It wasn't just the Stringtown bunch he was concerned about. Missouri had entered the Union as a slave state, not long before Lin, Micah, and Griff were born. In the years since then, cracks in the national edifice had become virtual chasms. Some of the most extreme firebrands were predicting open warfare in less than a year.

State against state.

The rending of social constructs a century old. More, the rending of families.

Brother against brother.

A few months before, Lin would have shrugged off such predictions as hyperbolic nonsense.

Before he was betrayed by his own. Before he learned Oscar Bruhn, his mentor in the Rangers and his own maternal uncle, was deeply embedded in the Order of the Ivory Compass, a not-so secret society whose goal was to secede from the United States and form a new nation based on slavery and trade between a circle of territories from the American South, Mexico, and the Caribbean.

Never before had everybody's future been so uncertain, and strangers openly traveling with an African through a slave state would most certainly bring questions if they met up with the wrong people.

"Best we keep moving," said Lin. "I imagine our friend will catch up. Greed will spur him along."

Lin slowed his horse to cross a rocky outcropping, and Micah followed. Once more they dropped into a steady gait across an open pasture hemmed in by shag bark hickory trees, walnut, and elm. The stony ground was pock marked with badger dens and sink holes, the limestone ridges they passed, spackled with sun-tanned minerals.

They were crossing some damned rough country, and the ubiquitous hardwood forests, rocks and cliffs felt like iron bars hemming them in on both sides.

Lin ground his back teeth at the pace but allowed his horse to choose his own way. A broken leg now would upend the entire apple cart.

He couldn't wait to get done with this end of the job and roll back down to Texas.

Before long, Griff's quiet buckskin sidled into place between Lin and Micah, and the riders could easily converse.

"I've considered the matter further, and I have to admit, you've got me curious," said Griff. "First tell me how far we've yet got to travel."

Lin tilted his head back, tried to gauge the position of the mid-afternoon sun. "Another little bit to Syracuse. If we're lucky, we'll arrive just before the train."

Griff nodded. "Tell me, who robs a train for zero reward? This isn't for some kind of public spectacle, is it? Perhaps a stunt of some kind? A joke?"

"No stunts," said Micah.

Lin abruptly changed the subject.

"How about you tell us about your relationship with Hart Prescott," said Lin.

"What makes you think I know Hart Prescott?" said Griff.

"Because I know you know him. Now stop pretending."

"He's the founder of an entire railroad as well as being candidate for Missouri's Governor in this year's election. I should think a great many people know him. Why ask me?"

"You've worked in his Jefferson City office for the past few months," said Lin.

"People tell me you might not be happy there," said Micah.

"I'm not?"

"No, sir," said Micah. "Not happy at all."

"Well, it's news to me. I should think if anybody knows whether or not he's happy, it would be—"

Lin pushed back his hat. "Aw, hell, Griffin. You act like we don't know the time of day. I've spent the last month and a half learning all about you. About how you and old Mother Stackpole came across from Cornwall to Virginia, then followed the trail to Ohio where she worked in various houses of ill repute."

"I...um...am sure I don't know...uh..."

Micah's eyes flared, and he made a buttoning gesture over his lips.

Griff fell silent as Lin continued. "After your old mum was put behind bars, you came to St. Louis and went to work for Prescott in his shipping yards. You did well enough supplementing your income with petty thefts and odd jobs for wrong-headed people. When Prescott moved to the capital city, you followed him. Most people say you're a good man at heart—the complete opposite of your boss. But they also say you spend too much time with pasteboards and booze."

"Who are these oh-so knowledgeable people?" queried Griff.

"Nearly married, twice, but can't commit," said Micah. "Enjoys onions on a pork sandwich and drinks far too much beer—yet always attends Anglican mass on Sunday. Has the confidence of the wealthiest land baron in the state but disagrees with almost every policy in the man's campaign platform."

"Sum it up for you?" said Lin.

Griff absorbed everything he heard with good natured ease. "You men certainly make a gent feel important." He bowed his head in acknowledgement. "Imagine spending so much time getting to know me."

"You want to hear more?" said Lin.

"Not particularly."

"There was an incident with a girl from Tipton?"

"Enough," said Griff.

As they conversed, the horses slowed to a walk and together as one burred off toward the trickling path of a spring-fed creek branch. Lin gave his mount its head, and before long they were taking a break on the banks of the Sorrow River while the horses quenched their thirst. Under his jacket, Lin felt the ticking of his pocket-watch against his ribs like a hammer.

But there was nothing to be done about it. Horses need water.

Dismounting, he stood next to his saddle and reached for his saddlebag and the makings of a smoke.

While he measured a sprinkle of leaves across the black licorice paper, rolled it tight, licked, twisted, and scratched a lucifer to light on his bootheel, he explained the situation to Griff. "Here's what you need to understand. My uncle, Oscar Bruhn, is currently behind bars in San Antonio. He won't be there as long as I'd like." Lin inhaled the rich, dark smoke. "Do you know why he won't be there as long as I like?"

Griff shook his head. "Do tell."

"It turns out Oscar's a head muckety-muck in a militia group called the Order of the Ivory Compass. How about it? Does the name ring any bells for you?"

"Unfortunately, it does," mumbled Griff. "An entire church steeple full of them."

Lin was on the right track. He inhaled again, then blew a long stream of smoke into the air. "The thing is,

Uncle Oz, he talks a lot. He's not afraid to answer questions. In fact, he's proud to talk about the Ivory Compass. He says men of honor got nothing to hide. He says the Compass offers direction. It points toward the future. You get what I'm saying?"

"You're saying he's told you all about Hart Prescott."

"He told me there's a confederacy of men whose aim is to secede from the United States and set up a new nation. Men who intend to profit from human trade."

"I assume your uncle also identified Mister Prescott as another—what's the word you used?"

"Muckety-muck?"

"Yes, *muckety-muck* in the organization," said Griff. "They are in...cahoots."

"He did. And they are."

"The Ivory Compass has a great many goals," said Griff. "Some more honorable than others."

"Are you one of them? Do you believe the same things they do?"

Griff held his tongue, and Lin continued, "Because we heard you don't. In fact, we heard you're opposed to them."

"These are extremely powerful men," said Griff. "Prescott's home near Blackwater is comprised of more than two thousand acres of corn, tobacco, wild mustard seed, and cattle. He buys and sells entire armies."

Lin struggled to read Griff's expression.

"You're scared of him, aren't you?"

"I've been secretary to Mr. Prescott for quite some time."

"Answer the question."

Griff squeezed the bridge of his slender nose

between thumb and forefinger. "Then you also must know—yes, of course I'm frightened of him. I'm opposed to their entire way of life. But in my position, as someone who knows certain things, it's much safer to keep one's personal feelings to oneself."

Lin breathed a sigh of relief. "Good. I just wanted to hear you say it."

"We also know you've tried to leave Prescott's employment more than once," said Micah.

When Griff's composure let go, it was loud and emotional. "He won't let me go. He says he values me too much. He says I'll be a rich man in the new order. He says history will remember us as visionaries. The truth is..." Griff turned his back and walked a dozen paces before he turned around to say, "hell, I don't know what the truth is."

"Yes, you do. But you're too lily-livered to say it," said Lin.

"You're out gambling in Stringtown trying to make some money to escape," said Micah. "Hoping to sneak away and start up someplace else. Somewhere where nobody knows your name. Where no one has heard your story."

"How do you know so much?"

"I know all about wanting to escape."

Griff nodded. "If it were possible, yes, I'd escape." Griff chose the words with care. "What your dear uncle may not have explained is how once you're a part of the Order, you can never be anything else. It's a lifetime membership. This goes for anyone with any confidential association, of any kind. It's like..." He groped for the words.

"Like being a slave?" said Micah.

"Exactly like being a slave."

"We can help you," said Micah.

"To be honest, I don't care about their damn agenda. But neither do I care to fight it."

For a second, Lin thought Griff would stamp his feet.

"I just want to be left out of the entire mess. It's not as if I'm some kind of wild-eyed *abolitionist*." Griff gazed into Micah's sober countenance and stopped himself. "I'm sorry. I shouldn't have said it. What I meant to say—"

"You know what your real problem is, Griffin? Deep down, you're too brave to be the coward you want to be." Micah looked at Lin. "He wants to go hide under a rock, but his soul won't let him."

Lin recognized the symptoms. The stuttering speech, the pale skin. The beads of sweat breaking out in a cool breeze.

"Caught between two worlds. It's a hell of a place to be."

Lin offered his hand, knowing Griff was afraid of what it might represent to take it.

"Freedom from your boss. Freedom from the Ivory Compass," said Micah.

"An early death."

"Every death is early to the fella who's dying."

"Damn it all," said Griff.

"Freedom is a bitch of a responsibility," said Lin. "If you don't want it, we'll leave you alone right here and now."

"And just who the hell are you?" said Griff.

"We're just a couple hellbenders," said Lin, "and we're going to Syracuse to rob the train of $10,000 in Ivory Compass money."

"And pray tell, what will you do with this money once you've got it?"

"There's an emancipator's way station down in

Texas. It's a little place called Emberville just south of Lambert's Ferry. It's a place where runaway slaves can find help getting across the border into Mexico."

"Now you know why your take is zero," said Micah. "None of us are getting a cut. At least not until we get our coach down the trail to Emberville."

Lin added, "Emberville's an independent station located on a spur off the main-traveled trail. Without frequent visitors or Butterfield Overland support, it needs financing to keep horses, food, and coach repairs. It needs money to buy silence and pay people to look the other way."

Griff licked his lips. "Would you mind very much making me one of those cigarettes?"

Lin handed over the makings. "Help yourself."

"The way it works, we win twice," said Micah. "Not only do we cripple part of the Ivory Compass by taking their money, but we turn around and use the money for a cause they are against."

"And again, you trust your uncle about all this? What does he gain by selling out Prescott?"

"Less time behind bars. Plus, from what we can determine, there's something of a shakeup going on in the Ivory Compass. Some men in the party believe war between the states is imminent. They're ready to fight. Others aren't so sure. They would rather work behind the scenes. My Uncle Oz backs the former. He and his hawkish friends have no use for Prescott."

As he smoked, Griff's voice was steadier, but he was still confused. "Why me? If you know where the money is on the train, and you have the means to escape with it into Texas, what good can I do?"

Lin hated to answer him.

Such a pity.

They'd been getting along so well the last few minutes.

"We don't know where the ten-thousand dollars is. We don't know the man who's carrying it. Uncle Oscar says you do. He says you're our man. You'll be robbing the train by yourself."

CHAPTER 5

Beside the spoked front wheels of her forest green stage line coach, Reece waited for the train on the graveled shoulder of the railroad grade, soothing her anxious horses with soft murmurs. The team of four was a lovely bunch of chestnut driving mares, young and energetic, procured from a friend of a friend in San Antonio.

Like Reece, they'd been idle too long and needed to be on the move.

With learned expertise she examined each animal's harness, pulled on the collars and martingale, checked the breast straps—not too high—checked the tail cruppers, traces, bridles, and reins. She patted her lead horse on the nose, running her knuckles down the narrow white blaze. "Just a little while longer, Meg," she said.

Reece named all her horses, Meg. Made it easier to get it right.

All she had to do was wait for Lin and Micah to join her with their special cargo. Then they'd hightail it down the Texas Road through Missouri, Arkansas, and the Nations, changing horses at stations like Mulhaven, Wynot's Dairy, and Plummer.

Reece was eager for the run, her third trek down the trail.

Reece walked around the wagon, giving it one final going over. The big, green Concord was so named because of its place of origin, the Abbott Downing Company of Concord, New Hampshire. Similar to the coaches used by the Butterfield Overland Express, Reece's conveyance was slightly smaller with less brass ornamentation and thicker bracing.

The front wheels of the carriage were painted black and came up to her chest, the back wheels to her shoulders. In between, a folding step led to the carriage doorway. The window there and to either side of the hatch were covered with canvas side curtains. The thoroughbraces stretching along the underside of the carriage were three-ply leather. The rear boot was packed with gear. Add to it, Reece carried a stout wood trunk up top. It too, was full of supplies.

The cabin held up to nine passengers. The center seats folded over to make a rough bed.

She walked back around to the side of the coach where she started.

When Lin arrived, there wouldn't be much time. On this run, they would be freighting stolen cargo.

They'd need to leave Syracuse in a hurry.

From down the street, the low whistle of the oncoming St. Louis train sounded, and Reece saw the big totem of rolling black smoke rising against the sunset. Within minutes the big locomotive would pull into the station.

Flood Tyner was right when he said the people of Morgan County considered the arrival of the St. Louis train to be old hat. Six o'clock on an April evening and fewer than two dozen people populated the narrow, peaked roof depot and surrounding boardwalks.

Reece got the impression community excitement here at the terminus of the line had never been as great as the railroad hoped. Now, eighteen months after the first launching of the line, the whole endeavor seemed to be a bigger splash for the people back east than for the heartland settlers.

The cool evening air smelled of fried liver and onions from the saloon across the town's wide-open square, of tin-roofed box shanties and pole barns. On a regular schedule, the train brought in a sack full of mail, and a variety of supplies. A welcome service to be sure, but nothing to get in a tizzy over.

Another sounding of the whistle and the churning rush of steel wheels came louder.

For Syracuse, the train had become part of the routine. Tyner had said most times the town marshal didn't even show up.

The liver and onions caused Reece's stomach to rumble, and she craned her neck to see past the train depot and watch the road into town.

With a steady clop, clop, clop, Flood Tyner rolled up with his commercial carriage.

"Meant to compliment you before on your wagon, Miss Reece," he said as he wiped dust from his forehead with a red handkerchief. His eyes played over the silver words painted across the top of the carriage door. "The Jarret-Sinclair Line," he read aloud.

"Your rig must've cost a pretty penny."

Reece couldn't help but think about her home. All she and her dad had gone through to make the Sinclair rancho flourish with the transition from a traditional crop of sheep to the new, more lucrative cattle business.

She would never forget how the Texas ranch was almost lost to her thanks to a horrific insurgence of militants under the command of a greedy man named Cardoza. Thanks to Lin Jarret and Micah LeMay, she still retained ownership of the most prosperous land in the Rio Grande Valley.

Right about now, her ramrod, Stick Carvell, would be bedding down the mares for the night.

"I'm good for it," she said. And she was.

"Yes, of course," Tyner said hastily. Then, as if prodding for an unspoken truth, "You're taking on passengers today?"

Her answer was laced with innocent charm. "As a matter of fact, I'm awaiting three young men from Jefferson City."

Tyner pulled a concerned face. "Family? Siblings perhaps?"

Had he combed his hair since Reece had seen him last? And she smelled the distinct odor of a fresh application of bay rum cologne.

"I'm an only child," said Reece.

With his next query, Tyner's voice cracked, "Husband?"

"It's not any of your business, now, is it?" The old fella was pushing pretty hard, but Reece's heart went out to him. The life of a wagon drummer had to be a lonely one.

"Gracious me, no. No, of course not. It's only...I hate to see a young woman left all alone."

Reece toed the dirt and batted her eyelashes. "I'm sure they'll be along."

As if on cue, the Prescott-Missouri-Pacific Railroad company's big locomotive thundered into town hauling a tender of hardwood, three freight cars, and a passenger coach.

Reece watched the train pull into the station beside the tall water tower. Quickly the railroad men fell in line and lowered the spout down to the locomotive to fill the tank for the return trip to Jefferson City, then back to St. Louis. Someday the rail would extend on to Kansas City, but not for a while yet.

"If you'd like, I'd be delighted to keep you company while you wait," said Tyner. "Perhaps I could show you my inventory." He sat back and made a show of admiring the heavy Sinclair coach. "You certainly are well built."

Reece let his words hang in the air between them. Tyner's face went from pink to red.

"Er...rather, what I meant to say is, your wagon is one of the tightest...I mean, um..."

"Maybe next time," said Reece.

"Maybe you're right," said Tyner. The old man gave her a hasty salute, then swished the reins and drove his rig on down the street.

The poor devil.

Chuffing steam and taking on a full, fresh tank of water, the heavy locomotive had been parked for less than ten minutes when Reece heard her name being called.

"Miss Sinclair?"

Reece looked up to see Matt Price pushing a two-wheeled dolly along the board walk in front of the depot. A dirty gray canvas sack reclined on the conveyance like a baby elephant.

The St. Louis to Fort Smith mail.

Price was the Division Manager for the Butterfield Overland, and the meticulous job of balancing coach schedules and keeping dozens of way stations supplied with goods, personnel, and horses, suited his priggish nature.

He pushed his burden along casually as he approached, refusing to show any sign of strain, confronting her with an air of nervous authority. "Has Mister Jarret arrived yet?"

Reece curbed her temper and smiled to herself. Price never would get used to a woman driving a stagecoach, and preferred speaking to men.

"He has not," said Reece, "but I'll tell him you asked for him."

Price held a clipboard with a pencil tied to it and nodded as he continued on past. Reece watched as he delivered his burden to the Butterfield Overland stage, saw the driver toss the sack to the top of the coach, and sign Price's receipt.

Before the other stage arrived at the first station, Reece intended to be hot on the trail behind.

If Lin and Micah ever showed up with the package.

Assuming the Ivory Compass money hadn't already been transferred right under her nose and be aboard the Overland coach, rolling away down the trail in the custody of a passenger or hidden inside the sack of mail.

But Reece didn't think so. At least she hoped it wasn't.

Oscar Bruhn said the transfer of money from Prescott's office was to be made overnight in Syracuse and travel down the trail to Texas at a later date.

For what it was worth, she hadn't seen any young men leave the train and board the Butterfield Overland. And Oscar had been absolutely clear Seth Coombs of Prescott's Jefferson City office would see to the transfer of the money personally.

But Oscar didn't know Coombs, had never met him, and consequently hadn't been able to describe him.

He'd suggested employing a known fugitive— Griffin Kale—who worked in Prescott's office, who did know what Coombs looked like.

Which is why the Hellbenders needed him.

Leaning against the door to the Concord, Reece murmured to her horses once more and chewed her lip.

Her mind kept rolling back to the same nagging worry.

What if Lin and Micah couldn't convince Griffin Kale to help them?

———

IT TOOK Griff less than ten seconds to turn-tail and leap for the saddle of his horse.

Lin's suggestion he single-handedly secure Seth Coomb's $300,000 parcel didn't appeal to the gambler's sense of adventure.

Lin was more than disappointed. Oscar had described the gambler as a man with more grit.

When Lin caught Griff by the jacket collar and spun him around, he nearly punched him in the mouth.

"Listen here, you—"

He'd forgotten about the brass boxlock pistol hidden in Griff's sleeve. Three inches long with a lightly engraved frame and walnut grip, it held a single charge and percussion cap.

Griff produced the gun as if by magic, and he jammed it into Lin's face.

The barrel looked fit for a .36 caliber ball—plenty of lead to tear into something vital, especially at close range.

"I've gone along with you this long, Ranger, not because of my sympathies for your cause," said Griff, "but because the idea of my employer losing such a great sum appeals to me."

"So what the hell are you doing," said Lin. "Let's get on the move."

"I won't go up against Seth Coombs alone."

"The idea was to catch him off guard as he disembarks from the train. He won't expect you to be in Syracuse. You gain his confidence; learn how he's carrying the money—"

"You don't know Seth Coombs. He's just like his brother, a born killer. Trust me, these men are lunatics."

"You're talking about Logan Coombs?"

"Logan Coombs of Springfield, yes."

"My uncle told us his name too," said Lin. "He's the recipient of the ten-thousand dollars. Funding for the Ozarks chapter of the Compass."

Griff said, "On this end, the three of us together might—just might—have a chance of taking Seth Coombs. But alone? I wouldn't chance it by myself in seven Sundays."

"All right. How about this," said Lin. "Your familiarity with him will allow you get close enough to slug him."

"Slug him?"

"Then Micah and I rush in and pack up the money."

"I can't imagine such a scheme would work."

Micah tapped Griff on the shoulder and handed over a trim silver flask. "Have a drink."

Griff took a sip, grimaced at the burn, and swallowed hard.

"Gads, are you trying to poison me?" he said, with a pronounced rasp.

Micah shrugged and took a pull from the flask. "I

hate to bring this up," he said. "But you do owe me your life."

"What? Are you talking about when you shot the rope above my head?"

"Saved you from having a stretched neck."

"Don't be daft," said Griff. "I never would've been in such a situation if you and your friend here hadn't been present."

"It's not quite how I remember it," said Micah.

"There was a matter of cheating at cards," said Lin.

"And Baldy was plenty jumpy about those stolen horses."

"I've been in and out of worse scrapes."

Lin slapped him on the back. "Mister Kale, my pocket watch is breaking my ribs with its ticking. How about you ride with us to Syracuse and point out Seth Coombs. Afterwards...we'll see how it goes."

Griff took a second drink.

"I'm telling you, Seth Coombs is a madman."

"You've convinced me. We'll handle him together."

Griff seemed to be pondering the offer. Finally, he said, "As long as I don't have to go up against him alone. It's rumored he killed two men up Chicago way."

"I've killed a few men in my time," said Lin.

"How many?" said Griff.

Lin didn't answer him.

Somehow, it didn't seem like a good way to win the argument.

CHAPTER 6

LIN JARRET RODE INTO SYRACUSE ON A SIDE ROAD AND hid his horse between two crooked storage sheds. One of them had an open door and was half full of dry ear corn. A mouse scurried along the threshold and dropped down over the edge to disappear under a rotting foundation.

Across the street, Griff and Micah rode in. At the saloon, they looped the reins of their horses to a hitching post.

Boots on the ground, Lin tied his Butterfield Overland mount to the door handle on the grain shed. Before they left town, he hoped to talk to the division manager about Stringtown's stolen horses.

He didn't look forward to seeing Matt Price. The man was a stuffed shirt, and Lin didn't like the way Price talked to Reece.

First things first.

The big locomotive was already pulling in as Griff and Micah left their saddles.

The mouse reappeared at the side of the shed, and Lin followed it across the street into a litter-strewn alley. He met Griff and Micah behind the noisy saloon.

A toothless man in a round kepi hat and overalls was propped up against the rear wall.

"Train's a little early," said Lin. "Hope we didn't miss our man."

Toothless raised his brown bottle to the three of them. "Salute," he said.

Griff ignored the old drunk. "My guess is Coombs will be one of the last passengers to disembark. He's quite secretive in daily life. I would expect him to be rather stealthy about this entire affair. In fact, I wouldn't be surprised if he's waiting for his man to come to him."

"What about the money?" said Lin. "Ten thousand dollars is a lot, even if it's paper money. How will he carry it?"

"Quite obviously they would never attempt to transfer such an incredible sum of wealth in gold. It would be too heavy, too bulky. They'll absolutely want to avoid attention."

"So how else would they send it?"

Griff shook his head. "I'm not sure. Stock certificates, bonds, something unobtrusive. It would need to be something the members of the Ivory Compass can easily trade between themselves. Perhaps they would keep it in a traveling case of some kind."

"If it's easy to carry, maybe Coombs wouldn't transfer it. Maybe he'd personally deliver it to his brother by way of the Butterfield Overland Stage? Springfield is one of the stops on the stage."

"I don't think so," said Griff. "As long as I've been working there, Coombs never leaves Mr. Prescott's office unattended for more than a day. In fact, I saw him sitting at his desk this morning when I checked in before riding over to Stringtown."

"The St. Louis train passed through Jefferson City and picked him up...when?"

"The train stops at Lohman's Landing on the riverfront just before lunch."

"You said he won't want to leave his office long. In such a case, we have to imagine he'll ride the train back tonight. Somebody must be meeting him here."

"We need to get to him first," said Griff.

Lin cracked open the lid of his pocket watch, checked the time, then addressed Micah. "Reece should have been here a while ago. She'll be waiting at the appointed spot."

"Th'as a mighty fine-lookin' watch," said the old drunk. "You mind tellin' ol' Dalton the time? I got's somewhere I'm s'posed to be."

Lin offered the man a sour look and shuffled his friends away toward the street.

"You two wait here and watch for Coombs. I've got to run over to the Division Manager's office."

"One thing," said Griff. "You said you called yourselves Hellbenders? In Prescott's office they mentioned the name a time or two. We always heard Hellbenders was nothing more than a laugh, some group of misfits run by a deranged girl down near the Rio Grande."

"It isn't a laugh," said Micah.

"My apologies," said Griff.

"But you've got the deranged girl part right," said Lin.

"I'm gonna make sure to tell her you said so," said Micah.

"Once we're on the stage headed to Texas, you can tell her anything you want," said Lin. "Come to think of it, I just might tell her myself."

———

THE OFFICE OF MATTHEW PRICE, division manager for the Butterfield Overland line smelled like rancid cigar smoke and overcooked coffee.

Lin felt right at home.

The Ranger's ease of bearing annoyed Price, Lin could tell, but the manager was nothing if not a proud bureaucrat.

He wasn't about to let on.

"What can I do for you, Jarret?" said Price, peeling a sheet of paper from a pile on his desk. "If you're wondering about Miss Sinclair's whereabouts, I saw her near the train station."

Lin gave Price his most polite expression. "Yeah, that's not what I'm here about."

But he was relieved to know Reece was in town and ready to roll as per the plan.

Behind his spectacles, Price blinked at least ten times and moved to the window of his office. He glanced outside, then turned around, pale as goat's milk. "I see, I see," he said, suddenly flustered in his threadbare salt and pepper suit. "Well, how then may I help you?"

He arranged a few items on his desk. He moved his coffee cup to one side. Then he moved it again.

Lin was puzzled by the man's behavior.

"What's your trouble, Price? You'd rather sponge wash a rattlesnake than talk to me," said Lin. "Why so jumpy?"

"I'm not jumpy."

"I'm here on Ranger business."

Price knocked over his cup of coffee.

"I see, I see," he said, using his coat sleeve to mop up the spilled grounds.

"Told you," said Lin.

Price practically roared back with defiance. "Oh, all right. You've got me dead to rights."

"I do?"

"You do," he said. "But you'll have no good luck proving it, and you won't find many to support your claims. This isn't Texas after all. You don't have so much pull here."

Lin put his fingers to his chin, wondering what in thunder Price might be confessing to. Here he'd come in simply hoping to report a crime, and the little despot was coming all unglued.

"Most foolish thing I ever heard of—a law man masquerading as a stagecoach owner simply to ferret out a few petty horse thieves."

Ah-ha.

"It's simply preposterous."

Lin chose his words with care.

"No masquerade about it, Price. I've wanted to run a stagecoach for several years now. It's sort of a...well, a dream if you will."

"I've never heard of a Texas Ranger running a stagecoach."

"There's Rangers who farm, Rangers who run mercantile shops, Rangers who work as blacksmiths. Why not a stagecoach operator?"

"Nonsense."

"Anyway, as you say...I guess I've got you dead to rights."

Lin was eager to hear more, but Price wasn't talking.

"I refuse to say any more about Stringtown without my attorney present."

Or maybe he was saying more than he thought he was.

"Funny thing," said Lin. "Did I mention Stringtown?"

The Ranger walked to the window, hooked back the curtain with a curled finger. From Price's office, the stolen Stringtown horse with the BO brand was clearly visible.

"Something about my horse upset you, sir?"

Suddenly a loud blast from the train split the Syracuse air. This time it was Lin who jumped.

"Last call for passengers to depart the train," said Price, absently.

Lin slapped his britches and reached for the doorknob. "Son of a gun," he said. "I gotta go." Then he leveled his index finger at Price's chest. "But you and me, we'll resume this conversation later."

"Not without my attorney."

"By all means, but here's an idea: why not use the telegraph line to turn yourself in to the postmaster at Fort Smith and things might go easier for you."

"W—w-well, I should th-think we..."

"See what your attorney thinks."

"I...don't know."

"Fort Smith," said Lin, charging out the door to find Micah and Griff. "The man there is named Wilber."

CHAPTER 7

CAREFUL TO STAY IN THE SHADOWS, THE THREE MEN walked behind the buildings of the town square and approached the train from its rear passenger car. At the back corner of a brick hotel building, they encountered an odoriferous cloud carrying whiffs of skillet fried meat and whiskey. A pair of boys, no more than five or six years old played with a handful of marbles in the dirt.

The Prescott-Missouri-Pacific engine with its tender, freight, and two passenger cars was stretched out in front of the long white depot across the street like a sleeping black dragon. While Lin watched the rear coach, a few teamsters drove past, and a red van advertising Tyner's Firearms wheeled forward along the length of the cars.

"What kind of man are we looking for?" said Lin. "Tall, short?"

"Regal," said Griff. "Aloof. An immaculate dresser."

"I wanna punch him already," said Micah.

"He's rather like me, I suppose," said Griff.

"Now I really wanna punch him."

"He's blond with a part down the middle. Clean

shaven, with spectacles. He speaks with a clipped German accent."

Lin scanned the boardwalk in front of the depot. None of the people departing from the train came close to Griff's description.

One of the boys hurled a big marble against the rock foundation of the saloon with a loud crack. Lin watched the kid retrieve his prize. "How well do you and Coombs get along?" he said.

"If you're trying to suggest some great comradery between us, there is none. Neither is there any enmity. I suppose you would say we're on friendly terms."

"Friendly enough to invite him to the saloon for a drink?"

Griff considered the possibility. "Yeeesss...possibly. Though he'll wonder what I'm doing here in Syracuse. I'll need a good story. He's quite clever, and his suspicions will be aroused."

"Tell him you're visiting family."

"He knows my backstory almost as well as you do. I have no family here."

"How about tell him you rode over behind the train in order to convey a message from the office. Tell him Hart Prescott has something important to tell him."

"What could be urgent enough I'd ride all day to intercept him here?"

"Make something up."

"You'll remember I said Coombs is quite clever."

A quartet of laughing travelers rounded the back of the train, one of them carrying a canvas duffle, another with a heavy trunk on his back. For a second, Lin tensed.

The two men were obviously lending a hand to a couple ginger-haired members of the fair sex.

Sisters.

"Best liver this side of the Missoura," said one of the men. "If you can stomach liver," said the other man. "This fellow here has enjoyed it for his entire life. Steals it off my plate if I give him the chance."

"Says you."

"Yeah, says me."

Brothers.

Lin relaxed and watched the quartet mount the boardwalk in front of the saloon. As soon as they disappeared inside, Lin urged Griff into the street.

They couldn't wait any longer.

"Now or never," he said.

They rounded the back of the train.

Except for a portly old official with a railroad cap and uniform, the opposite side of the track was deserted. Even the platform in front of the depot was quickly drained of life as the last of the travelers met their contacts.

As they closed in, the old porter called to them. "Hope you folks aren't riding the stage line. The Butterfield is just set to pull out."

Lin heard the rumble of the big wheels across the crossing ahead and saw the shiny black Concord wagon lumber over the rail crossing and head out of town. He waved at the porter and whispered under his breath. "If Coombs or his man is on the stage, this could be the end of the entire affair."

Micah pulled away from Lin to stare into the reflective squares of the passenger coach, it's glass awash with the warm pink and orange of a mid-Missouri sunset. "I saw a shadow moving inside. I'm betting our man is still on board the train," said Micah.

"It'll only take a moment to see," said Griff.

The three of them hurried to the front of the car

where a series of iron steps led up to the entrance. "Go ahead," Lin told Griff. "We'll wait here."

This time Griff didn't argue. Nodding, he took the steps in one quick jump and stood at the threshold of the car, peering inside.

Withing seconds, a second man rushed forward carrying a heavy leather satchel.

"Dalton?" he said.

"Mister Coombs, isn't it?" said Griff.

When Griff spoke up, Coombs jerked back like he'd been stung by a hornet.

As Griff had promised, the German was tall with a splendid suit and wire spectacles. His three-piece woolen wardrobe was perfectly tailored with a light pinstripe. He wore a black ribbon tie around the heavy shirt collar, double breasted vest, and polished shoes. His attire conveyed not only wealth, but unquestionable taste.

The satchel at Coombs' side was equally fine, made of dark leather and outlined in gold thread with fittings of brass.

"By God, Griffin, is it you?" Coombs was honestly surprised to see his office mate.

"Why, yes, old man," said Griff. "Indeed. Thank heavens I've found you."

"Found me? I don't understand. What is it?" As Griff had promised, Coombs' voice conveyed instant suspicion. When he turned and saw Lin standing on the boardwalk next to Micah, his tone was even more wary. "What's this all about?"

"We're a tad conspicuous, don't you think, Ranger?" said Micah.

Lin's response was a quickly improvised growl. "I told you we'd miss those damn girls if we didn't get here on time."

"Girls?" said Micah.

"Yeah, *the girls*," said Lin, shifting the heel of his boot onto Micah's toes. "The *girls* we're here to meet."

Micah caught on to the charade. "Oh, *those* girls."

Lin looked up at Coombs. "Say, buddy, you haven't see two red-headed beauties leave the train have you? A couple of sisters?"

Coombs' gaze was hard and cut through Lin cold as a winter wind.

After what seemed like an eternity but was only a few seconds, the German looked away, motioning them back down the boardwalk and across the street. "Yes, yes. They left with two men. I think they were going for supper somewhere."

Lin's gratitude was genuine. "Got it. Thanks a million, friend." He waved, but Coombs' attention was already back on Griff.

Lin and Micah held their ground, but turned their backs to the train, nodding their heads together as if in deep conversation. On the passenger car balcony, Griff told Coombs, "I have a message for you from Prescott. It can't wait."

"Surely you didn't ride all the way from Jefferson City today?"

"I did," said Griff. "It's important."

"Then, you had better tell me."

"Let's find someplace a bit more private. Maybe have a drink first."

From the corner of his eye, Lin saw Griff move toward the steps. Coombs put his left hand on the center of Griff's chest. "Let's have it now, shall we?"

"Here, let me carry your satchel, old man," said Griff, reaching for the case Coombs still held on to with his right hand.

"I can manage," said Coombs.

"But...with your arm as it is," said Griff.

Arm as it is? Lin snuck a glance over his shoulder. What in thunder was Griff talking about?

"I said I could manage," argued Coombs.

"And I said, let me." Now Lin saw Griff had a firm hold on the satchel's handle and was putting all his weight into procuring it.

"In the satchel," said Lin. "There's the payout."

He pivoted on the heel of his boot and sprang to the bottom of the steps with Micah behind. Above them on the train, Griff used both hands to wrench the satchel free from Coombs' arm.

If not exactly free from his grip.

Because the bag Griff held tight in his clutches still had a free-floating hand attached to the handle.

The prosthesis was exquisitely carved from a soft blond wood, the curled wooden fingers a precise match for the real thing. When the hand popped free, Coombs gave an awful yowl.

Before Griff could make another move, the German savagely kicked his shin. Then he swung around, his coat sleeve pulled back to reveal a long wooden arm.

Coombs used his artificial appendage like a club, delivering an explosive blow across Griff's shoulders.

The Englishman lurched forward with a cough and dropped the satchel. It slammed into the second step down, bounced, and cracked open on the boardwalk in front of Lin.

In the dying light of the day, Lin saw a thick ream of paper inside, each page lined with heavy script and gold embossing.

Without a second thought he grabbed the satchel and pressed the latch closed. "Got it," he said. "Let's go."

On the steps above, the German's good hand had a death grip on Griff's neck, but Lin's triumphant cry distracted him.

Griff broke Coombs' hold and shoved him away.

Coombs again came around with his wooden arm in a terrific swoosh. This time, Griff ducked the attack, and the arc ended with Coombs slamming his wood into the side of the passenger car.

The impact gave out a terrific crack.

"Run," said Griff.

Lin tossed the satchel to Micah. "Find Reece," he said.

Griff tripped and fell down the last step of the car backwards, landing hard on the boardwalk. Lin crouched to help him up as an enraged Coombs charged toward them.

"I said, run, damn you."

Lin straightened his back and balled up his fists.

"I don't think so," he said, "I can't imagine I'll have much problem here."

CHAPTER 8

At seven years old, before his family moved to Texas, fighting was the farthest thing from Lin Jarret's mind. A peaceable kid living in Kentucky, he liked kittens and puppies and almost always released the fireflies he caught at night. A top student in his ma's one-room schoolhouse, Lin preferred serious books to petty squabbles, actual history to rumors and gossip.

He shot rabbits and squirrels for game, but he had a fierce hatred for snakes once he saw one of his friends lose a swollen puss-filled hand after an encounter with a copperhead.

In fact, Lin stomped every slithering thing he came across.

Which, in retrospect, might be why he wanted to stomp Charlie Wegner the first time he saw him.

After Charlie, fighting was on Lin's mind quite a bit.

Three years older than Lin, and standing a full 12-inches taller, Charlie moved into a cabin across the winding Ideal Creek with his pa and no ma. Rawboned with flaking pink sores on his face and crooked yellow teeth, the big boy had snake eyes and moved with sneaky purpose.

A purpose which soon became clear.

Whether sitting beside Lin in the one-room schoolhouse, where he would pinch him on the arm and pester his handwriting, or meeting Lin at the creek, where he'd push him into the murky brine, Charlie's only goal in life was to ruin Lin Jarret.

One day in December, Charlie cornered Lin on the banks of the frozen Ideal and told him—through a series of tortured phrases—to strip bare and jump into the ice water or face a trouncing. When Lin refused, Charlie pushed him over, sat on his back, and slammed his face into the snow. Over and over again.

Through a flurry of frozen blood and snot, Lin vowed revenge.

With all her books and fancy poems, Ma couldn't help him anymore.

Now it was pa's turn.

During the following weeks and months, Lin's father taught him how to fight. He learned how to scuffle, to cuff, to undercut, and gut-punch. He practiced his footwork, over and over like a mad-hatted dancer. He mapped his enemy's daily routes, and he knew Charlie better than Charlie knew himself.

Lin faced a multitude of options for a satisfying revenge.

He mapped out a half-dozen ambush points around the country, devised a handful of ghoulish weapons, and concocted hundreds of cruel, hurtful words.

When the time came, Charlie Wegner, the rotten skunk, wouldn't see it coming.

Then one summer day in 1840, the Wegner clan pushed on to the West.

As people do.

Some said the Wegners ended up in Wyoming. Others said Colorado.

Lin never saw Charlie Wegner again, but the old grudge still remained.

Charlie Wegner grew in Lin's mind to symbolize anybody who took advantage of people who weren't as strong as they were.

Lin intended to beat Charlie Wegner whenever and wherever he found him.

Standing on the boardwalk in front of the narrow frame train depot in Syracuse, facing the tall German, Seth Coombs, Lin saw Charlie Wegner's sneering face. He squared his shoulders and beckoned him forward.

"Let's have a go, then," he said.

But Coombs wanted nothing to do with it. His gaze was full of hot contempt for Lin, but his words were cold and neutral.

"I won't quarrel with you," said Coombs.

"Come again?"

"I will not engage in a public display of pugilism."

Griff scoffed and dusted his hands, "You've already engaged, old man."

Lin gnashed his teeth. Here he was all rarin' to go, and the big bastard wouldn't put up his dukes. After the way he'd tossed Griff around like a rag doll, there was no way Lin would let Coombs walk away unscathed.

It would be Charlie Wegner slinking off to Wyoming—all over again.

"Don't worry about him," said Griff, grabbing Lin's arm. "We got what we came for. Your friends are waiting."

At the end of the boardwalk, Micah emerged from in front of the locomotive. He held the satchel high so Lin could see it. Reece Sinclair was beside him, and the green Concord coach waited just beyond.

Griff dusted off his clothes. "Coombs wants to provoke you into doing something reckless," said Griff.

"I'm happy to oblige," said Lin.

Something here sure was off. Why wasn't Coombs directly trying to reclaim his property? Why was he suddenly so unflappable?

The German wagged his head and clicked his tongue. "Tch, tch. How little you understand me, *freund.*"

One of Lin's buddies in the Texas Rangers was a Lutheran transplant from the old Holy Roman Empire. He'd taught Lin enough German to get by.

In some ways, Coombs' mother tongue was more comprehensible than the man's heavily-accented English.

Coombs' thin lips stretched across his face in a grim smile.

"*Hast du gedacht, ich wäre alleine?*"

Did you think I was alone?

He gave his fingers a snap, and a horde of men poured out of the passenger car above him.

Lin counted at least six hardcase ruffians, each one as big and powerful looking as Coombs, each one snarling and out for blood. With Griff five steps ahead of him on the station boardwalk, Lin spun on his heel and ran like hell for the green Concord wagon, Coombs' rowdy pack whooping and screaming at his heels.

Badly outnumbered, there was no way for Lin and Griff to win a fight.

No time to do anything but get to the coach and escape.

Blessedly, Reece and Micah had climbed to their

positions above the front box of the coach and Griff had hold of the cabin's open door.

"Go, go, go!" shouted Lin. "Yah, yah," he cried at the harnessed Sinclair team.

Behind him, one of Lin's pursuers started slinging lead. Lin pressed his left hand against his hat as the other arm hooked around and reached for his Colt. He hated tossing bullets around in town with citizens afoot, but he wasn't going to go down without a fight.

Reece flicked the reins and her four horses lurched ahead, jerking the wagon into motion, dragging Griff off his feet. Lin churned through the dusty exhaust, following the wagon as it accelerated.

Another loud blast and this time a lead ball sizzled through the air past Lin's ear.

Lin pivoted, took careful aim with the Colt Walker, cocked the hammer, and pressed the trigger. One of Coombs' men windmilled to earth, a crumpled pile of pants and suit coats.

My-my, weren't they all dressed in splendid attire.

Jackets, suit-pants, string ties, and beaver-skin hats. Lin hadn't seen such a fine-looking bunch since visiting the bank in San Antone with Reece to secure financing for the Jarret-Sinclair stagecoach venture.

Lin turned around and kept running, ducking low, dodging from side to side whenever he heard a shot. Up ahead, Griff had managed to haul his butt inside the Concord and was leaning out the open door, yelling for Lin to hurry the hell up.

What did he think Lin was doing?

Blam! Another gunshot from behind had Lin pivoting around to hoof it backwards in front of the mob.

He didn't like what he saw. A heavy handful of men were nearly upon him.

As he leveled his gun at the lead man, another concussion hit the air, but this time the gunfire didn't come from him or the bunch chasing him.

It came from the outfit he'd seen before, *Tyner's Gun Service and Sales*.

Lin had to blink twice, then wipe the dust from his eyes with the back of his gun hand to make sure what he saw was real. The red van wasn't nearly as ornate as the Hellbenders' green coach, but it loomed over the street like a brick fortress, and the war horses pulling it were steel-gray Percherons.

Holding court from the driver's box, a barrel-chested man with white hair held a Remington .44 in each hand, and the muzzles were spitting flame straight up into the sky.

Rather than fire on Coombs' men directly, Mister Tyner seemed more intent on persuading them to give up the chase. With each score, the gunman laughed like crazy.

"At least one of us is enjoying it," said Lin.

Distracted by Tyner's lead barrage, Coombs' remaining rowdies were stopped short, allowing Lin the time he needed to catch up with his friends. Griff still held the door open, and when he was parallel with the cabin, Lin dove inside.

Frantic, Lin's hands latched on the first thing he could grip—Griffin Kale's trouser cuff. Griff clutched at the back of Lin's shirt with both hands and hauled him up and inside.

The coach hit an enormous chuckhole in the road, bouncing a foot into the air.

Both men were thrown headlong against the opposite panel, and the carriage door slammed shut behind them. Lin popped up first and almost lost his head as a crashing pistol blast came through the open back window and slapped lead into the upholstered interior.

Micah's query sounded from the bench seat above the din of wheels and hooves and creaking leather braces. "Are you hit? Are you alright?"

"We're okay," shouted Lin. "Drive like thunder."

An explosion from above rattled the coach.

It was Micah returning fire with his big Clayborne shotgun.

Griff crouched on the rear bench seat and peered out the rear view. "I think the old man with the Percherons has got them foxed," he said. "I don't see Coombs' men following us."

But with the sun dipping below the horizon, it was getting dark, and the coach was kicking up enough dust to choke a gopher. "Stay alert," said Lin. "We can't be sure they won't come after us on horseback."

Griff let out a breath of exasperation. "Bloody hell," he said. "That was something of a corker, wasn't it?"

"I have no idea what you just said."

"We're damned lucky to be alive."

"Ain't it the truth," said Lin, keeping watch out the side window with the muzzle of his Colt near his chin.

The wagon rocked back and forth and jumped again as the wheels slammed through a large chuckhole in the road.

"Who was the Good Samaritan? The man in the red wagon?" said Griff.

"Don't know, but I owe him a drink next time I see him."

"I wonder why he'd risk helping us?"

"Why not?"

"Why not? You bloody well know why not." Griff wagged a finger through a hole in the collar of his coat.

"My new buttonhole isn't due to moths," he said. "There was every chance of being killed out there."

Lin shrugged. "Good Samaritans. Guardian angels. They come in all shapes and sizes."

"It still makes me wonder why he would bother," said Griff.

"The sign on his van said Tyner's Gun Service."

"I suppose we'll never know his true motivation."

————

AT SYRACUSE, the men pursuing Reece Sinclair's green Concord wagon exemplified German efficiency. Within minutes, the dapper young men had picked up their dead and retreated to the train. By the time the town constable made the scene with a barber's bib still tied around his neck and his beard half-shaved, all the men had transferred to a buckboard wagon and wheeled out of town.

With a one-armed man at the reins, they fled in a direction opposite the Butterfield Overland stagecoach road.

Flood Tyner's wagon sat still just outside the town limits next to a jagged deep fissure in the middle of the road. From his comfortable perch on the box seat above, he watched Coombs' men disappear, then pondered the hollow spot.

It was the kind of chuckhole that could break a wagon axel in two.

Why the Butterfield Overland hadn't repaired it yet was beyond Tyner's reckoning, but everybody was strapped for cash these days. Everybody tried their best to save a nickel here or there.

With her gorgeous chestnut mares and sturdy chassis, Reece Sinclair had plowed over the cavity at full speed—as if money were no object. Leave it to a woman grabbing the ribbons.

Or...maybe she didn't need to worry about costs.

Tyner clucked his tongue against the roof of his mouth and fingered Reece's gold coins in his side coat pocket. She certainly hadn't been afraid to outbid Ned Brock when it came to the Walch Navy 12-shooter.

A noisy clomping of hooves and creaking leather drew Tyner's attention from the road. Tyner watched as Ned Brock, with two of his drover buddies on horseback, came together in the town square. The windburnt sodbuster sat in a worn saddle atop a swayback mule. Another man with long curly hair and no cap sat on a roan next to Brock. The tough gunslinger rode a snorting, black mare. Though Tyner couldn't hear them, he had a fairly good idea what they were planning.

They were going after Reece Sinclair.

Brock slapped his horse with a braided leather quirt and gave off a mighty whoop. Beside him, Curly matched the call-to-arms, and the three men rumbled past Tyner's wagon, leaping the chuckhole, and driving down the stagecoach trail without a second look.

Well, faint heart never won fair maiden.

Pursing his lips tight, Tyner navigated the immediate road with care, then flicked the reins and followed the posse down the road, still pondering Miss Sinclair's bountiful assets, determined to make sure Ned Brock's crew did her no harm.

Clearly, the trio of muttonhead train robbers traveling with her were next to worthless.

CHAPTER 9

In lantern light, Micah gripped the iron rimmed wheel and pulled himself out from under the coach. Clasping his hand, Lin helped him to his feet.

Micah dusted off before addressing Reece. "How far until Mulhaven station?" he said.

"I'd say six miles," said Reece. "Maybe seven. Fog's rolling in and I'm not sure exactly where we are."

They had made seven good miles over the winding Missouri trail at a high-speed gallop before the clattering shake of the Concord was too much for Reece to manage. As their workload grew more and more unstable, the horses were more increasingly quarrelsome.

Reece pulled over at the first gravel-lined shoulder offering adequate space to stop and look things over.

"The axle's in bad shape," said Micah. "Honestly, the whole beam ought to be replaced."

"You think we can make it into the station?" said Lin.

"Maybe. I did my best to shore it up with splints and your rope. But it's a bad break. I'm betting it started coming apart when we left Syracuse. We hit a pretty big hole in the road."

"Isn't this a fine predicament," said Griff. "Just peaches and cream, lovely."

Micah scowled down at him. "You want to crawl under there and take a shot at it?"

"I wasn't disparaging your work, sir," said Griff. "Rather, I was cursing our fate. The men who chased us out of town might well be on our tails. Coombs is nothing if not tenacious, and here we are limping away like a buckshot stray bulldog."

"How long until Prescott knows we've got his money?" said Reece.

"I expect he's got the message by now," said Lin. "There's a telegraph line between Syracuse and Jeff City."

"Prescott won't take it well," said Griff. "His rage is well known."

"Everybody you know and work with seems to be a lunatic," said Lin.

"To Prescott, the smallest slight can be worth a man's life," said Griff. "By slipping away with his delivery, we've put Seth Coombs into a horrific position of redeeming himself quickly—or paying the ultimate price."

"He'll be coming for us, directly."

"Indeed, he will."

"About the money," said Lin. "Back at the station, when I caught a glimpse inside the satchel, it looked to be filled with some kind of stock certificate?"

Before Griff could answer, Reece said, "Micah showed them to me just before we drove out. They're shares in Prescott's Colorado gold venture. Each certificate is worth ten shares at ten dollars a share."

"By such reckoning, there ought to be 100 certificates?"

"We haven't taken time to look at 'em," said Micah.

"What with dodging bullets and the stage falling apart, Reece and I decided running for our lives took priority over counting out papers."

"Let's take a closer look when we get to Mulhaven's," said Lin. "With what you're saying about the axle, we might be there a while."

Reece's voice was confident. "Mike Dooney is the station master there. If anybody can get us up and running, he can."

"If we make it," said Griff.

Lin shot him a dirty look. "If you want to go your own way, you're free to do so."

"Meaning what?"

"Meaning your part of this job is done, mister. You identified Coombs. We've got the payoff in our possession. Nobody's keeping you here, least of all me."

"You'd like that wouldn't you? If I simply walked off into the dark?"

"Yeah," said Lin. "Maybe I would."

"By god, I think you mean it."

The two men stood nose to nose.

"By god...I think I do," said Lin.

"Enough—out of both of you," said Reece. "It's been a long day for all of us, without the two of you taking time out to scuffle in the middle of the road."

"Lady, you don't know the half of it," said Griff. Then he turned to Lin. "Don't make me sorry for staying."

"Don't make us sorry for not leaving you here," said Lin.

Reece raised her voice. "Didn't I say, *enough?*"

"This has nothing to do with me," said Micah, tossing up his hands. "I'm out." He rounded the carriage to regain his position at the shotgunner's spot.

Beside Reece, Lin jerked open the carriage door

and swung his hand around in a big arc. "Your chariot awaits."

"I'm content to drive," said Reece.

"Not with a broken axle in the dead of night. You think I'd let—"

"A woman?"

"Okay, yeah. You think I'd let a woman continue to drive in such conditions? My daddy raised me better than to see such a thing happen."

"You two can argue all you like, but one thing's sure," said Griff. "I'm most definitely not driving." The Englishman clamored into the cabin and pulled the door shut behind him.

Before Lin could react, Reece snagged his arm, holding him back. "What's your problem with Griffin Kale?"

"Me? Why don't you ask *him*?"

"Him, we might still need. There's no telling what we'll face up ahead—or behind, as he rightly pointed out. He might know something about Seth Coombs and the way he thinks. Something beneficial."

"Oscar told us all we needed to know."

"Your uncle betrayed my father to his killer. He betrayed you to a bloody war for survival. I can't believe you're standing here defending him."

"I'm not defending him; I'm simply saying he told us all we need to know about Coombs."

"You can't know if he told us everything. Think about your uncle's vile heart and ask yourself what he may not be telling us."

Lin chewed on her question long enough to admit Reece made some sense.

"Fair enough," he said, "but I have no reason to trust Kale either."

"Lin," said Reece. "He just might save our lives."

"When he does, I'll be the first one to give him a medal. Now, are you going to let me take the ribbons?"

"Do I have a choice?"

The question hung between them for longer than it should've. Finally, Lin said, "We're partners. You'll always have a choice."

"Good." With renewed vigor, Reece spun around and hoisted herself onto the driver's box. "Strap yourself in with Griff," she said. "It might get bumpy back there."

Lin watched her grab the ribbons and snap off the brake.

"It's good to see you, too," he whispered.

———

In Jefferson City, the new capitol building of 1840, illuminated with lantern light, was visible from Hart Prescott's three-story brick office building. When August 6 gave him the gubernatorial reins, as he knew it must, he imagined parading through the streets of the Capitol city in a chariot of brass and black enamel, waving to his admirers, putting his enemies on their guard. In his mind's eye, he smelled the rich leather upholstery of the car, felt the sleek, comforting warmth of his otter's fur coat. The fantasy always ended with him presiding over the same desk he sat behind now but relocated to a better location inside the prestigious capitol.

He withdrew his attention from the north-facing window and considered his office as it was tonight. Prescott appreciated the dim radiance of his small, cut-glass lamp, its slender chimney magnifying the smoldering ember wick only so much before giving the shadows their due.

He sat in darkness, aware of the curled telegram on the desk before him, barely able to perceive it.

The diminutive messenger who brought the missive waited dutifully three paces toward the exit. Prescott thought it was all the little magpie could do not to pee on the expensive Persian rug under his feet.

"Such woeful news."

"S-sir?" said the magpie.

"How do you bear it, son? Carrying such woeful news?"

No answer.

Prescott cleared his throat, repeating the message just as the magpie had first read it to him. "Arkansas payment pilfered before delivery. Coombs." Flat, matter of fact, without emotion.

"It is exactly what the message conveyed," said the magpie. He slid a scrawny, black-clad leg toward the exit. "If there's nothing more, Mister Prescott, I'll just be—"

Prescott raised his eyes to the light.

"Don't you think I want to respond to the message?" said Prescott.

"I didn't know—"

"Don't you think I'd have something to say at such a loss?" Struggling to keep his voice under control. It wasn't the magpie's fault Seth Coombs was a pitiful imbecile.

"Don't kill the messenger," he whispered to himself.

The magpie stuttered. "A thousand pardons, I —what?"

"I said *don't kill the messenger!*" The scream was enough to force the pitiful child back two steps. Standing close to the light, Prescott saw the boy was trembling.

Pathetic.

He abruptly stood, his chair crashing into the wall behind him, and rounded the desk with a limp. He kept one arm outstretched, fingers staying in touch with the top of the desk. He tossed back his mane of long silver hair and stroked his glistening snow-white beard.

"Take my words back to your precious telegraphy machine and send them to Syracuse."

"O-of course, sir."

With his right hand, Prescott reached across and squeezed at his left shoulder. The pain in his chest was more acute than ever before. The numb sensation heavier, pulling his left arm down. "Three...words," he said against the agony. "I want you to send three words."

"Are you...are you quite alright, sir?"

"Three. Words."

"Yes, sir? What are they, sir?"

"Get. It. Back."

"*Get it back*. Yes, sir. Is that all, sir?" The magpie had half-turned, had one hand on the doorknob into the hallway outside.

Prescott nodded and turned away to lean on the desk with both arms. Staring down at the tracery of veins on the back of his hands, he struggled against his affliction. "Yes, that's all, damn you."

"Are you sure you're—"

"Get out!" he yelled. Then, softer, "God's blood can't you leave me in peace, you stupid nincompoop?"

When the door slammed behind him, Prescott turned his head to stare at the glass-covered portrait on display in his office. The likeness dominated the wall adjacent to the High Street window, and the gray-beard face therein glared at the ostentatious room. Matthias Byrnes O'Fallon, the philosophical founder of the Ivory Compass ideal, dead three quarters of a century, but a man whose legacy was only now taking shape.

A kingmaker whose phantom hand stretched confidently into the future.

And Prescott was determined he would be the king.

In the glass, Prescott saw his life's work reflected in heavy maroon curtains and expensive rugs. A mahogany sideboard and silver tea set. A selection of European crystal. And swimming amongst it all in the glass was Prescott's lion-maned reflection. At nearly seven feet tall, and weighing a multitude of stone, Missouri's next Governor forced himself erect.

Prescott would prevail.

The words had become his daily, almost hourly, mantra.

The pain was leaving him now, as it generally did after a few minutes. A wash of perspiration broke out across his forehead, and a feeling of exuberance flooded his system. The attacks left him weak, but strangely euphoric.

Like he'd beaten down the devil one more time.

Prescott combed his fingers through his long, thick hair and looked past his reflection at the visage of O'Fallon. It was Prescott who fate decreed would seize the reins from the old order. Prescott who would blaze a new trail and carry a cadre of chosen passengers into a new, better world.

With the fortune from his part of the Ponder's Peak gold mine, he could buy half the planet.

If he didn't lose any to the enemy.

Prescott's fist started to shake uncontrollably at the thought, and he slammed it hard against the top of the desk.

It would help to know who the enemy was.

Snatching up the telegram, he held it close to his face, reading the words he had only previously heard. It smelled of ink and cigarette smoke.

Springfield payment pilfered before delivery. Coombs.

Cryptic, with no further explanation. Typical of the German.

Pilfered before delivery.

How pilfered? By whom?

Prescott felt his lip curl into a sneer, and he crumpled the telegram into a tight-fisted ball.

The pain crept back into his shoulder.

CHAPTER 10

IT SEEMED LIKE LIN JARRET HAD ONLY JUST DRIFTED off to sleep when the coach crashed into the dining room wall of Mulhaven station on the Butterfield Overland way. Naturally, he thought he was dreaming, but the smell of cracked cherry wood and an arrow of pain at the base of his skull convinced him otherwise.

He blinked twice and rolled against the escape hatch as the Concord pitched over with a sickening jolt. Lin was sure the side panels would give way under his impact, but the sturdy construction held fast. Outside, the horses were blowing and squalling out a racket, heaving the stalled rig in three directions at once.

Braced against the far side of the rocking interior, Griff had been sleeping too. "What's happened?" he said.

"I knew I should've drove," said Lin, trying to make sense of the window's crooked view. He tore away the spool of canvas shade hanging in front of the window to stick his head outside. The big back wheel was gone, and the entire weight of the coach rested against the ruined siding of the station.

And the coach was slipping.

Above the din of the horses, Lin couldn't make himself heard. He tried yelling for his companions again, "Reece? Reece!"

Then a wrenching tug brought the coach forward, scraping the station wall, and the snap of heavy timbers told him the team was breaking free. He heard Micah's booming voice. "Cut 'em loose, dammit! Cut 'em loose," and a tremendous shudder went through the cabin. The horses sprang away with a burst of heavy drumming, and the painful squeal of the coach ceiling against the side of Mulhaven station had Lin seeing red.

The busted axle was bad enough, they didn't have time for a smashup.

Bracing himself against the forward passenger seat, he stretched an arm through the upper window and, reaching through, was able to twist the crank latch and fling open the door. Gripping the edges of the opening, he hauled himself through and dropped over the edge of the coach to the ground.

He was met by a quartet of lanterns in the hands of four children positioned in a half-circle around the wrecked stagecoach.

Mike Dooney's kids.

Before Lin could say a word, Reece jogged in between a little girl and a bookish-looking young man with a crooked nose.

"Are you hurt?" she said.

Lin performed a quick self-check. Other than the throbbing bump at the back of his head, he appeared to be whole. He fingered the goose-egg tenderly. "Sore, but I'll mend. You?" he said. "What about Micah?"

"We're both okay. When the coach went over, we both jumped."

"What the hell happened?"

"We couldn't see the steep approach to the station because of the fog. The horses were going too fast for the grade, and we hit bottom hard. When the axle flew apart, we lost the back wheel."

"And the coach fell over into the station," said Lin.

He reached for her, and she came into his arms.

"Just so you're not hurt," he said, pressing his lips to her hair. Her embrace was strong, her eyes clear when she pulled back to address him.

"We've been through worse," she said with a smile. "Haven't we, Ranger?"

"We sure have, Contessa."

"Discouraged, but not defeated," she said.

Griff crawled free of the wreckage carrying Seth Coombs' leather satchel, then joined them in the arc of flickering light. "By the by, I'm fine, thanks for asking."

Reece laid a hand on Griff's arm, but Lin ignored him. He was more concerned about the horses.

"How did the team fare? Those mares are fine stock. I'd hate for anything to happen to 'em."

"Micah's tending the horses. They didn't seem to be injured," said Reece, "just startled with the commotion."

"We needed to swap them out here anyway." He looked over his shoulder at the precariously positioned Concord. "We don't have time for this kind of delay."

"At this point, I don't think it's up to you," said a good-natured voice.

The man who clomped to stop beside them walked like a pack mule, and his voice was full of the blarney and brough.

Lin acknowledged Mike Dooney with a nod.

"Howdy, Mike," he said. "Feel like patching up a wagon tonight?"

Dooney grinned and scratched his chin. "Might be able to help you," he said. "But this is a hell of a way to drop by for a visit, Lin. You could've knocked on the front door instead." He smiled at Reece and tipped a wide-brimmed hat away from his scalp. "Miss Sinclair. It's good to see you, again."

"How long do you think it might take to fix?" said Reece.

"Gonna depend on how much damage you've done and the good grace of the Lord above," said Dooney.

"If it's all the same to you, I'd rather put my faith in your two good arms, Mike."

Dooney cocked his head toward Griffin Kale. "Is this another one of your charity cases, Miss Reece?"

Lin and Reece traded glances.

"This man's part of our team," said Reece.

Dooney shrugged. "It don't make me no never mind."

Lin said, "But we are trying to make a schedule."

"If such is the case, we'd do well to get to work, hadn't we?"

Lin couldn't agree more.

Griff limped away, still clutching Coombs' satchel. "I'll just be inside if anybody needs me."

"The missus has hot coffee inside. You go ahead too, Miss Reece," said Dooney.

While Griff tottered off toward the entrance to the station with Reece close behind, Dooney instructed one of his kids to lead him around to the back of the wagon with Lin. "This is my boy, Kevin," he said.

"Howdy, Kevin," said Lin. "Ain't this the damndest mess you've ever seen?"

Glad to be included in the manly exchange, Kevin nodded with enthusiasm. "Sure is."

"Tell me what happened?" said Dooney.

"We think the axle split as far back as Syracuse," said Lin. "We're lucky to have arrived."

Kevin lifted the lamp as they examined the under-carriage.

"And what, pray tell, were you driving over so fast as to split an axle? The Overland's the smoothest grade around these parts. Like riding a Sunday morning milk-skinned lassy." Dooney furrowed his brow at his son. "Cover y'r ears, lad."

"We didn't leave the train station under the...uh, best of circumstances," said Lin.

"Is that a fact, now?"

"The truth is, if we don't get this cart pulled back together, we might all be in dutch."

Dooney's cheerful expression faded. He addressed his son as a cloud drifted over his face. "Hand me the lantern, Kevin, and then go on and join the others inside."

Kevin's face fell. Once again, he was relegated to the house with the rest of his younger brothers and sisters.

"Aw, Pa, I can help fix this thing."

"Mind your pa, lad."

Lin watched the reluctant boy trudge slowly toward the house and close the station door behind him.

Once everyone was inside, Dooney turned on Lin, his voice thick with anger. "Sure and you know I ain't pleased to hear what you're telling me, Jarret. It's one thing we agreed to open our home to you and your friends on account of the Overland line giving us a little extra in the coffers."

"But you don't deserve to see your kids in danger."

"That's for damned sure."

"I understand."

"Do ya, now?"

Dooney stood three inches shorter than Lin, but was twice as big around the chest, and his arms were forged iron. There was no arguing about his strength. Hosting the first station on the line—and the last for coaches coming in from the West—was a terrific strain.

Every stopover came in the dead of night, and passengers were nearly always at an emotional high— eager and excited to be underway or exhausted after a 2,500-mile trip. Dooney and his family provided food, drink, comfort and bedding. They maintained a remuda of horses and prepared fresh teams for transit. They were often called on for medical advice, wagon repair, and simple encouragement.

They were a vital part of the Butterfield Overland mail.

They deserved better.

Dooney wasn't a man to mince words. "If any harm befalls my family because of your arrival here tonight, I'll kill ya myself."

Lin didn't blame him. He slapped the man gently on the shoulder and agreed. "If such a thing happened, I'd hand you my gun. Now, let's get to fixing that wagon."

CHAPTER 11

THE BUTTERFIELD OVERLAND STATION AT
Mulhaven was a two-room frame house with a peaked
roof layered in shingles. The main dining hall featured
a central table seating eight and two smaller tables
toward the back of the room close to a pot-bellied
wood stove. A door beside the stove led to a back
kitchen and storage room. The cookstove was there,
and smells of hot beef and potatoes, gravy and stewed
tomatoes, fresh baked bread and fresh butter made
Reece homesick for her ranch on the Rio Grande.

Through the open door into the kitchen, Reece
watched Louise Dooney, her yellow hair pulled back in
a bun, prepare a pot of coffee with rich, black grounds
and broken eggshells on top before turning to look
outside into the night.

A strong woman, thought Reece. Stronger than
most people could ever imagine.

Yet she was friendly and kind. Caring in the way
some women simply exuded warmth.

It was something all the bad men and road agents
had yet to understand. On the frontier, friendliness
meant survival. Bad manners and uncouth behavior

were a sign of weakness not to be tolerated in polite company.

Louise Dooney was good natured.

But push her the wrong way and she'd knock in your skull with a frying pan, then set to fixing the bacon and eggs and hum a hymn while she did it.

The Dooney's living quarters, a sturdy house with an upstairs loft aglow with lantern light, sat ten yards further back on the 3-acre property, behind the station house. An enclosed corral with three or four outside haystacks was connected to house and station by brick lined paths lighted with luminary boxes.

It was 3:00 in the morning when Louise brought supper to Reece, Griff, and Micah at one of the corner tables. The warm tin plates were smothered with buttered grits, and the beans were laced with pepper bacon and sorghum.

For a long time, nobody talked, and the click of tin cutlery filled the space.

Louise carried coffee in, and Micah sopped the edges of his plate clean with thick slabs of corn bread before drinking deep from his cup.

"Another helping, Mister LeMay?" said Louise Dooney. Micah said he didn't mind if he did.

Louise smiled and topped off his coffee, then filled Reece and Griff's cup before returning the tin pot to the kitchen. "If you folks need anything, just holler."

Reece said they would, and the hostess disappeared into the adjacent room with three kids in tow.

After she was gone, Griff said, "About this Overland mail line, explain it to me?"

"Been active for three years, since March of 1857," said Reece. "The Postmaster-General opted for a trail along the 32nd parallel and solicited bids. After several schemes were proposed, John Butterfield won the opportunity to establish and equip stations with stock and coach repairs every 12 to 20 miles along the way."

Micah added, "There are two Eastern terminus points, both of them on the Mississippi River. One at St. Louis and one at Memphis. They join up at Fort Smith, then run through Indian Country, across Texas and down into the southeast territories all the way to San Francisco."

"Without these stations, the fast trip would take five times as long and be virtually impossible," said Reece.

While they finished eating, Reece thought about the dozens of stops, starting with Mulhaven, and moving on to Wynot's Dairy, Plummer's, Springfield, and all the others—all vital to the line's forward momentum. Each station supplied the rolling coach with new teams of horses and mules, fresh drivers, food, water, and other necessities of life on the road.

For independent travelers like Reece or the many immigrant trains using the road to reach Texas, the stations charged a modest fee for food and services.

She and Lin had made the division run twice before, carrying essential goods for the emancipator's station—from Syracuse to Fort Smith, through the Nations to the west side of Lambert's Ferry. At the Red River, while the regular stagecoach traveled on to Fort Chadbourne, Reece dodged south to Emberville.

Like Micah, Griff was busy cleaning his plate when Reece brought up the subject of the satchel. "While we have the opportunity, I'd like to look at one of those goldmine shares more closely."

Griff reached under the table, between his boots, and unclasped the ornate leather bag. He withdrew one letter-sized share and smoothed it out on the table.

It was a beautiful parchment piece, with a floral

border and a central illustrated vignette of a mining camp—complete with bearded prospectors panning for gold and swinging wood-handled picks. Unissued and not cancelled, the document was labeled as Number 24. According to the ornate script, it represented 10 shares of the capital stock of the Prescott Ponder's Peak Company at the fair value of ten dollars each.

"So this piece of paper is worth a hundred dollars," said Micah. He whistled softly, then said, "There's the Prescott name again."

"As in Hart Prescott," said Reece.

"As in the Prescott-Missouri-Pacific railroad. As in the next governor of the state," said Griff.

"Ponder's Peak played a big part in last year's Colorado gold rush," said Micah.

"Initially the vein hasn't proved to be as abundant the Pike's Peak strike, but there are mineralogist who claim Ponder's will ultimately prove to be twice as large," said Griff.

"So this is stock in a gold mine?"

"It's not exactly," said Griff. Certainly there's gold at Ponder's Peak, but it's not the only source of money in the venture. Hart Prescott took advantage of the gold rush last year, but not in the way you think. Rather than mine gold, he mined men."

"What do you mean?"

"He purchased a couple thousand acres of ranch land near the mines and set up a base camp town catering to the miners and their families. Several men have set up similar ventures, but Prescott's camp is the most heavily fortified. They sell everything the prospective mining family might need, and then some."

"With Prescott getting a cut of everything," said Reece.

"He owns an enormous amount of Missouri farmland, huge tracts of land all over the state, but rumor has it he's leveraged to the hilt. The potential fortune from Ponder's Peak promises a way out from under his debt, plus a healthy stake of funds for his next venture...whatever it may be."

"And now we can share the fortune with Emberville," said Reece. "Provided we can turn these certificates into cash."

Griff tapped his fingers on the table.

"How do you afford to do this? Upkeep on a coach? The horses, the food?"

"Call it a favor for a friend," said Reece, her eyes glancing over Micah.

Griff saw the exchange and questioned it.

Micah answered. "There's a woman who cooks at Emberville station. Her name is Sylvia. She's...special to me. Without an infusion of cash, they won't last another month, maybe two."

"I still don't see how you can afford to run the coach for charity. You must have some kind of backing."

"We do other jobs from time to time, freighting items other stage lines won't touch."

"What items?"

"Black powder."

"Eggs," said Micah.

"Phosphorous matches."

"Chickens," said Micah.

Griff wrinkled his nose. "Still, I can't imagine covering the expense."

Micah explained. "Miss Reece owns a ranch down at the Rio Grande. Ramrod there name of Stick Carvell runs cattle on some of the best grazing land in Texas. We get by."

Griff couldn't hide his surprise. "A slip of a girl like

you owns a ranch free and clear? I think I need something stronger to drink than coffee."

Reece clenched her jaw at the remark. She'd worked to reserve judgement, but maybe Lin had been right about this royal polecat after all.

It was clear he was being obstinate simply to get a rise out of them. Apparently, he didn't know any better.

If he wasn't careful, somebody was going to have to set him straight.

In this case, Micah came to her rescue.

"You wouldn't say what you said if you knew what Miss Reece has been through during the past year. She's paid for her ranch many times over with her own blood, and the blood of her friends and family."

"I fought for my ranch against the *Cortinistas*," she told Griff. "My father was killed. I survived." She shared a meaningful look with Micah. "We fought. We won."

Griff picked up the O'Fallon-Prescott share and quietly slipped it back into the satchel.

"I should think you would have had enough contention right there to last a lifetime," he said.

Then he drank his coffee in silence.

"Tell me, Mister Kale," said Reece. "If you don't believe in the goodness of the human heart. And you can't believe we would continue to fight after winning our first war...what is it you do believe in?"

Griff turned his hands over and inspected his palms.

"Aside from enough money to move me forward into tomorrow?"

"Aside from that."

He was quiet a while more. Finally, he said, "I don't believe in taking sides."

Reece finished her meal and pushed her plate back.

"But with your actions, you already have," said Reece.

Micah stood up, and Reece joined him at the door. She didn't think Griff was a bad man, just confused. And he warred against an inner cowardice which would one day betray him.

She recalled what she told Lin back at Dobb's Bend.

He just might save our life.

Or, she thought now as he sat by himself at the table, still looking at his hands, he just might get them all killed.

————

THE FOG HAD CLEARED when Reece walked outside to check on the wagon, and she found Lin with a cigarette in the moonlight. His hands were thick with axle grease, and his clothes were covered in dust. "Taking a breather?" she said.

Lin squinted through the illuminated blue smoke. "Dooney's still working on the wheel, but right now I'm just in the way." He scuffled the dust of the road with his toe.

"How goes the repair?"

"We should be out of here in a couple hours."

Lin flicked away the cigarette.

"You know you smoke too much."

"Likely so."

"Supper's inside."

"I'll get some before we pull out."

"They'll be coming for us."

"I know."

They stood together, staring up the lonely trail,

willing Coombs and his men to appear over the steep hill in a flurry of horseflesh and gunfire.

"Fog's cleared," said Lin. "We've got that much at least."

An owl hooted from a hardwood grove of walnut and cedar, and Reece wished for it to fly up into the air, so she could see it, so she could make a wish on its wings, as her mother had taught her.

She never saw owls when she needed them.

"One thing still bothers me," said Lin.

"Only one?"

"Who was the pickup man?"

"I'm not sure who you mean?"

"The pickup man. If the Ivory Compass payoff is traveling from the Missouri state capital to Coombs' brother, who was going to pick it up at Syracuse? If Coombs wasn't taking the money on the stage directly to Springfield, who was?"

"Griff has no idea?"

"Naw," said Lin. "I heard Coombs call him *Dalton* when they first met, but Griff says the name doesn't mean anything to him."

"Maybe this Dalton person got waylaid somewhere before making the pickup."

"Maybe so," said Lin.

He snapped his fingers, remembering the drunk in the alleyway behind the saloon.

You mind tellin' ol' Dalton the time? I got's somewhere I'm s'posed to be.

"Maybe so, indeed," he said.

"I asked Mrs. Dooney about the stagecoach ahead of us," said Reece. "There was a relief driving from the BO waiting here for them. She said the stage carried a mail agent and two female passengers."

"What about the Butterfield coach's first driver out of Syracuse? Have you talked to him?"

"No, but you have." Reece chuckled under her breath. "It was Mike Dooney himself."

Lin shoved both hands into the pockets of his corduroy pants and told her his suspicions about the Syracuse drunk named Dalton.

"There's an old saying about laying down with dogs and getting fleas," said Reece. "It looks like Prescott and Coombs never learned the old lesson."

"Guess not."

"If you don't mind me saying so, you're giving in to your moods. You ought to go get something to eat. You get grumpy when you're hungry."

"Aw, hell, Contessa. This one's got me all jangled up. Nothing's gone right since Micah and me got to Stringtown."

Standing close, Reece noticed the chafed skin around his neck for the first time. She reached out with gentle fingers, let the tips brush against the scraped, torn skin. "Lord, what happened to you?"

"Micah didn't tell you about the hanging?"

"Micah can be extremely reticent when he wants to be."

"He just doesn't want to brag."

When Reece didn't answer, Lin said, "He saved my life. Griff's too."

"Remind me to thank him," said Reece, and she lightly kissed him. "Not everything's gone wrong, Ranger. We have the payment. It's going to be a chore to convert to cash, but we've got it and the Order of the Ivory Compass does not."

"Not yet," he said.

"No. Not yet."

Lin put an arm around her back as Mike Dooney

called out across the yard. "You two lovebirds got time to smooch, you got time to help me set this crate upright," said the Irishman.

"Maybe we'll be underway sooner than we hoped," said Reece.

"Or maybe not," said Lin.

He dropped the embrace as an insistent thrumming of horses' hooves broke through the night.

Somebody was coming down the hill.

CHAPTER 12

AT THE CROSSROADS TO DOBB'S BEND, FLOOD TYNER had to make a choice.

He could forge ahead on a road lost to fog, or he could camp under a parade of stark white sycamore trees lining a nearby creek. Mulhaven station was at least six miles away, and it was already well past midnight.

Tyner had pushed the two old Percherons harder than he should have getting into Syracuse, and they weren't the only ones getting tired. The last hour had been an exercise in determination for all three of them as the steeds slowed to a caterpillar crawl and Tyner's head was filled with more clouds than the road ahead. Twice he caught himself nodding off, twitching to the alert only as he felt himself sliding from the spring bench of his wagon.

The Sinclair girl filled his thoughts, and he couldn't help but speculate about her and the passengers she was driving down the trail ahead of him. He didn't dare risk losing her. Couldn't allow her to get too far ahead of him. Had the green Concord arrived at Mulhaven's yet?

The train robbers would need to rest.

He ground his teeth thinking about them. If those jaspers had harmed a hair on the fair lass's head...

The scent of water lured the Percherons off-road, and the night air swarmed with the noisy buzz of spring peepers. Tyner had only just made up his mind to let his horses take the wagon into a clearing on the other side of the trees when he smelled hickory smoke. A brief flicker through the branches caught his eyes, and he peered between the trees at the healthy flames.

Where there was fire, there were men.

Tyner pulled back on the reins, reconsidering his course of action.

He supposed there was every chance the Concord had stopped here to overnight, especially given its reckless passage across the yawning chasm in the road at Syracuse.

Could he be so lucky? How fortuitous it would be for him to find the poor lass broke down on the road.

For an instant, he considered her companions and what they carried.

Tyner had seen them take the satchel from the train and wondered what was inside.

He'd seen the three robbers join the Concord—each one a unique specimen of masculinity. A cowboy. A gambler. And an African.

Each one of them younger than him. Each of them no doubt carrying a firearm of some kind.

No doubt the girl was an innocent pawn, her wagon hired by these muttonheads—whoever they were.

The heavy weight of the holstered Remington pistols on Tyner's belt, one dangling from each hip, gave him a sense of confidence old age threatened to take away. In his day, Tyner had been quite a lady's man.

And quite a scrapper.

He imagined himself at the rescue, delivering Reece Sinclair from the arms of her gun-wielding oppressors.

If he took them by surprise, he'd kill the three men and keep the girl for himself. Probably earn an award from the railroad on top of it. Maybe the two of them could retire to the country somewhere.

But then again, the campfire ahead might also belong to somebody else.

Tyner certainly didn't want to meet Ned Brock and his two coyotes in the dark. The gunslinger was somebody you needed to see in daylight, alone, with none of his crew saddled alongside.

He wasn't scared of Brock, hadn't been afraid to chide him during the auction.

But he knew better than to ride up on him unannounced.

Tyner weighed potential good luck against probable misfortune as his Percherons plodded toward the campfire. If it were Brock, how could Tyner turn the encounter to his favor?

When Tyner made the clearing, he held up both hands to show peaceful intent.

No doubt about it.

The camp belonged to Brock.

The hardcase devil squatted on a tree stump behind the flames, flanked by a man on either side. Except for a thick carpet of fallen leaves and scrub, the ground was bare, the travelers' bedrolls still string-tied and packed on their grass-hobbled horses.

A temporary camp. A place to stop for a bite and a quick cup of coffee before moving on.

They too were following Reece Sinclair.

Tyner had a sudden realization. Maybe a hired gun was just what he needed to fight train robbers?

Brock was the first to see Tyner approach. When he

did, he rose in one continuous motion, like a snake uncoiling. His hand was already on the tied-down gun at his hip.

Tyner kept his hands up as the horses brought his wagon to a stop not thirty feet away.

"Evening, Brock. Or should I say, good morning?"

Brock's failure to respond sent a spider scurrying up Tyner's back, and he wondered if he should fill the space with more talk or just wait the man out. His tongue wagged inside his mouth with indecision.

It wasn't like Tyner to vacillate. He was more worn out than he'd believed.

When the gunman greeted him, Tyner savored the tiny victory.

He was still alive.

"What do you want, Tyner? You following us, old man?"

In this case, the truth was the best defense. "I've run my horses into the ground," said Tyner. "If I don't let them recuperate, they'll not be long for the world. I...uh, saw your fire from the road."

"Uh-huh."

The doubt-filled affirmative rolled off Brock's tongue as if Tyner had delivered a half-hour expository on the benefits of Widow Maven's Liver Elixir.

The gunfighter followed up with a wary invitation. "How about you come over and join us by the fire, and we'll talk?" Then he drew his side iron. "But keep your hands in the air. Fair enough?"

"Fair enough, indeed," said Tyner, trying to sound grateful. He kept his head up as he climbed down from the wagon, taking into account everything he could concerning the three men.

What they were wearing (leather chaps, flannel shirts open at the collar, slouch hats, and boots). What they smelled like (rancid bacon grease, sweat, and horseflesh). Any distinguishing marks (the curly-haired one on the left had a jagged red scar across his throat, the wind-burnt sodbuster on the right, a port-wine stained birthmark on his cheek).

These were the same men Tyner saw when Brock rode out of Syracuse, but they appeared so much more villainous in the half-light of the fire.

As if the blaze burned away their outer skins to reveal their true natures.

"Take a seat on yonder hunk of driftwood," said Brock, and Tyner obeyed.

For more than a minute, the four of them sat in silence. One of the thirsty Percherons nickered with soft impatience, and Tyner's stomach rumbled at the smell of hot coffee. He nodded toward the tin pot next to Brock's hard leather boot.

"Would you spare a cup?"

Brock picked up the pot and handed it to Curly. "Pour Mr. Tyner a shot of bug juice," he said.

"I'm obliged," said Tyner.

After Curly handed over the mug, Brock spoke again.

"Why are you following us?"

Tyner wiped his lips with the back of his sleeve. "It's not you I'm following," he said. "It's the girl and the green Concord."

"Sweet on her, aint'cha?"

"I don't know why you'd say so."

"Hell with that noise. We all seen how you made sure she won the gun off me. You might as well have given it to her on a satin pillow."

"She paid cash money for it."

Brock rubbed his chin, thoughtful like. "Well, now

there's a good point," he said. "Thanks for reminding me about the money you're carrying."

Up until now, he'd balanced his gun with the butt resting on his knee, the muzzle pointing in Tyner's general direction. Now Brock zeroed in on Tyner's bread-basket. "How's about you share some of the profit with me and the boys? Call it payment for the coffee?"

Tyner slowly drained his cup. The holstered Remingtons still hung from his belt. But no man dared slap leather against Ned Brock in the best of circumstances. And Brock already had his weapon cocked and ready.

"A thought occurs to me," said Tyner, "wherein we might be able to help one another."

"I got thoughts too. The first one is you handing over the money."

"Oh, oh, don't worry about it. I will." Tyner was momentarily surprised by his own willingness to part with the cash. "I will indeed share. But first," he put down the cup and folded his hands. "If you'd like to take in even more lucre, let me make a proposition."

So far, confident in their boss, Curly and the Sodbuster had been content to watch Tyner verbally spar. At the promise of something more than what Brock suggested, they both perked up.

"What's lucre?" said the Sodbuster.

"Fancy way of saying *loot*," said Curly. "I think maybe you oughta hear this old boy out, Ned."

The pained expression on Brock's face was the same one Tyner had seen during the auction. The thinking loom inside his head was shuttling hard, back and forth, stringing together a decision. Unfortunately, Brock wasn't much of a weaver.

Tyner pushed ahead.

"The way I see it, boys, you're going after Reece Sinclair because you'd like to fire off that Walch-Navy." He winked at the Sodbuster. "Or maybe you'd just like to fire-off?"

"I sure do think the Sinclair gal is purty," said Curly.

"Shut-up," said Brock.

"What's your idea, Tyner?" said the Sodbuster.

"I did me some talking to Miss Sinclair after the auction. Turns out she's got dispensation from the Butterfield Overland to run her Concord as a passenger wagon. Tonight, she has three men on board. These jaspers have stolen something from a ticket-holder on the St. Louis train—a wealthy gentlemen from the looks of him. If you fellows were to help me get back whatever it is the trio of robbers stole, I'm sure this gentleman would be most generous. We might even earn something from the railroad."

"You mean, there'd be a reward?" said Brock. "How much?"

"I have to imagine it would be quite a bit more than the pittance you're asking for."

"You'd give us the...uh, *pittance* now, as a down-payment on our share of the reward?"

Tyner made a show of considering it, but the conclusion was foregone.

"You'll need to split it up between yourselves," he said. "I'm not responsible for what goes on between the three of you."

If he wanted to rescue Reece Sinclair from the train robbers and secure his just desserts, he'd need help.

"But first, how about another cup of coffee?"

CHAPTER 13

SOMEBODY WAS RIDING IN TO MULHAVEN STATION, and the hoofbeats grew louder as the shadowy form closed in on Lin and Reece.

Was it Coombs, following up on the Syracuse heist? Could it be one of his men?

Or maybe it was somebody else? In the back of Lin's mind, he was still on the lookout for Baldy, Dale, and Sour-milk Verna.

Lin stepped forward, his arm in front of Reece, the rider nearly upon them. "Stay behind me," he said.

"You're kidding, right?" Her voice didn't cover the double click of her guns' hammers, and curiosity at the plurality made Lin hazard a glance.

"What the ever-lovin' God is that?"

The pistol Reece held was built with a strange extra-long cylinder, a pair of stubby triggers, and two side-by-side hammers. He'd never seen a weapon like it. "You sure you can lift such a beast?"

But then the rider was at the bottom of the Mulhaven hill, and Lin flung his gun-arm around even as Reece covered him with the big iron in her fist.

The trotting horse veered sideways as the man on

its back flung both hands toward the stars. "Whoa, hoe-there. Stop, stop, stop." The man's round-top hat fell back as he hauled in the strings on his nag. "Don't you shoot at me, you young son-of-a-bitch."

Lin jabbed his gun forward. "State your business."

"I'm with the Butterfield Overland," he said. "Division superintendent and part-time driver. Who the hell are you?"

"Tell me your name, old timer?"

"Burt Sullivan. Like I say, super-in-tendent, and you ain't answered my question."

"You ain't told me your business."

"Part time driver. I handle the route between here and Wynot's' Dairy."

"The Butterfield stage took outta here more than two hours ago. I expect the real super would know it."

Keeping his hands in the air, Burt slid off his blanket, plopping to the ground like an over-ripe apple from the tree. "Overslept," he said. "Figured on wakin' up whenever it got dark. Guess I goofed it all up."

Lin stood his ground.

"You ain't never overslept before?" Burt hocked a wad of phlegm at the road. "No, a'course not. Snot nose piss-heads like you got the entire world by the balls."

The dark horse was a scrawny devil, its ribs showing like the slats of a washboard, and the raggedy blanket thrown across its back had trailed through the mud between its staggering hooves. Burt was as thin as his mount, with a heavy coat and worn-out gloves allowing his knobby fingers to poke free.

"Where'd you come in from?" said Lin.

"Got me a claim 'bout three miles back," said Burt.

When Lin didn't answer right away, Burt took offense. "You don't believe me? Get your damn ass over there, and I'll show you. Kitty-wompass from the walnut grove. Me and the missus get by with farmin' a small patch. Got corn and some potatoes. Small grain too."

"Awful hard work," said Lin.

Burt agreed. "Hard to raise a crop in this rocky ground. Fillin' in with the stage puts an extra dollar in my pocket." He pushed back his cap and rearranged his tangled mop of white hair.

"You still ain't said who you are, snot-nose." Burt leaned over sideway to address Reece. "You too, missy. I don't cotton to you wavin' that flippin' hog-leg around."

Burt's face was a scrimshaw picture of age. A thousand dark lines, each with a backstory pressed deep in ivory flesh presented themselves to Lin. It wasn't age, but scars from a life of turmoil and abuse.

Lin felt an inadvertent sigh of relief escape his throat. He actually believed the old rascal.

Lin saddled his Colt inside its holster.

Likewise, Reece jammed her heavy artillery into the space between her belt and hipbone.

"I'm waitin' for you two to explain yourselves. Where the hell's Dooney?"

Lin told Burt his name, then introduced Reece. "We've had some trouble of our own. Lost a wheel and axle. Mike's working on it now. You good at repair work on a Concord?"

"Repair work? Hell, I used to build the damn things over in Mary's Home before they started shippin' them in from out east."

"Sounds like you're the man we need."

"I could've told you that if you weren't wastin' my time showin' off your hardware."

"My apologies, Mister Sullivan," said Reece.

"Shore could stand to wet my whistle," said Burt.

Lin nodded at Reece. "You wanna take our friend in for a drink, while I help Mike with the wheel?"

Burt shook his shaggy head. "Naw. Forget it. I'll get a sip later. If you got wagon trouble, you no doubt want to get on the road. I'll just wander down to the shed and check in on Mike." Lin followed him to where Mike was working, and Burt said, over his shoulder, "I'll catch up with the bottle later."

Then he added, "And I ain't your friend."

"I ought to go help," said Lin. "It's my wagon."

Reece cleared her throat.

"It's *our* wagon," he said.

It was true, after all.

When the opportunity with Reece came up, he hadn't been able to refuse—he was still an active Ranger, but he'd always wanted to run a stage line.

He reached for her long sleeve. "I just hope Mike can get the damn thing roadworthy again."

"If not, it sounds like our new friend can build you a new one by morning."

"In his dreams."

Reece put her hand on top of his, holding it against her arm. "We haven't seen each other for three weeks. We need to catch up."

"I don't s'pect they'll miss me for a few more minutes."

He took Reece into his arms and kissed her.

"Other than your misadventure in Stringtown, how was the trip up from Texas?" she said. "Are you and Micah getting along?"

"He's a good man," said Lin.

"He is," agreed Reece. Then her voice took on a whispered hush. "It must be so hard for him."

In the dead of night, Micah had escaped the Texas

rancher who held him in slavery to seek out Reece Sinclair's Rancho de Jada, a haven for runaways seeking refuge in Mexico. Instead of sanctuary, he found Lin and Reece in the middle of her Cortinista war.

The three of them came through the fire. Together, they forged a new unit. With the Concord wagon, they found a new mission.

"Just about everybody who ever knew Micah thinks he's dead," said Lin. "In some ways, I envy him. It's not often a man gets to make a fresh start, and for Micah, it comes with freedom."

"You're saying it's not difficult?"

"I'm saying it's better than it was. And he's got a new life now with the Hellbenders. A new family. I'm proud to call him a brother."

"Me too."

"And there's this gal down in Emberville waiting for him."

"Sylvia."

"Hope it works out for them."

They held each other in the moonlight, letting the turmoil of the day wash away. Lin felt his body relax and nearly sagged to the ground.

Gads, he was tired.

"I'm thinking about the satchel," said Reece. "Shares in a gold mining company are not what we hoped for."

"Gonna be hard for Emberville to trade stock shares for the basic essentials they need."

"It would be better if we could find somebody willing to exchange them for cash money."

"Oh, is that all?" he laughed.

"Any ideas?"

"Not a one," he said. "We've still got a lot of road to travel between here and there. Fort Smith, Lambert's

Ferry. We haven't even crossed the Osage yet, and I hear the river is up."

"A chance to wash off the road dust."

With a quick peck on her cheek, Lin turned from Reece to join Mike and Burt at the coach. "See if Mrs. Dooney will pack us a little extra food for the road?"

Behind the house, Lin was pleased to the see the coach back on all four wheels as Burt watched Dooney tighten the lug. He'd procured a silver flask from somewhere and was sipping with contentment as he worked.

"Don't turn it too tight. You'll shear the damn thing off."

Dooney offered Lin an apologetic shrug. "I'm being careful. I get a little too enthused sometimes."

Lin squeezed Dooney's shoulder and walked around the rear of the coach.

The round-belly Concord had set Reece Sinclair's father back $1000 when he purchased the thing on a lark a year before. Since uncovering it in a sheep herder's line shack and blowing off the dust, Lin and Reece had dropped a second sizable chunk of cash into getting it ready to run.

Lin had made some modifications of his own to the original New Hampshire model. New leather thoroughbraces had cost more than $10 a piece, and a voluminous back flap, the rear boot, set them back twice as much.

The Sinclairs already had the tack necessary for the four pulling horses, but Lin insisted on a new whippletree, new hounds, and a strong pole.

Lin ran his hand along the painted enamel side panels and brass door fittings.

Reece had the rear boot and top of the coach stocked with bed rolls and warbags with a change of clothes for each of them. She'd packed coffee, hardtack, and salt pork, but Lin hoped Dooney's wife would sell him a few cans of peaches. Dooney had tied a half-dozen oak trekking poles to the roof, and Lin knew they would need those to help cross the Osage.

"If you think she's sound, we'll soon enough be out of your hair, Mike."

Dooney wiped the grease from his hands onto a rag. "She's sound, but don't push her anymore. Far as I know, we're the only station on the line before Springfield with tools and supplies to properly mend things."

Answering Lin's dubious expression, Mike continued.

"Been some trouble with bandits." When he lowered his voice, Lin leaned close to hear. "I don't have to tell you this whole country's fallen to shit. Everybody's angry about everything nearly all the time, and there's constant talk of uprisings. Ain't like the old days. Tools, food, whatever you've got, goes missing soon as somebody gets wind of it."

"Winds of change," said Lin. "Got everybody in a dust-up."

"It's hard times coming, these next few years, you mark my words."

"What do we owe you?" said Lin.

Mike told him, and Lin paid the tab with a sack from the rear boot. "Here's enough more to cover some canned peaches and eggs."

The two men shook hands. "I only wish you were coming along to drive," said Lin.

"What'd you say, son?"

"Said I could wish for a driver. Each station, the Butterfield gets a new driver and new set of horses. Mike's got some fresh animals for us, but looks like it's up to me to push ahead to the river."

"You ever crossed the Osage before?" Burt drank from his flask.

"Twice before, yes."

"How full was she? Runnin' water? Strong current? Or did you cross durin' our last drought when you could hop from gravel bar to gravel bar."

Lin had to admit the way had been fairly dry.

"Ain't dry now," said Burt. "She's a real live river out there today. It'll be sunup 'fore you get there. You're lucky you ain't doin' it in the dark," said Burt. "Bad enough in daylight. Three, four hours, dependin' on what kind of time you can make, but if you get there before dawn, you wait to cross." Burt nodded at the trekking poles on the coach. "Good you got some sticks along. You'll need 'em."

Mike nodded. "You listen close to this old buzzard, Lin. He's forded the river dozens of times."

"Don't cross directly at the trail's end," said Burt. "Too narrow. Go upstream about 100 feet. It's wider there and not as deep. Current's not as fast."

"Will do," said Lin.

"And you're gonna want to cross at angle. Head downstream, but face upstream, leanin' into the current, steppin' at an angle. Of course, if you're leadin' the team across, you'll have to play with them critters."

"You ought to ride along with them, Burt," said Mike. "Share your expertise."

"I don't think so."

"Why not? You missed the Overland coach anyway," said Mike.

Lin stifled a yawn. "I like the idea, Burt. How much will you take to drive for us?"

"Won't take a goddamn penny."

For a minute, Lin mistook the old timer's reluctance for generosity. "I'll pay you twice what the BO would've."

Burt's frown turned the valleys of his face into dark, craggy canyons. "It ain't about the money."

"Then what?" said Lin.

The old man turned his head ever so slightly, let his eyes shift just enough toward the front walk of the station house. There in the doorway, walking out ahead of Griff and Reece was Micah LeMay.

Burt looked back at Lin. His voice was flat and dripping with scorn. "I don't ride with his kind."

There it was.

The too common prejudice ripping the soul of the nation in two.

Living and working in Texas, a slave state, Lin had encountered racial discrimination more often than not. It was a continual background irritant, like mosquitos on a summer evening, or a constant, biting cold wind in the winter. Narrow-minded idiots had always been a fact of life, and Lin hadn't really questioned them.

He didn't share their beliefs, but he'd learned to exist alongside them and go his own way.

Now, since working with Reece and Micah, his threshold for intolerance was practically non-existent. He couldn't stifle the frustration in his voice.

"You'd turn down three-day's pay because of a man's skin color?"

Burt answered immediately.

"I'd turn down three, yep." Then he narrowed his eyes, took a drink from his flask. "Guess I'd take six, though."

Lin felt the knot in his stomach tighten. It was all he could do to hold his anger in check.

If he weren't so damned tired.

Reece and Micah were exhausted, too, and Griff would sure enough get them all drowned.

"You'll drive us to the Osage, help us to the other side, and on to the next station for double the pay?"

"Ay-yuh, guess I would." Burt sipped at his flask like a rat sucking down your last egg.

Lin felt the tension build up in his temples. Tasted the bitter scratchiness of his throat.

He realized he still needed to eat.

"It's a deal," he said, but when Burt held out his hand to shake, Lin ignored it.

"Work with the others to hook up the team. I'm going to get some supper."

"I'll work with the bearded man. I ain't workin' with no woman, nor the other one. You understand me?"

Lin stalked toward the house, irritated and suddenly ravishingly hungry.

He understood too well.

Maybe the old man would drown while crossing the river.

It wasn't a bad thought.

CHAPTER 14

FLOOD TYNER DID HIS BEST TO SLOW THE Percherons' descent into Mulhaven station. Whatever imbecile had determined the bottom of the steep hill was an opportune place for a stopover was either the sorriest road grader alive or a man who liked a joke. Either way, gravity had the last laugh, and Tyner slid the wagon and horses in like a folding jack-knife as the first light of morning grayed the eastern tree line.

He dropped from the bench seat and walked along the side of the wagon on wobbling legs, cursing himself for a novice. He should've remembered the incline from his last visit less than a year before when he'd first carried in a load of black powder for the Overland stage.

At the wagon's rear hatch, Tyner flipped a wood latch and Ned Brock's men tumbled out. First came Curly, followed by the Sodbuster. Finally, Brock himself stumbled out the door. "Awful rough ride," he said with a whine of annoyance.

The smell of cooked eggs and fried pork sausage filled the air.

"Breakfast is on me," said Tyner. In his experience, stage-line meals ran fifty cents to a dollar. He dropped five dollars' worth of coins in Brock's open palm. "You're welcome to eat your fill."

Brock's smile was almost as wide as Carly's head of hair was long. "You're a better man than I figured, Tyner," he said. "C'mon boys." The two lackeys fell into lockstep behind their boss as he marched toward the front door of Dooney's place.

Tyner shook his head. Brock was a strong man with a gun, but money made him weak.

Tyner took a thorough survey of the station.

Tyner's Gun Service and Sales was the only conveyance at Mulhaven, but a holding pen in back of the station house contained a tight bunch of mares. A young man, maybe 15 or 16, was pitching hay into the pen.

Mike Dooney's oldest boy. Tyner tried to recall his name.

Kevin.

Tyner picked out four familiar chestnut mares with ease. Reece Sinclair's horses.

So the green Concord had been here, swapped teams, and moved on to the Osage.

Tyner wondered if she'd taken on a new driver. Or left anybody behind.

The good thing about Mulhaven was its hostess was a gossip. Louise Dooney would answer his every question about her recent guests. Better yet, she'd answer some questions he wouldn't even think to ask.

But first things first.

Fingering a few more gold coins, he called out to the boy, who came running. "Tend my horses, won't you, son?" He flicked the currency through the air. "I'll need a couple replacements if you've got any to trade."

"Other than a couple old broomtails, we don't have any fresh horses right now, Mister," said Kevin. "Two coaches came through in the night and wiped us clean."

Tyner nodded to himself. "One was the Butterfield and Overland," he said. "Was the other a green Concord?"

Kevin said it was.

Tyner was right about Reece Sinclair.

"Tell me about the broomtails," he said. "Maybe I can use them."

"One of 'em is a neighbor's old swayback. I've also got a couple gouch-eared mules available. They ain't much, but they're younger than the swayback."

"Would the mules pull my wagon across the Osage?"

Tyner could tell the boy appreciated the consultation. The query made him feel like an adult.

Kevin poked out his lower lip, stretched his neck to look past Tyner's shoulder at the wagon, then nodded just a little bit too quick. "I reckon they'd get you to the other side. The next station after is Wynot Dairy, five miles on. You'll be pushin' 'em hard to make it. I'd be sure and let them rest after the river crossin'."

"I'll take them," said Tyner, "with plans to return for my Percherons in a week or so."

The deal was adequate as far as Kevin was concerned. "I'll double check with my pa before hitchin' up the mules," he said.

"That'll be fine."

"Y'all need breakfast, Ma's got it cookin' inside." Again, Tyner savored the scrumptious smells.

"She's fryin' up a passel of doughnuts this mornin'," said Kevin. "Maybe you'll want to take a sack along for the ride," said Kevin.

"Maybe so," said Tyner, feet following his nose.

But before he made three more steps, a bustle of hooves clattered down the hill behind him, and he spun around.

Tyner liked to think of himself as unshakable—a man of the world whose business acumen and financial wherewithal kept his nerves at bay. As one of such skill, nothing rattled him. Nothing took him completely by surprise.

Until now.

The erect figure of a one-armed blond man in suit-coat astride a wild-eyed roan and the lusty howls of the rough quartet behind him, set something to fluttering just south of Tyner's gizzard.

All the riders were dressed like the blond man who Tyner recognized as the victim in the Syracuse train robbery. As the dour horseman swarmed his wagon, Tyner was more than nervous.

Actually, he was afraid.

The blond had a dark malevolence about him, affecting everyone in his radius. Tyner could see it as Kevin stood frozen, waiting for the tall man to descend from his mount like some kind of barbarian king.

"Is this Mulhaven?" said the man with a curt, German accent.

"Uh...y-yes it is," said Kevin.

"Have you serviced a green Concord carrying a girl and three men?"

Once more Kevin stuttered, "Y-yeah."

"I see."

"Can we help you, sir?"

"My name is Coombs." His high forehead reflecting the pink glow of dawn, the blond seemed to notice the red gun service wagon for the first time. From the legend on the side, the German's black gaze traveled in an uninterrupted arc around the station yard to finally intercept Tyner.

The grimace of recognition was like a grip of ice.

"Tell the matron she'll have five more at table," said Coombs, jerking up and out of his polished ebony saddle. "We'll stay for breakfast."

Kevin pivoted around and took the news inside while the newcomers dismounted. The men were all dressed alike, which is to say, identical to Coombs with gray jackets, single-breasted vests, pressed trousers, polished boots, and flat-crowned wideawake caps. They dressed like bankers.

Except each man carried a big 1847 Colt Walker on his hip.

"Flood Tyner, isn't it?" said Coombs, scratching a cleft chin with his wooden appendage.

Tyner took pride in keeping his voice low and even. "I don't believe I've had the pleasure of making your acquaintance, sir."

"You men, go on inside," Coombs told the others. "Find out what you can about Griffin Kale and his companions." Lips pressed into a determined smirk the German returned his attention to Tyner. "As I told the boy, my name is Coombs. I'm on the trail of some stolen property."

Stolen property, thought Tyner. The words made his guts dive low and swim in circles.

Even with Remington pistols on both hips, Tyner felt naked and vulnerable next to Coombs. The German towered over him.

"The property I speak of was taken from me aboard the St. Louis train in Syracuse. My men pursued the blackguards." Then Coombs let his tongue run along his lower lip.

Not unlike a snake.

"I saw you drive your gun wagon in front of my men, hampering their pursuit. I asked around regarding your identity."

"I assure you, my interference wasn't deliberate," said Tyner, lying. "A bumbling accident."

"I don't recognize accidents in my business, Tyner. Nor do we accommodate bumblers."

Tyner swallowed hard. There went his stomach again. If things went any further south, he'd need a fresh pair of pants.

"What exactly is your business, Mister-ah...Coombs?"

"Sedition, Mister Tyner." The German's voice had an edge like a barber's hot razor.

When Tyner didn't react to the comment, Coombs seemed disappointed.

"Me, I'm a simple drummer," said Tyner. Even as he said it, he felt foolish, "A gunsmith by trade. You have nothing to fear from me."

Coombs' top lip curled.

"Another thing we don't recognize is *fear*," said Coombs. He prodded Tyner with the false hand, moving him to one side. "We'll refresh our horses and continue on. I trust this time you will stay out of our way."

Tyner scraped a dry tongue against the dusty roof of his mouth. "I'll certainly do my damndest," he said.

————

"MAKE WITH THE POTATOES, SISTER," said Curly.

Brock, at table: "Bring the hot pot along."

Coombs, standing impatient beside the front door: "You will fill our flasks, first."

With both ovens fired up and the Dooney family

falling all over one another to deliver coffee to Coombs' men and plates of food to Brock, Curly, and the Sodbuster, the interior of Mulhaven station was nearly too much for Tyner.

It was a symphony of clanging cutlery and wet mastication. The steady background sizzle of fried meat from the kitchen, the percussion of boiling, bubbling water, the vocalized clearing of throats and murmurs of table talk.

Tyner counted nine guests, including himself.

Coombs' men were reluctant to sit, though a few of them finally took a bench. The German remained standing, tapping a wooden finger against his chin.

Of the four men in suit coats, three of them shoved eggs and burnt toast into their mouths, while one standing next to his boss abstained. The staid German made five.

Brock and his voracious men added three more.

Tyner was number nine, and his guts were too churned up to eat.

The place was full of devils.

Kevin's little sister hefted a two-gallon tin coffee pot into her brother's arms, and he set about filling orders while Louise bustled around the front room between the men, servicing both sides of the long table at once, filling cups and flasks with coffee and warm beer, juggling platters filled with fried eggs and sausage links.

At the back of the cramped front room, Tyner sat alone on a short stool, cradling a tepid tin cup in his lap between two hands, sea-sick on the ocean of activity.

Even as Tyner counted the men one more time, the station's front door cracked open and three more jackalopes pushed into the noisy room, skirting Coombs' impatient figure.

"'Scuse," said the lead man, a heavy-set hombre with a flannel shirt, ripped pants, and a droopy old campaign hat. Behind him, a short bald man and a buxom blonde followed. The blonde smiled at Coombs, but the German sniffed and flinched away, as if struck by a bad smell.

Only a few men noticed the newcomers, and the raucous cacophony of consumption continued. There were more calls for drink, orders for eggs, bacon, sausage, and toast.

Somebody dropped a cup, and the Sodbuster turned over a jar of mulberry preserves with a thick crash of broken crockery.

Tyner watched Baldy and his friends squeeze past a suit-coat and take the last open place in the station, a barren table with only two chairs. The woman and the bigger man sat down. Baldy picked up a fork and started banging on a tin plate.

Bang, bang, bang.

"I'll be with you in a minute," said Louise Dooney, hustling past with a stack of vittles.

"Could I have everybody's attention?" said Baldy. "Everybody?"

Most of the crowd ignored the little man's voice, but Tyner smiled at his persistence. After consulting his friends, he again drummed the tin plate, but this time, the heavy man did the shouting.

"We're looking for a green Concord wagon," he said. "A woman named Sinclair might be driving it, and one of the men aboard is a Texas ranger name of Lin Jarret."

Brock set his cup down and found Tyner's eyes across the room.

The gun drummer came to attention. *Texas Ranger?*

The German stopped tapping his finger.

Louise Dooney spun around on her heel.

The room was immediately silent as a tomb.

Baldy's grin was self-conscious, and his voice faltered under a dozen sets of flaring eyes.

"M-maybe you've heard of them?" he said.

CHAPTER 15

SEVEN MILES OUT OF MULHAVEN, THE OPEN ROAD had narrowed to little more than a cow trail through the dense hardwood forest and weedy rock-strewn hills. In skinny straights between impenetrable stands of elm and shag-bark hickory, Lin wondered how the heavier Butterfield Overland coach could have possibly made its way through, only to watch from his shotgunner's perch as his own coach squeaked through the gaps.

"Hard to believe how much these woods grow up in a short time," said Lin.

"Yes, it is," said Burt.

"Last time I was on this road it was daylight."

"Good thing we're outta the fog," said Burt, sitting next to him on the spring bench, the reins loose in his callused paws. "You don't wanna ford this river in a fog."

Or if it's snowing.

Or blistering hot.

Or with a herd of cows.

During the past few hours, Lin had heard more warnings and remonstrations than a boy in short pants heard from his Sunday school marm.

If Burt didn't have an even ten commandments, he wasn't far off.

Once full of water, there didn't seem to be any way alive to cross the wide Osage River.

"Yet, the Overland stage manages the miraculous and crosses here at Meadow's Ford twice a month," said Lin. "Once on its way to California, and once coming back."

"Do you have any idea how many coaches them burrhead drivers have lost for us?" said Burt.

"None I've heard of," said Lin.

"'Course you never heard," said Burt. "You don't think they'd let word of somethin' like that get out? What kind of ignoramus are you, anyhow? Oh, wait—I already know the answer to that."

Lin clutched Micah's scattergun between two hands and buttoned his lip.

With the rancid hash Burt's mouth was slinging, Lin wondered if the old man would even make it to the river before Lin gave up and bashed his brains in.

When they topped the last hill before the river valley, the pink globe of the sun was just peeking over the horizon beneath an onrushing plane of heavy clouds.

Red sun at morning...

The scurrilous sky promised a long day ahead.

A day made longer every second Burt Sullivan rode with them.

Once they crossed the Osage, Wynot's Dairy was only a few miles off, maybe then they could be rid of him.

After would come Plummer's, then Wicker Station. Surely, they'd find a new driver at one of the stops before arriving in Springfield near midnight.

"Another thing you never do, never reach for a

floatin' stick or branch on the Osage. Fella I know did so once and damned if the thing wasn't a cottonmouth snake. You shoulda' seen the ol' boy's arm. Blew up the size of a watermelon."

Lin thought about the boy from his childhood. "I've seen it firsthand."

"Not like this you ain't," said Burt.

Of course not.

"Looks like we're gonna get some rain on top of it," said Burt. He made a show of breathing in the dawn air with a loud sniff. "Stinks of storm drainage, don't it?"

The Ozark foothills weren't the only thing stinking.

What Lin wouldn't give to trade places with Reece, Micah, or Griffin Kale.

Let them sit up here and smell the windbag's fetid breath while Lin slept in the passenger cabin behind.

As if sensing Lin's thoughts, Burt told him:

"Best stop here and wake up your friends. We got to be ready to make the ford. You don't wanna cross the river in the rain."

Before Lin could agree, Burt leaned down and started to pound his leather braided quirt on left side panel of the coach. "Pull up your pants and get ready to dance," he called over his shoulder. "Ain't none of us gonna stay dry."

With a loud hoot, he cast his long whip into the air above the new team of dun-colored horses, and they charged the last half mile through the trees. The winding silver ribbon of the Osage twinkled in the first of the morning's sun.

Before long, the road opened into a wide-open park dappled with the sooty evidence of old campfires and trampled grass. Burt brought the horses to an abrupt stop and pulled back the coach's brake lever.

In spite of his disdain for Burt, Lin felt sudden

apprehension at the sight of the wide river. When he made the run before with Reece, the Osage had been a benevolent source of water. A partner to the traveler, a friend to the daring wilderness adventurer.

In Lin's limited experience, it had never been more than a few inches deep. Now gallon upon gallon of water rushed headlong down the channel, carrying branches, sticks, and entire trees.

Disheveled, but still in one piece, the cabin's three passengers disembarked at river's edge to grumbles of thunder and skeins of lightning.

First came Reece, knuckling the sleep from her eyes before fixing her braid.

Then Micah stretched his arms above his head, threatening to split the taut fabric of his bib shirt. Lin had known strong men before, but nobody as powerful as Micah LeMay.

Seemingly the opposite in manly character. Griff jammed a balled-up fist into the side of his own hip. "I don't know what's worse," he said. "My aching muscles or my sour stomach."

"Gripe and moan," said Lin.

Reece explained the situation. "Before falling asleep, these two ate all the doughnuts we brought from Mulhaven."

"Louise Dooney is some kind of cook," said Micah. "I enjoyed every sugar glazed morsel."

Griff groaned again and stumbled off through the bluestem to disappear behind a row of mulberry trees.

"He gonna be able to make it?" said Lin.

Micah waved away the question. "Bumpy ride. He's not as bad as he makes out."

"He looked a little...ah, green," said Lin.

"Not as green as those clouds," said Reece.

"Hailstorm," said Burt, standing up to retrieve

the long wooden poles fixed to the top of the coach. He traced the long wisps of turquoise falling from clouds bruised indigo and black. "I'd say the storm's four miles away. Maybe five. We've got our work cut out for us now, and there's to be no slackin' off."

"You act like you've got a plan, Mister Sullivan," said Reece.

"Hell, yeah, I've got a plan. On the Meadow's Ford across the Osage, you better have a plan. You don't have a plan, you won't make it."

While he untied the twine strings, he outlined his strategy.

"Jarret, you take the right lead, next to the front horse by her collar. Get'cha one of these poles." He handed one down and Lin caught it. "Hold on to it with one hand and the mare with the other. Grab her by the nose band if you have to in order to help guide her."

"She won't like it," said Lin.

"She won't like it at all, but you show her you mean it. Grab the side check if you need. I'll take the other side," said Burt.

"What about us?" said Micah.

Burt ignored him, answering the question as if Griff had asked, addressing the Englishman alone. "You guide the rear horse, behind Jarret. Same thing, only instead of the nose, hang on to the trace. Better balance that way."

Perched on the wagon seat, Burt scraped a hunk of wax from his ear and wiped it on his pants. "The missy stays inside the coach."

Lin stepped in. "Micah will take the lead opposite me. Burt, you stay in the rear with Griff."

"Don't go tellin' me my business."

"You heard me," said Lin, grabbing the lead mare's collar to gently walk her forward. "C'mon, Micah."

Micah moved to the front of the team without a word and took control of the other lead horse. Lin tossed him his pole, then turned to Burt. "Need a second pole here, old timer."

Burt hurled the wood down at Lin from atop the wagon with a scowl. Lin caught the pole in mid-air. "Thanks," he said.

Griff took up his position, holding the trace behind Lin, leaving the opposite space, behind Micah open.

Burt climbed down. As soon as his sloppy worn boots hit the grass, Reece clambered to the driver's bench and sat down.

"You'll do better to ride inside like I told you," Burt told her.

"I'll stay as far from the water as possible, thank you."

"Humph," grumped the old man. "Suit your own self, girlie."

"Get into position, Burt," said Lin.

Burt argued. "As driver of this outfit, I think I ought to take a lead position. I know the river. You're gonna need the man knows the river when the storm hits."

As if to emphasize his declaration, the clouds pounded out a dramatic beat.

Lin dismissed them both. "As co-owner of this outfit, and the one paying you, I'm telling you to take the position that's open."

Burt cast a sullen expression at the spot behind Micah and reluctantly shuffled in next to the second horse on the left where he gripped the animal's leather loin strap.

Carefully, and with Lin's soft coaxing, the rig moved ahead.

On the muddy, slick banks of the river, Lin expected the horses to balk, but Micah's sure hand and his own unyielding demand pushed them forward. The water was murky and olive brown at the end of the trail and smattering of pale orange oak leaves floated across the surface of the edge waters like pond scum.

Wheel ruts showed from the passage of the mail coach less than a few hours before.

Lin thrust his pole into the river ahead. The tip met bedrock with a reassuring thump.

The first dollops of rain hit the river and ripples spread out in concentric circles.

Out toward the river's center, the more prevailing current was swift, but not nearly as fast as Lin imagined. Here the course was even slower, a foamy drift splashed by sprinkles, washing gently to the east.

When the horses stepped out, the water was cannon-high, half-way to the knee. The Concord rolled ahead, smooth and unobstructed.

"The way here is solid limestone rock," said Burt. "Slippery, but passable if you keep to the ford. Cast your poles ahead at a slight angle, probe the depth. Remember I said to angle slightly downstream but face up. The ford ain't a straight line. We're headed for them sycamores across the way."

Over the expanse of running water, on the far bank, Lin saw a pair of bone-white trees, their twisted limbs twirling high with fresh sprigs of foliage. The ground between them was dark and devoid of grass. The Butterfield Overland trail winding its way on to Wynot's dairy.

Lin told his horse, "Aim for the space between the trees, Meg," and let his weight pull against her.

Micah's horse was a tad more reluctant to move, but together the men kept the two leaders walking.

For twenty paces, the water stayed at their knees, flowing at a leisurely pace as pillars of clouds bunched in the sky above and spit steady drizzle.

"At this rate, we'll have time to dry off and enjoy an early lunch at Wynot, maybe make it to Plummer's before dark," said Lin. He called over his shoulder "How's the sky-view, darlin'?"

"You're drifting too far left with the current," said Reece.

"I'm on it," said Micah.

"Keep proddin', boy," growled Burt. "Chuck holes and river trash will trip us up faster'n a slick pig."

Griff stumbled, went down on one knee, but caught himself on his steed's harness.

"Don't get lost under the hooves, son," said Burt. "Damn critters can be calm one second and skeered bald-headed the next."

"I'll...remember it."

"You okay, Griff?" said Reece.

Griff told her he was, and Lin mocked her under his breath. "You alright, Griffy-poo?"

But Micah overheard him, and the big man flashed a wide smile. "You gonna be sorry I shot that hanging rope," he said.

"I'm already sorry," said Lin.

"Hell, Ranger, I wasn't talking about Griff. I was talking about you."

"Hell, Micah," said Lin. "I was talking about me too. I'm better off feeding the buzzards than listening to sweet talk."

Micah's laugh was contagious, sweeping away Lin's aggravation.

"Let's get this team across," he suggested, "and I'll take you out of your misery."

"Always good to have some incentive."

In the morning breeze, the river was a living, moving satin plain. Like an unleashed bolt of gray blue material rolling along a quarter-mile wide channel between pollen-thick springtime forests, the Osage was full of potential.

For good and ill.

They were halfway across the river when a burst of wind tossed a wave into Lin's face and the air was filled with spatterings of heavy rain, like pellets of glass, cold as ice.

Lin's lead horse made a misstep and tipped sideways.

A gale shook the Concord and one corner flap of the rear boot slipped free, fluttering like a stuck bird.

With a flurry of splashing high-steps, Lin jerked his horse back around to the fore, but his boot slipped on the bedrock and buckled under his weight.

Lin fell like a pole-axed side of beef.

In going under, his stick swung back up to pop against his mare's flank. Rearing up, she lurched down-stream, forcing the other three horses away from the underwater rock-way.

With slashing bolts of lightning, the storm cut loose.

Desperate to roll clear of Meg's thrashing hooves, Lin crashed into a furious deep current. Lungs explod-ing, he fought against the torrent to rise up and catch ahold of the frenzied team before they dragged the coach too far off-course.

Between the rush in his ears and the peals of panicked steeds, Lin heard Burt cuss the other men, "Hold them animals, dammit."

Hands clutching for horseflesh or leather, which-ever came first, Lin found little security in the churn-ing, soft mud of the river bottom. The deluge threatened to dunk him again, and the crazed look in his steed's eye had him on the defensive. Chest-high in water, legs furiously spinning for purchase, Lin could do nothing but struggle to hold a slippery, twisting harness once he caught it.

Saving the coach and team of horses was up to the other three men, and Lin had no idea how Micah, Griff, or Burt fared against the turbulence.

Water cresting over the hubs and climbing, the coach floundered, turned into the direction of the stream, and pulled Burt Sullivan under.

The old man screamed, caught between the pounding hooves of his horse.

There was nothing Lin Jarret could do but watch him die.

CHAPTER 16

An eternity of seemed to pass before Lin found his way out of the maelstrom and once more had a firm hold on the team's lead mare. Striving against the exhaustion of his limbs and coughing on sour river bile, he pulled himself around to the opposite side of the coach where Micah labored alone against the wind and rain.

His voice was loud above the churning water, "Stop fighting, blast you," and Lin first thought the command was directed at him.

Then he saw Micah's right arm submerged deep in the river while his left fist still clutched the throat latch of his mare. He fought to tame a crashing whirlpool between the lead horse and its follower, seemed to be losing the battle. "Stop fighting, I said."

Entangled in the reins, and trapped underwater, Burt Sullivan thrashed at the river's surface between a frantic mashing of hooves. His only lifeline was Micah's strong arm, his only chance at survival was the grip pulling him free.

But Burt struggled against it.

He rolled and bounced up, he spat and jerked away.

His face momentarily rose above the surface of the river. "Leggo, you sumbitch...ain't about...to be saved... by no black man."

Lin struggled between pitching in to help Burt get free or kicking the old bastard back under.

"Lin, grab his shirt collar. I got the reins." Micah was more committed to benevolence.

Or so Lin thought.

When Micah reached for his belt and withdrew his big fixed-blade knife, he wasn't so sure. Clutching the nickel-plated handle of his blade, Micah tore into the tangle of reins, rending the leather without a care.

His only goal, to free the man who despised him.

A fresh volley of thunder rolled across the sky, scaring the second horse.

Lin shouldered into the skittish mare's ribs, reaching down to yank Burt up and clear of the team.

While Lin and Micah worked to get the old man free, Griff secured their position on the other side as best he could. More than the other two, the Englishman had a good foothold facing upstream.

But as veins popped from his forehead, and he bared his teeth in agony against the weather, the strain was showing.

He was slipping.

Before Lin could object to her actions, Reece tumbled down from the wagon into the fray, anchoring herself to the river bottom beside Griff, holding to the horses' tack, adding her strength to the fight.

The effort paid off, allowing Micah an extra few seconds to cut the reins and set Burt free.

Lin hauled the old man out of the water with both arms, and when he did, the horses righted themselves back in the direction they needed to go.

Soaked to the bone, battered, and bruised, nobody

said a word as they trudged back onto the limestone ford. Again, assuming their positions, and with Reece helping Burt shove along, they dragged themselves inch by inch through the rowdy river storm until they made the far shore.

Between the two sycamore trees, the four Megs stopped and shook themselves free of excess water. Lin propped himself up on a short plum tree next to Burt while Micah led the team toward an open orchard less than forty feet away.

Once the animals were situated, he rejoined the others.

The rain fell away in curtains traveling down the river, descending beneath the cloud bank's swirling theatrics. Lin couldn't help but think they should've stayed on the opposite shore and waited the storm out.

He almost wondered if Burt hadn't delivered them into the fray on purpose. But then he recalled the old man's battered form and thought better of it. No man would take such a stupid risk on purpose.

Like the rest of them, he simply assumed they could beat the storm. And if there's a storm, it's always good to be on the right side of the river.

Clear of the coach, Lin's eyes immediately found Reece, half-drowned, but slender and beautiful, radiant for having survived the crossing.

"We made it," he said.

"We did." She nodded.

Griff slumped against one of the sycamores, mopping hair from his eyes as he gazed across the gray expanse of water. "Let's not do that again any time soon," he said.

"You...young idiots...lucky I was along," said Burt. He took two steps out into the open space between the two trees and shook his fist at each of them in turn. "If you think you're gonna make me feel guilty, like I owe you something..."

Lin shook his head. "You old fool," he began.

Reece said, "What in heaven's name are you even talking about, Mister Sullivan?"

Burt's lower lip poked out and he raised both arms in petulant anger. "I told you to leave me. Told you I didn't need no help."

"I wouldn't leave a blood-leech to the river," said Lin. "You want to kill yourself, you'll have to find a different way."

"It ain't about killin' myself. It's about bein' beholden to *him*." Burt swung his head in Micah's direction.

"You'd prefer Micah let you drown?" said Reece.

"I'd prefer to be saved by one of my own kind."

"Go to hell, Sullivan," said Lin.

"You drove us to the river," said Reece. "I think we can take the ribbons from here."

"You'd leave me here?" said Burt. "I almost died gettin' you across and you'd abandon me?"

"You can walk to Wynot's dairy. It's not so far," said Lin. "How does that sound to you, Micah?"

Cool, stoic, the target of Burt's hate had stayed quiet until Lin's query. Now he grinned and gave his friend a nod. "Sounds fine to me."

"That's how it's goin' to be, eh? Leave an old man to die on the trail?" Burt stepped into the space between the sycamore trees and shook his finger. "Just you remember one thing. If anybody asks, I ain't got a good word for any of you. If anybody asks, I ain't about to say I'm beholden to one of them damned—"

Before Burt could finish his vile tirade, Lin was astonished to see a red blossom grow from the old man's sternum just below his collar bones.

Then he heard the echo of a powder-driven boom.

Burt's head flew backwards, and the old man crumpled into a heap, his life blood draining with huge gouts from the hole in his chest.

Griff dived for cover as another loud report crashed across the surface of the Osage.

Lin took two steps and jumped, wrapping both arms around Reece Sinclair's waist as a third shot whistled between the trees, thumping into the wet earth, digging up a divot of crumbling clay.

They landed together in a patch of bluegrass, lucky to be alive.

Micah reported what he saw. "Four riflemen lined up on the far shore."

Another volley tore through the camp, slicing the bark off a walnut tree and knocking down a few early maple leaves.

"We need to move on away from here," said Lin. "As long as we stay here, they can take shots at us all day."

"I can barely move," said Griff.

"You're doing better than Burt."

"I'll grant you," Griff agreed.

"There's a curve in the trail ahead. We get beyond it, they won't be able to see us. We'll be out of range, and they'll have to cross the river before they can come after us."

"It won't take them as long to cross as it took us," said Reece. "We'll need to keep rolling in order to stay ahead of them."

"How far to the next station?" said Griff.

"Wynot's dairy," said Lin. "Couple miles up the road."

"Let's be off then, shall we?"

He bent over and grasped Burt's body under both

arms. "Help me get him to the wagon."

Under the barrage of four more explosions, they made it up the trail and around the curve into the woods.

———

HARDWOOD TREES and cedar saplings sprouted from a floor of wet leaves and underbrush on both sides of the Butterfield Overland trail while rotted logs dotted with white fungus and green moss lined the first clearing after the bend of the river. Rising up perpendicular to the trail, a twenty-foot-tall sheer wall of limestone and granite dominated the immediate horizon.

The road dipped into a low creek branch at the base of the cliff and spiraled back out, around a sharp grade with mossy rock walls pitched high on at the curves. Under the shady cover of oak boughs and hackberry, Lin drove the team of mares hard as he could without risking injury to animal, wagon, or the three passengers he carried—which is to say, they covered hardly any ground.

Switchback after switchback forced them up out of the river valley to a highland prairie where they could make like spring deer for the next station. But slogging up the incline was taxing the horses and tearing up Lin's nerves. Each ten yards was worth a quart jar's worth of sweat, and every ounce of his concentration stayed on the reins.

Finally, he had to ask Micah, "Build me a smoke, will you?"

Beside him on the bench with his feet propped next to Lin's on the coach rail, Micah put his shotgun between his knees and pulled the makings from Lin's shirt pocket. Once he had the paper rolled, he scratched a lucifer on the side of his boot and lit up. Handed the cigarette to Lin.

Burt's lifeless cadaver rode along behind them on the roof of the coach.

"Thank you."

"You think we're gonna make it?"

Lin mumbled around the burning leaf. "Wh'tcha mean?"

"To Emberville with the money?"

"Heh," Lin coughed. "I'm not too worried about Texas. Gotta stay alive long enough to get to Wynot first."

"I ever tell you about Sylvia?"

"Not a lot. You said you met her soon after you left the farm in north Texas."

"I heard about Emberville. Lots of us did. We knew it was a place to go."

"You stopped there on your way south, before we met?"

Micah nodded. "Sylvia helped me. Got me food, water for my horse. She's a tough gal."

"You're worried about her."

"Last letter she sent to Rancho Sinclair...things didn't sound so good. They're running out of everything—from grain flour to lye soap. Add to it, folks around the Red River are less friendly than they used to be. More folks than ever suspect Emberville of harboring runaways."

"We'll make it."

"What then?"

"Then we see."

"You think it's Coombs back there behind us?"

"I imagine so. Who else could it be?"

Micah counted on his fingers. "Three or four possibilities there. Our enemies are adding up."

"Point taken."

"Wouldn't hurt to have some kind of plan," said Micah.

"Guess not."

Lin thought ahead.

If they could make it to Wynot's station, there would be spring water and shelter. If the Osage crossing slowed Coombs down, the Hellbenders would find cover and concealment at the dairy.

Enough time to avoid a confrontation?

Likely not.

Lin's thoughts were grim.

"We could set up at the dairy. Maybe spring an ambush?"

"You know the people who run it?"

"Kindly old Swedish couple with twelve or thirteen kids."

"This old Swede good with a gun, is he?"

Lin tried to imagine old Iver Carlson triggering a six-shooter. "I'd say he's better with a frypan than a firearm."

"Hate to drag innocent people into our problem," said Micah.

"Yeah."

The Concord creaked along the final span and when they rounded the precipice of road, an enlivening view of grassland acreage spread out in front of them. Purple henbit and yellow coneflowers, butterfly weed, and swelled patches of wild onions and garlic scented the air with a ruddy mix of encouragement.

In the distance, a scattered string of frame buildings bordered the road.

"Yah, yah," cheered Lin, and the horses lengthened their stride, grateful for the chance to finally stretch.

Lin hoped it wouldn't be their last.

CHAPTER 17

WYNOT'S DAIRY, ESTABLISHED IN 1827, LINED THE left side of the trail with four long, low frame buildings with broken shingles. They all looked the same from Lin's vantage point, rectangular structures, chipping with old paint. Flat gray plank walls with no windows and no doors. The tired limestone foundations crumbling under a smother of weeds. The hail-broke shingles patched with rusty tin, red and brown.

The Carlsons produced milk for stations a hundred miles in each direction. Meat too, remembered Lin, and the station was well known for its scalloped potatoes and beans. This time around, they'd miss the noon meal, and Lin cursed his unlucky stars. The breakfast of Mrs. Dooney's doughnuts had worn off a long time ago.

Across the road from the main farm, an open flat carpet of lime green buffalo grass was a haven for an enormous herd of Guernsey cows, short-horned with hair the color of wet sand. They nosed the dirt behind a rickety split-rail fence, then flung their heads up and to the side when spooked by the sound of Lin's team.

Strings of saliva floated on the breeze and mashed cud dropped from wide open jaws.

The startled cows gave Lin an idea.

At the end of the line, he careened into the pasture's gravel driveway and rushed up to a loose section of fence which doubled as a gate. A passel of chickens scurried away from the Hellbender mares, and the Concord rolled to a stop, mud dripping from the coach's undercarriage.

Lin counted a handful of donkeys mixed in with the cow herd.

From here to Fort Smith, the way was more rugged, and as the road rose into the Ozark mountains, a good jackass was more valuable than the finest thorough-bred. Like the hot lunch he knew was simmering inside Wynot's station, he coveted the mules, would've gladly swapped the mares for them.

But there was no time.

He looked over his shoulder, back down the road toward the last switchback where a low rumble was gradually increasing in volume. No doubt Coombs would be upon them within minutes.

He hoped his plan worked.

Turning to Micah, he said, "Help me with the fence."

As the men jumped down to the soft earth, Reece poked her head out of the carriage, her fingers wrapped around the Walch Navy 12-shooter the way some women might cradle a fine piece of jewelry. "Why'd you stop? You do realize we're being pursued," she said.

Ignoring her, Lin spoke to Micah, "Grab the other end," he said. Micah shouldered his half of the top oak fence rail and they moved it to the side and dropped it.

In less than half a minute, they removed all the

planks and knocked aside the supports. The wide grazing lot was open to the trail.

Lin pointed at a line shack in the distance. "Take the coach and ride hell for leather across this field. I remember the shed from the last time I was here. It sits on a parallel road winding into the hills."

"We're leaving the Overland trail?"

"Unless you want to fight it out here and get somebody killed?"

Micah looked across the road at the row of buildings and the station house with its washtub of wildflowers sitting beside the front door. The station's only window was a paper-covered square hole devoid of glass, and the door hung half open on a rusty hinge.

"I think we've seen enough killing today," said Micah.

Lin nodded. "I'll catch up with you."

While Micah leapt aboard the wagon and took the reins, Lin removed his hat and sprinted past a close pair of straggling bovines to circumnavigate the herd.

"Be careful, Ranger," called Reece.

Once the Concord trundled out of the way toward the horizon, Lin began to flap his arms and methodically drive the skittish dairy cows toward the gate.

"Hey, hey," he yelled, zigzagging back and forth, racing one way and another as individual animals scrambled into a charge through the open gate. The noise of hoofbeats was louder still, almost immediately the riders came into view.

It was a problem of motion and geometry, not unlike when, as a child, his pa taught him to shoot at rabbits. In this case, the rabbit was a quintet of murderous horsemen, and his gun was a pack of spooky dumb animals. The trick was forcing them to meet up at just the right time.

"Yah, yah," said Lin, scampering through the cows like a madman, making one or two snort and gallop.

He drew his Colt, pulled back the hammer and triggered a black powder charge into the air. The first explosion made four cows jerk and shy away, the second and third sent a dozen of them into snorting, bawling throes of terror.

Lin triggered the gun again and again. In a crazed dash for the gate, four, then eight, then sixteen cows crashed sideways into the standing fence. Where one led, the other animals followed, trampling planks into the grass, spilling thousands of pounds of jostling, frantic beef into the gap.

As Coombs came into view on his lead horse, haughty spectacles flashing in the mid-morning sun, the herd stampeded, startled by the animals and men headed their way.

As one bawling mass, the cows flowed from the range of buffalo grass into the road, inundating the horseman at the precise moment they made the gate, turning their steeds away. Coombs struggled to wend his way through the fray, rearing his horse's head high, but she bared her teeth and fought against him, compelled to the follow the herd.

Lin counted four men with Coombs, each of them caught up in the torrent of cows swarming around them, each of them hanging on for life. If a man lost his saddle in such a storm of horns and hooves, he'd be trampled to a bloody pulp within seconds. A good ways behind the herd, with dozens of animals between him and Coombs' men, Lin turned in the opposite direction and made a mad dash across the acreage.

The green Concord was a bouncing fly speck in the distance, far away.

Lin pounded boot leather, running like he hadn't

run for twenty years, cranking his elbows, adjusting his breathing for the long haul.

Gunfire erupted behind him, and Lin heard a man's voice yelling above the frightened din of charging cows. But he didn't take the time to look back. Everything important was a half-mile in front of him, pulling away fast. His entire life was wrapped up in the bobbing black spot on the horizon.

At the last minute, one of the mules, a straggler, but healthy and strong, crossed his path. In fact, they nearly collided.

Grabbing a fistful of mane, Lin threw himself across the burrow's back and slapped his rump with the barrel of the Colt, pushing him away from the remnants of the stampede. Behind him, somebody lobbed off a last ditch shot. Then another. One arm around the animal's neck, cheek to withers, Lin ducked and jostled over the spotty spring grass as the slugs whined over his head.

He kept his eye on the shape of the Concord, clearer now as the donkey approached at a quick clip. In fact, he was gaining on them.

Had Micah stopped the coach before arriving at the line shack?

Lin sat up and waved his friends forward, "Go, go," he whispered, and the donkey swerved and bucked, threatening to throw him.

Reece was hanging out the window, motioning for him, but Lin continued to wave her away. They had to make time while they could. The cows would only hold Coombs back for so long.

But the coach didn't move, and when he got within shouting distance, he cried out. "Damnation girl, get on the road."

"We can't!"

"Why can't you?"

"One of the horses..." Reece answered, but the remainder of her explanation was lost to the wind. By the time Lin pulled up beside the wagon, the problem was clear.

The four mares Reece had acquired at Mulhaven's were exhausted beyond measure. Not only had they traveled more than twenty miles total, but after fording the Osage, they'd been forced around a series of ever steeper grades, then made to run flat out. Covered in foam and blowing hard, the two lead mares rocked back and forth, reminding Lin of a house built from playing cards.

"But that's not the worst of it," said Reece. "We went over some pretty rough ground back there. Badger holes, some soft mole runs. I think Meg turned a hoof."

Micah sat tight on the bench seat, waiting with reins in hand, and Griff hung out the side door window, his face almost as green as the turf underfoot.

Reece knelt a few feet behind the four mares, level with the rear horses' knees, doing her best to ascertain the problem.

"Each time she steps, her head bobs down and she deigns to put any weight on the foot."

Lin slid from the mule and let it lope away. The far side of the field was still a roiling dark mass of confusion, and Lin was temporarily relieved to not see any sign of Coombs.

He turned back to Meg. There was no arguing the mare was sweating more than her companions, and she had a deeply troubled look in her eyes.

"I don't think her leg's broken," Reece said, "but we can't make her go on."

"We'll have to leave her here," said Lin. "The Carlsons will find her. Care for her."

"Swap Meg out," said Micah. "Use the donkey."

Lin nodded, lifted his chin to the sun. "I don't know if we've got time."

"Go with three," said Griff. "Don't take any chances."

For his part, the donkey had already forgotten the rude charge across the pasture and seemed content to snack on a nearby clump of weeds.

Lin took a last look over his shoulder, motioned for Micah and Griff. "Let's swap 'em out," he said.

But when Griff tumbled from the cabin, Lin wondered who was in rougher shape.

"It's the jostling of the coach," Reece explained. "Griff gets sick from the motion."

Lin couldn't help but grind his back teeth together. Considering he'd just fled from a quintet of mad gunnies looking to perforate his hide...

He walked up to Griff and hauled him to his feet by the shirt collar. "We're running for our lives here. Toughen up, man."

Apparently eager to oblige, Griff punched Lin in the face.

CHAPTER 18

Lin had enough problems without fighting a half-dizzy British dandy, but somehow, it's the situation he found himself in as Reece and Micah got busy switching out Meg for the wild donkey.

Resting his butt on the cold spring ground, Lin wiped a trickle of blood from his lower lip. He narrowed his eyes and put as much menace into his voice as he could manage. "You might want to think about what you're gonna do once I stand up."

Griff was undeterred by the tone of Lin's voice. "You might want to consider the same," he said. "I'm through being bamboozled by the lot of you, do you understand?"

"That's the sick tummy talking, right there," said Micah.

"Not entirely," said Griff. "It's more. I've asked Mr. LeMay several times, and he's refused me, and now I'm...well, now I'm demanding."

Lin listened to the tirade and slowly rose to his feet, weighing his options, more puzzled now than angry. "What is it—exactly—you're demanding?" said Lin, dragging the back of his hand across his fat lip.

"I want to drive the coach."

"You...want to...drive?"

"I've asked several times and been turned down, but I absolutely think it best. It's the only way I won't continue to be sick, you see, and..."

"He wants to drive," said Lin.

Micah held up his hands. "I didn't think it was a good idea."

"With everything we've been through, I believe I have earned the right to—"

"Hell, I don't care," said Lin, dusting off his pants.

"Are you sure?" said Reece.

"Give him the reins," said Lin. "Give him your fancy gun, give him any damn thing he wants. Just get the damn donkey hitched up, and let's get the hell away from here."

Griff smiled like a boy at Christmas. "It's my stomach is all. I just—"

With Reece and Micah back at the team, Lin pressed in close and, lowering his voice, stuck a finger directly into Griff's face. "If you ever hit me again, I'll make you wish you were dead."

Griff cocked his head and replied. "If I ever have cause to hit you again, I'll save time and fill you with lead."

Lin held Griff's eyes and couldn't help but smile. "Goddammit, I think I'm starting to like you, English."

"That makes one of us."

———

A FEW MILES later they pulled into a natural campsite beside a shallow wide creek in front of a tall granite facade. Surrounded by a thick hardwood forest, the way they followed was nothing more than a meandering path established through the seasons by any number of critters, predominately deer. "You see where they've rubbed the bark off this tree?" said Lin. "Wouldn't mind getting a shot off at some venison today."

"You're making my mouth water," said Griff.

"We've got salt pork in the rear boot," said Lin, "Plenty of beans, and don't forget those peaches I got from Dooney."

"We'll stop here, then?"

Lin patted Griff's shoulder. "Just to tend the animals."

Griff nodded and climbed down from the driver's seat.

Behind him, Reece and Micah left the coach and went straight for the horses.

Lin joined them next to the team. "The donkey did better than I expected."

"You talking about this donkey," said Micah before pointing at Griff, "or the one standing over there behind the poplar tree?"

Lin smiled. "He did fine at the reins." Then Lin motioned for Micah to walk with him.

After they were a good distance away from the others, he said, "We're going to have to deal with Coombs."

"We don't stop him, his crew gonna dog us relentlessly."

Lin looked around the clearing, studied the tall, granite cliff bordering the creek.

"We'll stop him here."

"Like pulling a sliver before it gets sore."

Micah was right. Coombs would never let up. He'd trail them until they were dead.

If they didn't stop him once and for all, the end would be as exhausting as it would be inevitable.

It would be the end of everything.

"Let's get ready," said Lin.

————

IN THE SEDIMENT-STAINED face of the granite rock wall, a series of fractures came together and made a handy cubbyhole to hide in. The cave was just big enough for Lin to fit inside, but not high enough to stand.

Just deep enough for concealment, but hardly enough to shield him if things got too hot.

MICAH HAD PARKED the coach in the middle of the cow trail, just out of six-shooter range, facing toward Lin.

Here's hoping Coombs' rifle stayed in its saddle boot.

After setting the brake, Micah positioned Burt's corpse in an upright position at the bench, the reins dangling from his lifeless hands. From the mouth of the cave, the old boy looked as alive as anybody.

And if the smell of death bothered the donkey or the mares, they didn't show any sign. Carefree, brushed, and watered, they snoozed in the dappled woodland sunlight in front of the coach, their eyes half-closed.

Lin didn't think Burt would mind being used as bait for the men who killed him.

A woodpecker flickered past, and swarms of gnats rose in the heat of the noontime sun.

To the right of the stagecoach, a giant oak tree held

to the banks of the gurgling creek, its girth like three whiskey barrels.

Two to three feet deep, the spring-fed water flowed over a series of gravel bars and compact rock falls.

The place was a miniature version of paradise.

A holy place.

As good a place as any to meet your maker, though Lin fervently hoped today wasn't his day for introductions.

Micah, Griff, and Reece held still in their agreed-upon spots. Invisible to anybody coming up to the wagon.

Invisible to Lin.

The day wore on.

Lin did his best to stay quiet.

After a while, it was hard to keep awake.

He prayed the others didn't succumb to slumber.

When Coombs and his men finally showed up, they left their horses alone at the curve and approached the Concord on foot.

They were quiet, too.

From his high rocky hollow, groggy and tucked in behind, he raised his freshly charged and loaded Colt, Lin watched the party of five encroach on the scene.

By the time the German recognized the trap, it was too late to back out.

Coombs worked to maintain his regal composure, but from his concealed spot, Lin saw the signs of an internal struggle. With two of his men in front, and two behind, his head was on a constant swivel.

The quintet stopped less than twenty feet from the coach and fanned out around its backside.

When Burt didn't move, Coombs shot him twice.

The cadaver shook with the impact, then tumbled

over from seat, crashing to earth as the startled horses jostled back and forth.

"*Sehr gut*," called Coombs into the surrounding woods. "Heir Ranger, are you listening? Are you watching for me? You've managed to lure us in—what now?"

Lin tightened his grip on the Colt but held his fire.

Coombs would hedge his bets.

After all, there was always the chance Lin and his friends were hiding inside the Concord.

Coombs nodded and, at the signal, all five men started blasting away at the coach. Powder smoke erupted into the air and waves of raw percussion filled the clearing as crash followed crash, one after another.

Even as secluded as she was, it was likely Reece Sinclair was counting off the shots. So acute was her hearing and her mind so attuned to numbers, she often did it without thinking.

Lin lost track after the first five or six explosions.

Fist-sized hunks of wood and splinters of enamel, leather, and brass spun through the air as gouts of hot lead chewed into the Jarret and Sinclair conveyance. Riddled with holes, the body of the car shook under the drubbing.

Five men with six shots in their handguns meant thirty balls of lead. When the deafening echoes died away and only a prolonged ringing remained, Lin figured Coombs and crew had spent at least half their firepower.

Now he felt more confident.

He stepped out from behind the edge of the rock to the lip of the cave. At this distance, he made an almost impossibly small target for a sidearm.

"It's over, Coombs," he called. "Leave us now or die."

The German whipped around, saw Lin, and pointed him out with his wooden arm.

Two of his men took aim and fired, sending their bullets crashing harmlessly into the base of the cliff.

"Give it up," he called. "You can try all day."

Unfortunately, the same was true for him.

But not for Micah, Reese, and Griff.

"Drop your weapons and live," he said.

Two of Coombs' men tried again, lifting their guns, each of them triggering off a carefully aimed shot. The lead slugs tore through a series of tree branches, knocking off a fluttering chaff of leaves.

The air was thick with the smell of pollen and powder smoke.

Micah stepped out from behind the gnarled old oak and unloaded both barrels of his shotgun into the two gunmen, nearly cutting them in half.

Coombs' two other gunnies had their sidearms swinging into position before the dead men hit the ground.

They were a split second too slow.

Up from under the water of the creek, having retrieved her Walch Navy wheel-gun from the leaves on the bank, Reece triggered off six rounds in rapid succession, punching holes into both men, sending them into jangled death spasms.

Coombs fell into a crouch, arms over his head, and duck-walked to the back of the coach for cover.

Behind him, Griff sprang up from the forest floor where he'd been buried in a pile of dead leaves and pine needles. His hair full of brambles, and his black suit coat covered in burdock stickers, he held Reece's old No. 5 revolver in a limp wrist at his side.

But at the last second, Coombs saw him and beat him to the draw.

Keeping his office mate at bay with a big Colt .44, Coombs told Griff to "Drop it".

Shocked by Coombs' speed, Griff obeyed. The No. 5 revolver hit the ground, and Griff raised his hands. "Don't shoot," he said.

Lin groaned. The dang-blasted idiot!

From his vantage point, Coombs' smile was a bright as the sun. Waving the Colt, he motioned for Griff to come around to the back of the wagon and join him.

Griff complied. "Aren't you forgetting something?" he said. "Or should I say, *somebody*?"

Coombs cocked his head, then followed Griff's outstretched arm back to Reece.

She stood at the edge of the creek, her big iron still leveled at the German. Micah stood just behind, at her left.

Her expression was smug amusement.

From his vantage point above, Lin whispered, "Don't get cocky. Just shoot the bastard."

Coombs held his pistol carelessly in hand and laughed. "I heard about you at Mulhaven station. Frau Dooney told us all about you. How you help *his* kind." Coombs sneered at Micah. "To think you would use money earned honestly by admirable men for such as *him*."

"I don't think of the men in your organization are to be admired."

"You might be surprised, *liebchen*. We are better men than the Rangers of Texas, no?"

"Who said anything about Texas Rangers?"

"Word gets around. We know all about you."

"What is it you think you know?" said Reece.

Coombs licked his lips. "How you are good with numbers. Some say you can count bullets as they fly through the air." Now his smile was mocking, his face full of contempt. "I too, have a similar skill. For example, I saw you put your gun to my men. Quite clearly you murdered them in cold blood. Quite clearly, each of them took three shots to the chest. By my own count, you now will need to reload."

Coombs lifted his gun. "On the other hand, I have a full cylinder."

"You lose," said Reece, confident in her trick twelve-shooter.

She pulled the trigger on a cap and powder charged rear cylinder. Shot number seven.

Nothing happened.

She tried again.

Lin's heart raced into his throat. The damn goofy gun had fouled itself.

He should have taken the thing away from her first time he saw it.

Now Coombs was gonna kill her for the mistake.

"No!" shouted Lin, firing his Colt as a distraction, scattering lead into the leaves in front of the coach even as he hustled down from his perch to charge across the open space between them.

But there wasn't time.

Coombs shook his head, aimed the pistol at Reece. "I'm sorry, *Fräulein*."

Griff's arm came up.

The little brass single shot revolver fell from his sleeve into his palm, barking loud at point blank range.

A pink cloud of debris erupted from the side of Coombs' head, and he toppled over.

When Lin slid to a stop in the loose underbrush, Coombs' lifeless body was still kicking, and Reece had her arms wrapped around the Englishman.

Damned if Griff hadn't saved her life.

CHAPTER 19

AFTER LIN AND MICAH LAID OUT COOMBS AND HIS men in a straight row beside the creek, they rejoined the others on the trail closest to the rock wall and Lin's cave. Reece and Griff had the horses and mule out of harness and were leading Coombs' animals forward. Aside from a spattering of new, round bullet holes and a mess of splinters, the Concord appeared to be roadworthy.

"A gal could drain the water off her potatoes with it," said Reece, "but I think it'll stand the trip to Plummer's station."

"Albeit a bit drafty," said Griff.

"Drafty, I can live with," said Micah. "Sleep, I can't live without."

Lin felt the same way. His shoulders ached from the arduous river crossing, and his eyelids were like iron weights pulling down his whole face. "We need to make camp someplace. Everybody get some food and a nice, long nap." Hooking a thumb back at the line-up of dead men, he said, "But not here."

"Are you planning to leave Burt's body with the others?" said Reece.

"He's a BO division man. I think it's best we bring him in to the next station." Lin indicated the five mares near the coach. "Coombs' horses aren't in much better shape than the ones brought us here."

"Not much, but the river crossing wasn't as hard on them, plus they haven't been lugging a wagon. Overall, I say we put them together as a team and let our animals trail." She motioned for them to set to work. "How about we tie Burt over the mule's back?"

Once the new team was in place, they set out in the rough direction of the Overland trail. The way was rougher now, with too many trees and rugged hills of thorny vines. In the occasional open field, puffy, purple henbit gave way to the wavey emerald-gold summer hay, and cyclone clouds of buzzards circled lazy in the sky.

After a while, they found an old Indian trail, mostly straight and devoid of obstacles. Soon, with Griff taking a turn at the reins, the drowsy afternoon had Lin dozing on the bench, waking now and then to the occasional buzz of flies and bite of mosquitos. The air was still and smelled of rich loam and spicy pine needles, cedar pollen and silver maple dust.

Seven miles cross country from their run-in with Coombs, they came to an abandoned barn with a fresh-water spring oozing from a limestone hillock. A lonely foundation of bedrock showed where a cabin once stood, and a broken, dented coffee pot sat rusting beside a pair of steps. Griff piloted the parade of coach, horses, and cadaver mule into camp, setting the brake, then dropping to the ground with an audible sigh.

They stood on a hill in the shadow of the tall, two-story gambrel roofed barn frame, its occasional gray siding faded in the lowering sun, most of its hard oak beams naked to the elements. Lin stared up at the broken edifice in wonder.

No, not broken.

Unfinished.

Such an enormous building here, so far from any main road and miles from abundant water was an ambitious undertaking, now gone hollow. Forever incomplete.

Lin felt an odd kinship with the place and decided to bed down.

"We'll make camp this side of the barn," he said. "Let's get these horses situated, fed, and watered."

Draping an arm around Reece's shoulders, he said, "How about you rustle up a fire?"

"Okay, boss, but what exactly are you going to do while the rest of us follow orders?"

Lin pulled his Colt from its holster and put the muzzle against the brim of his hat. "I'm gonna walk the perimeter looking for snakes."

After the journey they had, he wasn't counting out the two-legged variety.

———

AFTER A TEN-MINUTE WALK FOLLOWING a thick path of daisies along the woods' edge, Lin found two graves tucked away in a cottonwood grove. Almost hid by a heavy stand of buffalo grass, the twin stone markers were crudely shaped with one name chiseled across each face. The markers stood barely knee high, their foundations covered in grass.

Lin literally stumbled over the first stone, coming to ground beside the second. From his spot stretched out on the sod, he reached up and tore away the strands of creeping jenny, brushed away the hard green and gray moss.

Lin let his fingers travel over the inscriptions.

Kelton.

Underneath the name, a crucifix was scored into the rocks.

There was nothing more.

Both stones were identical.

No beloved mother. Or trusted father. No dates.

No mention of siblings or geography.

Just two lonesome stones and a name.

Were they a married couple?

Sibling children?

How did they come to be here? "They certainly didn't bury themselves," said Lin.

The wind kicked up a skiff of dust and a passing cloud covered the evening sun.

Lin couldn't help but think of his parents, both passed within the last several years. And Reece's old man, too soon gone. Lin and Reece were alone in the world, just as these two must've been, and his pondering stirred up something deep that wanted children and a family. A place to belong.

A legacy to remember.

The soulful emotions had him pulling again at the vines covering the tombstones, had him using his shirt sleeves to scrub the flat surfaces free of nature's remnants.

Lin knelt at the foot of the first stone and dug weeds with bare fingers, pulling away the stickers and thorny vines, packing dirt up under his nails and slivering his fingertips. Then he did the same for the second rock, sprucing up the marker, tidying up the plot.

Back at the barn—the Kelton's barn—Reece had a fire going. Lin smelled the heady hickory smoke.

Griff and Micah would care for the horses.

Burt would still be dead, forever roaming the shadowlands.

Maybe he'd say hello to the Keltons. Or maybe ol' Burt had gone to a more fiery place where folks like the Keltons, with a cross on their markers, would never see.

It didn't matter.

Oddly enough, right now what mattered most to Lin, more than anything in the world, was his service to the Keltons' memory. Later, he would tell the others his hard work was given in thanks for camping at the homestead. Deep down, he knew it was something more.

A sense of inexplicable kinship for two souls all but forgotten.

In a hundred years nearly all of us are forgot, thought Lin. The least he could do in return for the night's shelter was maybe add a year or two to the life of the little cemetery he'd stumbled into.

He dug harder at the base of one of the markers, ripping away the grass, breaking his fingernails before he found the locket.

———

AFTER A MEAL of pork and beans, bread and gravy, and plenty of coffee to wash it all down, they sat around the campfire under the night's sky full of stars. Lin and Reece next to each other, smoking, Micah and Griff across the crackling flames, the barn's tall vertical timbers flickering orange in the distance. Even more than Mulhaven station, the Kelton place offered a sense of security.

Lin hadn't felt so much at home since leaving Texas.

He held up the locket he found at the gravesite and let it twirl in the firelight.

"It's clasp locket," said Reece, reaching to retrieve the brassy oval on its thin chain. "It has a hinge on one side."

With great care, she worked to open the piece. "It's tarnished," she said. "Rusted shut."

When it popped open, Reece looked inside. "There are two miniature ink drawings. A heart and a butterfly."

"Doesn't tell us much about the Keltons," said Micah.

"Wonder how long the jewelry's been out here?" said Reece, handing it back to Lin.

"Since the burial, I would suspect."

"Who do you think it belongs to?"

"Next of kin?" said Lin. "I doubt we'll ever know."

Lin passed the locket to Griff who shared it with Micah.

"The frontier is full of mysteries. Forgotten souls whose fate will never be known." Micah passed the locket back. "Stories never to be told."

Lin gave the locket to Reece. "For safe keeping," he said. "My big clumsy hands will lose it before tomorrow."

She tucked it away in her trousers pocket.

"Speaking of tomorrow, I'm ready to turn in," said Micah. "If y'all will excuse me."

Lin watched him stand up and carry his blanket a ways away from the fire to a flat, comfortable spot in the grass. After a final swig of coffee, Griff soon adjourned to a clearing, bedding down nearby.

Alone by the fire, Reece pressed her back against Lin's chest, reclining into him, snuggling her head of ebony hair into the crook of his neck.

It felt good to be quiet together, thought Lin. To be the two of us here, under the stars, alone with our thoughts, yet joined by the care they felt for each other. They were more than lovers, they were family. Lin had said it before, and it was true.

"We're all family," he said, in a low, husky tone.

"We are."

"You ever think about it?"

"About what?"

"You and me. Getting properly hitched. Start a family?"

For the briefest of instants, she stiffened in his embrace, then relaxed again and sighed. "Not now, Ranger. Not with the way the world is going. I can't imagine bringing a child into this divided nation."

"Other people are."

"Other people have less to lose."

He buried his lips in her hair and kissed her. "I don't think that's true," he said.

"I had a dream the other night," she said. "Do you want to hear about it?"

"I suppose so. If you feel like telling."

"I was walking down a sunlit road when all of a sudden, a devil jumped from behind a tree."

"A devil? Y'mean with horns and a pitchfork? Tail and everything?"

She slapped away his chuckling. "Stop it. Yes, a devil—it scared the liver out of me. Before I knew it, out popped another, and another. There were seven of them."

"You were all alone with these devils?"

"Not for long. You and Micah showed up."

"I imagine we whupped them seven devils all the way to Sunday?"

"No," said Reece. "You didn't. We ran from them. We ran, and eventually, they caught up."

He felt her trembling and squeezed her tight. She whispered. "They caught us, Lin. We...we didn't make it."

"Shhhh," he soothed her. "It was only a dream. Right now, you're safe here with me. There ain't no devils here."

"You promise?"

"I promise there ain't no devils. The Keltons will make sure of it."

"Are they our guardian angels?"

"Why not? I told Griff before: they come in all shapes and sizes."

The flames fell away to embers while they watched, and Reece's breathing deepened. Lin closed his eyes and listened to her snore softly against his chest, wondering about the future and the things making her afraid.

CHAPTER 20

PLUMMER'S STATION WAS A BUSTLING DEN OF activity when Lin drove the Hellbenders' team into the front yard. The grassy acreage with its well-maintained network of gravel-covered roads was three times the size of Mulhaven or Wynot's Dairy and centrally occupied by a two-story frame hotel and restaurant. Lin couldn't help but breathe a sigh of relief at the welcoming red outbuildings, generous tilled garden already green with light produce, rhubarb patches, raspberry vines, and a spry apple orchard.

It was like coming home. The hotel was longer than it was deep, with a porch above and below and a central door with windows on either side. Whitewashed and clean with hewn wooden shingles and two tall brick chimneys on either side, the house was fronted by a stand of lilac bushes and gardens of blooming daisies. Three border collies, friendly and alert, swaggered over to sniff at the Concord. One of them sent up a welcoming, quick bark.

At a two-story pole barn, one side open to the elements, a pair of muscular young men tugged at a long length of leather, talking, laughing, joshing with each other as they prepared the long belt for use on a big-wheeled steam engine filling the immediate space in front of them. It was rare to see such a grand machine, and Lin wondered what they were using it for today. Milling? It was situated in such a way so the wheel turned perpendicular to the building. Lin saw a framework of steel populated with wheels and cranks, and a pile of logs extended along the downhill slope beyond. A sawmill?

Closer to the coach, a dark-skinned fellow loaded a buckboard wagon with flour sacks, alternating his load with a white man who packed aboard iron-banded whisky barrels. Behind him, another wagon was full of coarse, long-cut lumber.

Lin imagined Plummer's was the kind of self-sufficient ranch Wade and Almeda Kelton had dreamed about when they started building their barn. Had they abandoned their dream when the final stage route passed them by? Or was it something else brought an early end to their ambition. Maybe somebody here in Plummer's would know about their history. Lin would ask around about and find out what happened to them.

Behind the hotel, a round woman with red hair hung clothes on a long line of rope tied between two hackberry trees. Lin didn't remember her from the last time he and Reece stopped at the ranch—didn't recognize her at all.

Scurrying around the woman's fat hips in a concentric spiral, a trio of cats played together. Ducking in and out of the pinned laundry, they teased each other, falling over to roll on their backs. When the unfamiliar lady saw Lin, she waved, and he waved back.

"Go on inside," she called. "Lunch is on the table."

It was ten o'clock in the morning.

At Plummer's station, breakfast had come and gone hours ago.

Lin stretched, listened to his muscles popping, and rubbed the stitch in his neck. The ride from the Keltons' abandoned barn had become increasingly circuitous and hard to navigate. Right-angled corners dropped off into steep ravines, and everything was set at a dramatic uphill grade.

Just another tension-inducing piece of Missouri road—there seemed to be a lot of them here in the far southwestern part of the state.

As usual, this many hours into a trip, Lin felt mighty stove up.

On the good side, the night's rest had been restorative, and Lin's complaints were nothing a good walk-around and home-cooked meal wouldn't cure.

"Good to have made it this far," said Reece, joining him. She breathed in. Breathed out. "Fresh baked bread. Clean linens."

"A hint of cow flop," said Griff, coming up behind.

"Griffin Kale, you could bring down a baptism, Easter day," said Micah. "Plummer's station is a major landmark. Fact we made it this far is cause for celebration."

"I'll celebrate when we're free of those damned stock certificates," said Griff. "Until then, you might as well paint a bullseye on this wagon of yours. You got a cigarette, Lin?"

Lin handed Griff the makings.

Then he turned his attention to their sorry cargo.

Walking past the Concord down to the end of his string of horses, Lin said, "Micah, please untie Burt from the mule. Griff, help Micah lay the old man out under the old oak tree over there."

Burt was an awful old bastard, but nobody deserved

to have their remains treated shabby. Even the most foul, egg-sucking snake deserved a Christian burial.

And Lin hated snakes worst of all.

Griff made his shaky smoke, spilling more tobacco than he needed to. Lin took back his leaves and papers, turned to Reece. "Let's us go see who's in charge."

"Last time we were here, Plummer's was run by Tom Plummer," said Reece.

"The old badger," said Lin. Nodding at the fat redhead walking toward the hotel, he said, "Looks like times have changed."

"Old bachelor?" said a voice like an iron rasp coming around behind them. At the front of the rig stood Tom Plummer. "If you said old bachelor, my reply to you sir, is—not anymore, by the grace of God. Since last you kids were here, He's delivered my Annie to me."

Tom Plummer was around fifty years old with only a little over the same number of miniscule pounds to his lanky skeleton. Skinny as a broomstick, Plummer flung out his boney, callused hand like a whipsaw in greeting.

Lin shook it, careful not to pull the old boy over, but Plummer held his ground. He was stronger than he looked. Reece shook his hand in turn.

Plummer wore heavy boots with spurs and tough woven braces over his shoulders that buttoned to dark canvas trousers over a red flannel shirt. A mound of scattered dark hair, like a birds' nest held up his wide-brimmed hat, and his eyes were robin's egg blue the size of cow orbs behind thick glass spectacles.

Plummer welcomed the four travelers with a brown-toothed smile, then coughed into his fist. "I wasn't expecting you, but it's good to have you here."

He tilted his chin up to examine the stagecoach, wrinkled his nose at the splintered paint and bullet holes. "Looks like you hit some rough weather."

"Nothing we couldn't handle. But what's this about you no longer a bachelor?" said Lin. "Tom, you told me last time we were here you took the oath against marriage."

Plummer couldn't hide his blushing cheeks, nor the nervous glance he shot back toward the two-story frame hotel building.

"Annie come upon me one night, lost and alone. I give her a place to stay. Two weeks later, she's took the whole damn farm by storm. By God, she did."

"Congratulations, Tom," said Reece. She put her hands on her hips, surveying the grounds. "The place looks beautiful."

"Yeah, y'can credit my Annie with the improvements. She's a corker. Brought in lots of improvements to the place. Saw things she didn't like and started in with new...uh...ideas."

As he said it, Plummer had looked past Lin to assess Micah and Griff's labor. "Holy Mary, is that jasper dead?" he said. "What the hell happened, kids?"

"Lead poisoning."

"You don't need to try to be funny. You need me to mind my own business, Lin, you say so."

"Mind your own business, Plummer."

"Sure's some kind of goddamn friend you are."

Lin smiled to himself. "Okay, here's the story."

Without going into too much detail, Lin told Tom about the harrowing trip across the Osage and how a hunter on the far shore had apparently taken out Burt with a long rifle slug. "Must've been an accident," said Lin. "Ol' Burt never knew what hit him."

Now that Coombs was dead and their pursuers thwarted, Lin felt a weight off his shoulders. He saw no reason to borrow any more trouble.

The less Plummer knew about their trip, the better. "We're looking for some grub, Tom. We'll need fresh animals, too. Have you got four good mules for us?"

"Grub, we've got—and plenty of it. For mules, you'll need to go on up the road a piece. There's a donkey remuda up there. Some Butterfield Overland stock, plus a few of my own horses. You ride up there after lunch and take your pick."

Plummer shook his head over Burt's cadaver. "Burt Sullivan and me, we had some good times in our wayward youth." Plummer sucked at his bottom lip, coughed again, and spat. "Of course, I'm a reformed man now. Annie's made sure of it. I've accepted the Lord and look at the world in a whole new way."

After they got Burt stretched across the lawn, Plummer peered through his glasses at the cadaver. "I'll send him back home on the east-bound stage. It's due sometime next week."

"I 'spect the people on the stage would prefer you just put him to rest here and send word back."

"Nope," said Plummer. "No, sir. Plummer's Station's only got so much ground allocated for our perpetual cemetery. Annie wouldn't like me upsetting things."

Lin got the feeling there were more things Annie liked and didn't like than anybody could keep track of.

"Besides, ol' Burt's got a wife back up the road near Mulhaven. She deserves to have him come home to her."

Lin couldn't argue with Plummer's logic.

"We're clearing a whole section of timber back to

the east there," said Plummer. The way he swept his arm along the green-spackled horizon, he might've meant all the trees to the Arkansas border.

"Looks like you've got the men for it," said Lin. "Equipment, too."

The two strong men had abandoned the long leather belt, turning their attention to the brass fittings of the steam engine itself. Looking for all the world like a train locomotive without rails, the big boiler tank sat on two high-wheeled trucks.

"We use steam to run our sawmill," said Tom. "The setup is a marvel of engineering. We burn sawdust for steam, and the tank drives a big mother of a piston." Tom held his hands up to form a circle with a wide diameter. "Pistons so big around with pert' near a mile-long stroke what spins the flywheel. The flywheel alone is 8 feet tall. We can rip a 40-foot cut in two minutes, and we keep three extry blades on hand. Hell of a thing —we can do the day's work of ten men in a single forenoon."

"I don't doubt it."

"Wish you could see her in action, but it will be a couple hours. The boys are just heating the boiler, now."

Lin admired the line of curling black smoke coming from the engine's stack. The monster was just getting started. "I'd enjoy seeing a thing like that make a go— but right about now, I'd rather see the lunch you told us about."

The comment produced an odd reaction in Plummer, and the station master's original smile turned south. Then Plummer put his hand to Lin's back, drawing him away from the others. "Something I need to say before you go inside, Lin. The thing is..."

"What is it, Tom?" Lin felt the need to keep his voice low.

"Like I say, before you all go in, there's something you need to know. I'm only telling you this because you and Miss Reece have been good to me when you stopped here before."

Lin wondered at Plummer's sudden dour tone of voice. "We've had quite a lot of company today," he said, clearing his throat.

"You're referring to the westbound stage? Came through sometime last night, ahead of us?"

Plummer nodded. "It did, but the Butterfield ain't who I'm talking about."

Plummer's voice took on a tone of deep suspicion. "I'm talking about some scruffy-looking varmints taking lunch in the kitchen. Annie says they're okay, but…"

"But? What is it, Tom? Spit it out, man."

"Maybe just get up on your wagon and pull on out. Go on up the road and get your mules. I'll tell Annie you couldn't stay for lunch."

Lin swiveled his head around, scanning the yard for horses or a parked wagon. "I didn't realize anybody else was here."

"They parked their horses out of sight. There's four of 'em, and a real secretive lot they are. I didn't get the picture as to why until after they sat down to eat. Said they didn't want anybody knowing they were here and getting spooked off."

"Anybody being us—Miss Reece and me?"

"Wouldn't you know they've been asking about you."

"These scruffy-looking varmints got a name?" said Lin.

"Not so's they'd tell me. All I can say is they asked

about you specifically. Texas Ranger Lin Jarett, they said. Something to do with a train robbery." Plummer patted him on the back. "I'm telling you to consider moving on right now. But like you say...I ought to mind my own business."

CHAPTER 21

"TELL ME MORE ABOUT THESE MEN WAITING FOR US inside," said Lin, but Tom Plummer had already turned his back. Traipsing past Reece, Micah, and Griff, Plummer said, "Annie's got fried chicken and turnips on the table."

He paused at Reece's and picked up her wrist in an awkward fashion. "I'll always remember you as a good friend," he said.

"I'm sure I feel the same way, Mister Plummer."

"Maybe come tomorrow, you might not," said Plummer. "Just remember."

Reece chuckled. "I'm sure your wife's cooking isn't so bad as all that."

Lin knew the puzzled expression she offered Plummer. "He's not talking about the cooking," said Lin. "It's something else."

Plummer shuffled away, and Micah said, "You're not gonna make me go get my scattergun again?"

Lin shared Plummer's warning with them. "Somebody inside wants to see us about a train robbery."

"Good lord," said Griff. "It never ends with you people."

Lin sighed and pulled his Colt. "Reckon you'd best get your scattergun, Micah."

"I figured as much." Micah jumped to the wagon seat and picked up the long gun.

"More of Coombs' men?" said Reece.

"Maybe," said Griff. "Coombs might have kept one or two to the trail when he went cross-country to follow us. If so, they'd be here ahead of us, waiting."

Micah said, "Or it might be Baldy and his stinkin' tin-plate sheriff."

"Or maybe it's somebody new from up ahead," said Lin. "Don't forget, there's wire between Syracuse and Springfield."

"Springfield is where Coombs' brother, Logan, lives," said Griff.

"The recipient of our leather bag. I know," said Lin. "Like I say, they might be coming at us from a new direction."

"We can't outrun the telegraph," said Micah.

"What if it's the law?" said Griff. "What if it's a U.S. marshal and his posse come to round us up for taking Coombs' grip off the train?"

Lin fingered his side iron. "What if it is?"

"Surely you're not planning to fire on them?"

"Depends if they fire at me, don't you think?"

Griff seemed to weigh the proposal, then agreed with Lin's perspective. "I will say I'm beginning to admire the way you think." Griff took Reece's old Number 5 revolver out of his waistband and spun the cylinder.

The four travelers turned away from the coach, each with a shooting iron in hand.

Reece lugged along the heavy Walch 12-shooter like a battle mace.

Lin said, "After it let you down yesterday, you're gonna trust that silly damn Walch?"

"I cleaned it and reloaded last night," said Reece.

"It's awful finnicky. I'd chuck it in a river someplace."

"I'm finnicky too," said Reece. "You gonna chuck me in a river? Besides, I've become quite attached to it."

"You never did say where you got it?"

"No, I didn't," she said. "Not to worry."

"I always worry about you, Contessa."

"Good to hear. Saves me the trouble."

They mounted the wide-open porch of the hotel, and Lin raised his hand to knock at the door.

Before he could land his knuckles, the entrance was open and the lady from the clothesline blocked the way. "The name is Mrs. Annie Plummer," she said. "You put your gun away right now, and you can call me Annie. You don't, and we're gonna have trouble."

Trouble from Mrs. Annie Plummer was the last thing Lin wanted.

She was the exact opposite of her husband in every way.

For one thing, Plummer's new wife was bigger than Lin had judged from a distance. Up close, she had four or five inches on him in height and double the size around the waist.

She smelled of lye soap and lavender, but her skin was oily and covered in bright pink pimples with yellow heads. Where Plummer was well-dressed for a man in his position, Annie's simple grey paper dress struggled to accommodate her heaving mass, and Lin couldn't help notice she was missing a toe in the center of her bare right foot.

Feeling like a scolded pup under Annie's gaze, Lin said, "We heard you had some company. We thought it prudent..."

"Prudent. Phooey. Everybody puts their guns away in my house."

"Everybody?"

"Wipe your shoes before stepping into the foyer."

So intent on learning the identity of the men inside, Lin hadn't noticed the heavy hemp mat laying at the threshold. He thought about it, then traded a questioning look with Reece. With Micah.

Micah shrugged. Reece nodded.

What could they do? The only option was to turn tail and run.

And the allure of fried chicken was too good to pass up, no matter who they had to share the table with.

Griff shoved his gun into his pants with a sigh.

Lin shuffled his boots across the rough fibers and re-holstered his Colt.

"Much obliged," said Annie, letting him pass.

The interior of the hotel was dark after the bright morning sunlight, and it took Lin a few seconds to adjust. The room he stood in was little more than an entrance to the rest of the house, though it contained a red upholstered walnut daybed. The wallpaper was a pinkish floral pattern, and the air smelled of lunch: chicken, cooked turnips, and butter rum cake.

The familiar warm feelings Lin felt upon first driving onto Plummer's ranch nearly overwhelmed him. Letting his hand fall to his belt, the cold steel of his Colt was an insistent reminder to be on guard.

He calmed his heartbeat by breathing in the fine smells.

He calmed his worries by reminding himself of who he was. What were the chances the unknown kitchen visitors would be quicker on the draw than Lin Jarret?

As Griff would say, it wasn't bloody likely.

The gambler came in next and a portrait on the left-hand wall, just above the daybed, caught his attention. While the others cleaned their boots, Lin stepped next to him, close to the painting. The graybeard in the picture wore an olive-green military style uniform, and his hair was long and unkempt. There was a wry look of madness about the fellow, but something familiar too.

As if Lin had recently seen the exact same picture.

"We need to leave," said Griff.

"I was just telling Tom what a lovely place you have," said Reece behind them.

"No thanks to him," said Annie, and her laugh was derisive. "You'd be surprised how much he relies on all the others."

"How many men do you employ here at Plummer's?" said Reece.

Annie's response cut to the bone. "Not near enough, dear. Not to satisfy me."

No doubt Annie was a hard one to satisfy. In all ways that mattered.

"We had a steady stable of a two dozen men. Half of them with wives and kids. Lost two last week. Brought three more on. It's a never-ending pain in my backside." The tired hardwood creaked under her weight as she rocked back and forth, and Lin noted the frayed wallpaper and worn pattern in the floor rug.

"It's a lovely place, regardless," said Reece.

The loud redhead continued to chide her husband. "Tom's got the saw busted down these last three weeks, and we lost two cows to the dirty lung disease."

Abruptly, she stopped as Micah approached the door. "About far enough for you, boy."

Lin turned from his study of the portrait to see Annie standing with a firm hand on Micah's chest.

He took a step back onto the porch. "Excuse me, ma'am?"

Reece stepped in between them. "Micah's with us, Annie."

"Not in my house, he ain't."

Reece's green eyes smoldered at the prejudiced affront. Lin didn't envy Annie. He'd been on the receiving end of such a glare, and it could sting like a bushel basket of hornets.

But Annie didn't miss a beat. "Aw, shucks, you all can carry some food out to him later."

"Or maybe we'll just switch out our horses and move on without partaking of your hospitality," said Reece.

"Suit yourself. I won't eat with animals."

In response to Annie's bigotry, Lin felt a familiar tension rise in him, a furious anger threatening toward violence.

Again, Griff said, "We need to leave."

This time, Lin answered him. "Indeed, we do."

Then somebody cleared his throat at the room's far side.

Lin turned to see three tough looking gents waiting in the doorway to the kitchen.

One of the men was built like a locomotive with a wide chest and shoulders narrowing to a slim waist. He wore leather shotgun-style chaps, a leather vest, and battered slouch hat. On his right hip was a leather holster rig, tied-down with a big Colt nested butt-forward for a left-handed cross draw.

A gunfighter.

With a bright red scrape, recently scabbed over, down one side of his face, beginning at the temple.

Lin felt a tingle run through his arm and his fingers twitched.

The gunfighter saw the reaction, carefully reached up and tipped his hat in Lin's direction.

His friend on the right wore his curly hair long, across his shoulders.

The tall wind-burnt man to the left had on a blue long-sleeved shirt and canvas pants over eggshell colored long underwear, like a farmer.

The sodbuster had a wine-stain birthmark on his face and made a show of picking a piece of grit from between his teeth with his dirty thumbnail.

Griff nudged Lin in the ribs. "We have to leave. Now."

Lin turned his attention to Griff and feigned a smile. Talking between his teeth, he said, "You're a little slow on the uptake, son."

But Griff wasn't looking at the men in the kitchen door.

In fact, if Griff had noticed the men at all, he didn't give any indication. Instead, his gaze held to the portrait on the wall behind Lin. He wiped his lips and Lin saw all the blood had drained from his face.

Still smiling for the gunman's benefit, Lin murmured, "You recognize the painting?"

Griff's only reply was to take a step forward and swallowed hard, his Adam's apple jittering like a junebug.

"Matthias Byrnes O'Fallon," whispered Griff.

Lin snapped his fingers. Now he remembered.

"It's the same fella is in the painting at Prescott's office," he said. "We saw it when we stopped by there looking for you."

"He's the founder of the Order of the Ivory Compass," said Griff.

"And I'm his grand-daughter," announced Annie.

CHAPTER 22

When Reece turned to look at the three men in the kitchen door, a fourth assailant appeared. He was shorter than the others, with a shock of white hair, and she smelled his Bay Rum cologne clear across the room.

It was the romantic gun drummer, Flood Tyner, and he held a pair of Remingtons in his curled mitts as he gave Lin a sneer.

Tyner still wore the same gray suit jacket and trousers as he had the day before, but now his cuffs were caked with mud. His button-up white shirt was dingy with road dust, but his nose was a shiny beet red.

As he addressed Lin and Griff, however, his voice was sober and straight-ahead.

"Look what we have here," he said. "We track you train robbers all this way, and we find a couple of art lovers. I declare, it's gonna be a shame to hang such cultured gentlemen."

Train robbers?

Reece spoke up. "You're making a mistake, Mister Tyner."

"I don't think so, dear."

Not to be shut out of the conversation in her own parlor, Annie piped up. "Mister Tyner told Tommy and me all about you." She planted a pudgy finger between Reece's breasts and poke, poke, poked. "He spilled the beans on all your rotten shenanigans."

"Is that so?" said Reece with a sickly-sweet smile.

She couldn't help but notice since directing them to the house, *Tommy* had vanished.

Reece addressed Tyner with venom. "When we met in Syracuse, Mister Tyner, I mistook you for a gentleman."

"You know this man?" said Griff.

"Flood Tyner," said Reece, "a gun drummer who I thought was my friend."

"You don't have to play along with these scoundrels anymore, dear," said Tyner.

"I'm hardly the one guilty of associating with scoundrels," said Reece.

She introduced Tyner's three associates to the others. "The long-haired coyote is called Curly. The other one is known around Syracuse as The Sodbuster."

"Ain't you forgettin' somebody, missy?" said the gunfighter.

She drew her finger down along the side of her temple, mimicking the path of the gunman's scrape. "Oh, yes. The ugly sonuvabitch goes by the name of Ned Brock."

"I told you once I might have to take you over my knee," said Brock.

"And I put you on the ground for it," said Reece. "Now who's being forgetful?"

"Mister Tyner has been a perfect guest," said Annie, interrupting the banter. "As has Mister Brock and his friends. You, on the other hand, Miss Sinclair, sound quite rude."

Tyner thanked Annie for the compliment with an affirmative nod. Then he told his companions, "Go get their guns, boys. We got these road-agents dead to rights."

"I really must emphasize our need to leave," said Griff.

"Don't tell me, tell them," said Lin.

Brock jerked his Colt from its home and came forward like a banty rooster.

Griff addressed the gunman. "Sir, if I may…"

"Shut your pie hole, ya twit," said Brock. Proud as Sunday mass, Brock told Tyner, "I learned that from a British whore. *Twit*—it means like, a fool, but in England talk."

"Excellent. Very good for you," said Griff.

"Exactly who do you think you are to hinder our travels? You have no authority over us," said Lin.

"Authority? A train robber speaks of authority?"

"Mister Tyner, stop and listen to reason," said Reece. But it was too late. Tyner's pride was on stage now for all to see, and he wasn't about to lose it.

"There, there, sweet thing. He may call himself a Ranger, but this fellow is obviously nothing more than a common thief."

"I'll sweet thing you," said Reece. She was close enough to swiftly kick the old man in the leg.

And she did.

Tyner gasped, as much in surprise as pain. He doubled over to grasp his shin and stumbled back, pushing Curly and the Sodbuster into the kitchen.

As soon as Tyner bent low, Reece saw Lin spin around on Brock to launch a rock-hard punch into his jaw. The gunnie barely flinched.

"Gonna take more'n a love tap to bring me down."

"Good to know," said Lin.

The Ranger's industrious arms hammered Brock's mid-section three times, driving him into the daybed where he struggled for balance. Griff was quick in backing Lin up, aiming the No. 5 revolver at Brock's forehead, giving the fight a moment's pause.

Long enough for Lin to crank a bone-crunching uppercut to his opponent's chin.

As Brock reclined on the daybed with a sigh, Lin hitched up his belt. "Now we're leaving," he said.

Reece showed him an affirmative nod and muscled past Annie.

But just as she made the door, Tom Plummer came in from the porch, shoving Reece back and holding high the leather satchel full of mine stocks.

"I found it, Mister Tyner. The bag was inside the Concord, just like you said."

"Plummer, you damned idiot," said Reece.

"Good on you, sweetie," said Annie.

Plummer's triumph was short-lived.

From behind him, Micah's dark blue bib shirt appeared at the threshold. The big man extended a long arm and grabbed ahold of the crossed braces at Plummer's back. Caught in Micah's unbreakable grip, the thin man wasn't grounded. Jerked off-balance, he dropped the satchel to the hard wood floor.

Again, Reece lashed out with a slender leg, kicking the bag into a slide toward Lin.

From outside came the sound of knuckles meeting bone, and Reece saw Tom Plummer hit the boards. One punch from Micah was all it took to put the slim man down.

Griff snatched up the satchel.

Tyner reappeared in the kitchen doorway, his twin Remies drawn and pointed.

"Stay still," he said, waving his guns in the air, "or so help me, I'll shoot."

Unsure where to direct his aim, Tyner's hands vibrated as if burdened by electric current. First, he aimed a pistol at Lin, then at Griff. Then he swung around to Reece. "I never considered you were in on this nefarious plot, lady," he said.

"If you'll put your Remies away, we could talk," she told him. "Maybe Annie here would make us a cup of coffee?" Slow, careful, Reece reached for the Walch Navy 12-shooter tucked in her waistband. "Wouldn't you like to share a cup of coffee with me?"

Her arm moved a fraction of an inch and Annie's hand shot out like lightning. She clamped her fingers like a vice around Reece's wrist and squeezed.

"It's a trick, Mister Tyner," she screamed, and yanked Reece off the ground.

Reece shoved at her opponent with her free hand but was outclassed by weight.

Annie yelled at her with a stream of obscenities. "You little bitch. Don't you think Tommy's told me who you are? I know all about you, *Hellbenders*! I know all about your crusade to help the heathen devils."

"You...don't know...anything," said Reece, snapping a heel into Annie's prodigious gut. The kick bounced off to no effect. Her second kick was equally pointless. The woman was a mountain of gristle, stolid and impervious, still holding Reece with a huge left hand.

Then Annie's right hand fell on Reece like an anchor. She wrapped the fingers of her right hand around Reece's neck and began to squeeze.

Micah tried to intervene from the porch, but Annie saw him from the corner of her eye.

"Stay there, boy. Or I'll snap her neck like winter kindling."

Reece had never felt such instant agony. One second, she had been breathing, the next second, everything stopped, the air in her lungs a burning, bursting thing, alive, pounding to escape. Her heartbeat a vicious, crashing thing in each eardrum.

Annie's voice was a syrupy sweet echo, a million miles away. "Gonna end your little crusade right here."

Sharp swords of agony lanced through Reece's forehead and down her jaw as she ground her teeth, fiercely fighting to break Annie's brobdinagian hold.

But she was stuck fast, and sparks popped and fizzled in her vision, alternating with floating circles of gray and black.

Her lungs screamed, but there was no sound.

No air.

"I must protest," said Tyner. "Let go of Miss Sinclair this instant. These three men forced her to drive them away from a train robbery in her coach. She's as much a victim here as anybody."

Annie's kill-crazed expression said different.

White knuckles, her fingers tightened, and Reece's eyes strained against their sockets.

"Let her go, damn you," said Tyner.

"Apparently you're confused as to who these people truly are," said Annie. "You talk to my Tommy. He'll tell you about the Hellbenders' unholy acts."

Reece felt an ugly gurgling come up from her belly. The bitter taste of bile flowed up, hit Annie's constricting mass. Her face burned with fire.

"I ain't gonna stand here and watch an innocent killing," said Curly.

Neither will Lin, thought Reece. He won't stand by. He'd save her...but the idea was fuzzy.

Reece saw Lin coming for her with both arms flailing.

As she knew he would.

But there were two of him. Maybe three of him. They all mixed together.

She fell limp, and felt the cool, sweet embrace of death.

And it wasn't so bad after all.

CHAPTER 23

LIN COULD NO MORE WATCH REECE DIE THAN HE could fly across the ocean. Gunfire be damned, he launched himself across the room at Annie and the air exploded with powder smoke.

Flood Tyner's aim was true.

The barking Remingtons punched twin holes into Annie's forehead. With an astonished expression, the fat lady sagged back into the wall, releasing her grip on Reece.

Lin caught her as she went down, cradling her head in both hands before it hit the floor. Her face fell to one side, revealing a line of ugly blue mottled flesh. She groaned, coughed and a quart of bile spilled from her mouth. Covered in filth, Lin hefted her close to his chest and stood tall in his boots.

Reece clung to him, continuing to retch, drunkenly trying to find her feet.

Lin carried her to the porch.

"I say there," said Tyner from inside. "Hold on, or I'll shoot."

"You do what you need to do," said Lin.

Lin reunited with Micah as a percussion cap went off inside the foyer.

Hot lead sizzled past Lin's ear and a second shot tore the top off the far gate post as he stumbled into the yard, his arm wrapped around Reece's waist.

"The next shot won't miss," warned Tyner, but two successive blasts flew sky high.

Tyner wasn't trying too hard.

Lin ignored the volley and stuck to his forward momentum. Reece needed time to recover, to heal. She lolled against his shoulder as he staggered toward the gravel ranch yard and the Concord coach. "Run ahead," he told Micah. "Get the team ready to roll."

"Give me a minute." Micah turned with his shotgun and triggered off a single blast in Tyner's direction, then another, lobbing shot into the porch floor close to the prone form of Tom Plummer.

Like Tyner, Micah wasn't aiming to kill, but he made his antagonists duck for cover.

From behind the hotel door frame, Ned Brock unleashed a screed of obscenities.

"Hold...up," said Reece, her hands massaging her neck, "Wait...a minute."

"You'll forgive me if I find us some cover, Contessa."

Lin hustled behind the wagon and propped her up against the back wheel. Reece put her hands out to her sides and steadied herself on the steel rim.

Micah scurried up to the bench seat while Griff backpedaled in, holding the leather bag up near his face for cover.

He still carried Reece's old No. 5 Revolver in one hand.

Griff tossed the satchel up to Micah. "Hot potato,"

he said, then turned to face the hotel and toss off another two shots.

"We need to stop fighting," said Reece, her voice stronger now.

"Are you okay?" said Lin.

She nodded, coughed, nodded again. "I'm...okay. Doesn't...doesn't matter." She directed her words to Griff. "Please, tell Griff to stop shooting. Mister Tyner is our friend."

"Not hardly," said Lin.

"He is. Dammit...if you give me a chance." She pulled away from Lin with a jerk and lurched sideways behind Griff, out from behind the wagon.

"Tyner," she rasped. "Mister Tyner!"

"Reece!" said Lin, but it was too late.

She stepped out from behind the wagon and another round of gunfire crashed through the air.

But this time the gunfire didn't come from the hotel.

It came from one of the two men Lin had seen working with the steam engine's leather belt. Responding to the gunfire at the house. Or maybe they had seen Tom stretched out on the porch.

The man was firing a small pistol and didn't seem to be sure of his target.

He blasted away, finally turning his attention to the wagon's driver seat.

Micah jumped from the coach as wood splintered under his seat, and Lin pulled Reece back behind the wagon and grabbed hold of the step rail. Another shot from the oncoming hired hand kept him and Micah both from claiming the bench, and the noise scared the team silly.

Already spooked by the raucous activity around them, the animals danced this way and that before finding purchase on solid ground, abandoning their human counterparts.

Unmanned, the team bolted ahead toward the sawmill, straight at the lanky pistol man who leapt from the path of the coach. He stumbled, and fell, rolling over in the dirt.

Lin watched the rig career toward the steam engine. The equines' forward progress was confused and erratic, swerving in a winding loop.

They weren't the only ones running willy-nilly.

From inside the hotel, Tyner with Brock, Curly, and the Sodbuster in tow, stumbled down from the porch, waving their guns high. At this point, Tyner's Remies had to be spent. Lin couldn't count shots like Reece, but the old man had lobbed more than ten since the first pair of bullets cracked open Annie's pate.

But why was Brock holding back on the triggers?

He still carried Lin's Colt, but wasn't shooting, and the other two men had weapons drawn, but likewise stayed still.

Lin looked across the farmyard and saw why they hesitated.

At the sound of gunfire, more working men at Plummer's station had gathered and were marching across the open yard with sleeves rolled up and farm implements in hand.

Long guns too.

The mob numbered ten to twenty concerned mugs, hard-faced men with furrowed brows and tight lips, coming up fast toward the hotel.

The white man Lin had seen working at the wagon led the pack. He carried what looked to Lin like an Enfield cavalry carbine. Another man had an older musket of some kind with a fixed bayonet.

Ned Brock and his two pals ran for their horses.

Two or three hundred feet away, the Concord stopped betwixt two barns, and Lin turned his attention back to Flood Tyner who was following Brock, hoping to make the horses. After the melee in the foyer, all the miscreants wanted to escape Plummer's—including Lin.

The Overland trail ahead was a flat run under a row of tall cottonwoods leading to the Ozark mountains' lofty blue-green horizon.

But none of them would make it to the main road.

Brock didn't even reach the stirrup before somebody shot the ground out from under him. Rock and dirt shot up like from a tiny volcano, and Brock landed on his butt, Lin's Colt wagging in the air. Curly reversed course, diving past Tyner, hoping to find cover in the house.

Halfway to the wide porch, a carbine shot echoed across the ranch. Punctured in the back, Curly's shirt sported a billowing red circle, and he hit the ground face first, flat out.

Tyner waddled like a duck out of water, his path leading straight for Reece. Griff held tight to the Number Five, pointed it above the heads of the mob and fired. Two men in the front line flinched.

But they kept coming.

Reece was too busy upbraiding Tyner to notice. "You idiot, do you see what you've done? Do you see what's happening? You stupid, stupid man. Two people dead because of your nonsense."

Twenty feet behind Tyner, the Sodbuster saw Curly's corpse and took his partner's death personal-like. Whirling out from behind Brock's horse, his gun blazed with fury.

Imminently practical, Brock used the diversion to mount up.

Solid in the saddle, he brought the steed around in front of the crowd, even as they mowed the Sodbuster in two with a powder-fueled salvo.

He pawed thin air, the port wine birthmark stretching wide with his open, silent scream. The Sodbuster's body collapsed at Reece's feet.

"Three people," she told Tyner, correcting herself from before. "Three people dead because of your nonsense. Shall we make it four?"

"Begging your pardon, ma'am, but we're out in the open here," said Micah. "We need to get moving."

It was an understatement if ever there was one.

More men were filling the ranks now, coming up from behind the sawmill and pouring out the door of a long building Lin guessed was the bunkhouse. A kid in dungarees with no shirt yelled, "They's shootin' up the house!" And a bearded gent next to him lifted a hickory club and replied, "Let's go get 'em!"

Lin recalled the history lessons he learned from his mom: citizens on a Holy Crusade.

There were at least fourteen to fifteen men from Plummer, every last mother's son hoisting a stick, plank, or club. Half of them carried firearms of one kind or other.

Some held on to pitchforks, and they called to each other as they came, encouraging each other's outrage, priming the fuse for violence. "There they are," said a tall black man with a pork pie hat. "Don't let 'em get away!"

"Kill 'em!"

"Make 'em pay!"

Lin was assured most of the crowd had no earthly idea what, or who, they were avenging.

The crowd ran ahead, overtaking Brock's unsteady horse.

The gunslinger left the saddle in an awkward position, feet facing heaven. For an instant, Brock disappeared in the circle of eight or nine men, each of them kicking and pounding at him, all of them yelling and losing control.

Coughing dust, with blood running down his face, Brock crawled free, scurried to his feet, stumbled, then ran straight for Lin and Micah. "Get to cover, goddammit," he yelled. "Find shelter, or we're all killed."

Tyner put his arm around Reece and ran with Griff across the open yard.

Lin, Micah, and Brock brought up the rear.

The six of them ran perpendicular from the mob, down the long, grassy incline to the branch valley floor. Tripping, skipping, and dodging gopher holes, Lin succumbed to the pull of gravity and fell, rolling back to his feet, pounding leather for the tree line ahead.

Tyner almost went down too, but Reece set him straight.

When Brock tripped over a stump, he wasn't so lucky. He went down hard, inadvertently crying out, and when Lin looked back, Brock was struggling to rise.

Lin changed the direction of his escape, went back, running straight at the group of men just beginning their descent of the hill.

"Can you walk?"

Brock snarled at Lin's charity. "Go on, don't worry about me."

Lin grabbed a handful of Brock's heavy shirt and jerked him upright, then got under his shoulder and hefted him up. "I wouldn't leave a dog to that bunch."

"You want dogs?" said Brock, "We got dogs right here."

The two border collies Lin met when they arrived had far outpaced the mob and flanked them in the grass on either side. One, a short black and white cur, was bolting on ahead, intent to capture Griff by the seat of his britches. Nipping, barking, chasing Griff like a rabbit, he was soon out of sight as Reece led him and Tyner into the trees.

The other dog, heavier than his companion, with brown hair and white markings was circling around in front of Lin. Lips peeled back, showing a row of white, snapping fangs, the dog wasn't fooling around.

Brock still had the Colt in hand and pushed it toward Lin.

"There's two shots left," he said.

"I won't shoot the dog, Brock."

"The first one's for me."

"Oh, for cryin' out loud."

"Do it, Ranger. Dammit, you'd do it to a horse was holding you back. I can't walk for piss."

"As if I don't have enough theatrics with Griff and my girl. Now I got a gunnie thinks he's Hamlet."

"Ham who?" said Brock.

"Just scare the dog away. Shoot in the air."

The collie stopped in their path, held its ground and barked.

Lin kept moving, but at the speed they limped along, they weren't getting too far. Brock was right, he couldn't walk for piss, and the first of the crowd was hot on their heels.

In the corner of his eye, Lin saw death coming. The reaper was a bearded man with a club.

Brock triggered the Colt into the air above the dog. The collie flinched, lowering itself to its haunches, but didn't exactly turn tail.

The distraction was enough to buy them a few seconds.

Darting off to the right and finally on flat land, Lin hoped to find cover. He aimed for a series of split-rail fences and peaked A-frame hog sheds planted along the tree line.

He was headed in the general direction of the sawmill, resting back up on the hill above. The Concord waited there, between two buildings. If only he could circle back up the hill and take command of the rig.

But what then? Where were Reece and the others?

Lin had no idea what became of them.

And he didn't have time to find out.

A sudden impact from behind sent him and Brock reeling.

A dull, heavy agony coursed through his legs, and his pursuer's club came once more across the back of his thighs.

Lin dropped Brock to roll with the blow, smacking his ribs into the hard prairie sod, and wrenching his neck. Doing his best to ignore the pain, he jumped to his feet and struck out at the bearded man with his left arm. He missed and took a thump of hickory to the shoulder for his mistake.

Swallowing hard, knuckling sweat from his eyes, he backed away, instinctively falling into the quick foot-work his dad taught him on the farm.

His opponent was smaller than him, but Lin had learned not to be over-confident.

Small men could be quick. It proved to be the case with this one.

A fast flurry of moves with the stick pushed Lin back to the edge of the tree line close to where Brock had landed.

The stick came at him again. Lin batted it away.

Again, and Lin slapped it.

The two combatants circled one another as three more men worked their way down the steep hill.

The fellow was no more than twenty years old, his beard a red peach-fuzz dusting. Close up, Lin saw fear in the callow pink face. He decided to use it to his advantage.

He decided to scare the kid.

He barked a command over his shoulder to Brock.

"Shoot him. Blow the kid apart."

With a befuddled expression, Brock held up both hands. Empty.

Well, hell.

"What happened to my Colt?" said Lin.

"Lost it when we fell," said Brock.

"What about your own gun?"

"Gone too."

So much for scaring the kid.

If anything, the verbal exchange had emboldened the stick.

Lin blocked the kid's next swing, then launched a kick into his breadbasket, knocking him back several feet.

Lin tossed a comment to Brock over his shoulder. "You aren't much of a gunfighter."

"You aren't much of a Texas Ranger," said Brock.

"Where's Reece?" said Lin.

"Seen her and Griff take Tyner up the other way into the trees."

The bearded kid came in again, faster than ever, swinging the hickory stick with all his might. Lin was winded from the run. Tired from carrying Brock.

This latest tussle needed to end fast.

Lin remembered Dad's instructions. Footwork was his friend. If he could step, step.

One more step. Fit in close.

Close enough to smell the boy's sour breath.

Catching the club on his forearm hurt like hell, but a withering combination right jab, left cross, right hook brought the smaller fighter to his knees.

The fear was back, plastered all over the kid's face. Lin finished him off with a boot to the head.

Almost immediately, a flurry of lead slapped the ground around them, tearing up divots of topsoil and showering them with bits of mud and underbrush.

The other men had taken the opportunity to reload their weapons.

Hefting him along, Lin carried Brock a couple hundred yards alongside the hog pen. Along the way, he spied his Colt Walker .44 half-buried in the mud where it had apparently landed when Brock went down.

Lin snatched up the weapon, dumped Brock, and inspected the cylinder. He dug hunks of earth from the iron and polished the action.

Plummer supplied his hogs with four, man-sized A-frame huts made of scrap lumber. When a rifle shot thundered in Lin's direction, he crouched down behind one of the shelters, counted to five, then spun out and snapped off two fast shots.

The last two shots he had.

A carbine crack split the air and whacked into the facade of the hog hut.

He and Brock were pinned down. Locked in place.

If only he more powder, lead balls, and caps, he could return fire.

If only he could catch his breath.

He was tired of feeling so damned helpless.

"Tyner's gun wagon is hidden somewhere around here," said Brock. "Tyner told Plummer to take it someplace and hide it from you. If they others find it, they can hold off a small army with the armory Tyner's got inside."

Another barrage erupted from the top of the hill and a pig squealed as a blast nipped his tail.

"Good for them. What about us?"

Brock showed his teeth, and the rotten smile sent a chill up Lin's spine. "Like I said, Ranger. They shoot horses, don't they?"

CHAPTER 24

REECE STRUGGLED AGAINST THE PAIN IN HER THROAT
as Tyner led her, Micah, and Griff down a wooded hill
and around a dilapidated old privy. The broken-down
structure was surrounded by a cloud of buzzing, biting
flies. They stopped behind the privy to catch their
breath.

Griff dropped the leather bag of stock certificates
to the moss-covered earth.

"Isn't this a fine destination for our travels?"

"I saw the wood structure," said Tyner. "I had
hoped my wagon might be stashed nearby."

The iron tang of blood washed across Reece's
tongue, and she breathed through aching lungs. Annie
Plummer hadn't managed to kill her off today.

But she wasn't sure about tomorrow and breathing
in the stink of the latrine was almost worse than not
breathing at all.

Far behind, in the distance, the sound of gunfire
split the noon-time air, and men shouted loud and long.

Reece felt a wave of panic threatening to well up
and overtake the self-pity she already wallowed in.
Where was Lin? Was he okay?

Time to nip all the self-indulgence in the bud, she thought.

Time enough to worry later on.

As she had so often done in the past, she clamped down on her emotions.

Tyner said, "Plummer drove the wagon in this direction...said something about putting it with the horses in the lower meadow. He said there was a clearing in the trees nearby."

"We wouldn't be in this mess if you hadn't been trying to hide from us to begin with," said Griff.

"I admit to asking Plummer to park the wagon somewhere out of the way, where it wouldn't be seen," said Tyner. "Apparently he was quite efficient."

"But you think he went off in this direction?"

Tyner said he did. "I distinctly heard him say, *a clearing in the trees.*"

"You all stay put," said Griff. "One can move more surreptitiously than four."

Griff handed the bag of stock certificates to Reece and forged off through the woods.

"You think we should let him go off alone?" said Micah.

"He's fiercely independent," said Tyner. "Efficiency minded. I'm impressed with him."

"You don't know beans about him," said Micah.

Reece turned on Tyner, scolding him like a schoolmarm. "His efficiency wouldn't matter if you hadn't been playing such a damn foolish game to start with. Griff was right. You've endangered us all. Hiding from us like...like children."

"It's you I was concerned with, Miss Sinclair. I didn't want them to spirit you away."

"Them, meaning us," said Micah. "Lin, Griff, and me."

Tyner spoke up for himself. "You can't deny you three men robbed the train in Syracuse. I saw it."

"Did you stop to think there might be a good reason for what you saw?" said Reece. "Didn't you ever consider I might be part of it?"

Tyner's face flashed red with embarrassment and his voice faltered. "I only assumed a young lass such as yourself..."

Young lass.

Synonymous with helpless, foolish. In need of protection.

Reece held back her temper.

Everybody always underestimated her. No matter how many times she proved them wrong. No matter how many times she showed off her strength.

"You assumed I was weak."

"You are, after all, a woman," said Tyner.

Micah let out a long breath at the comment. "Uh, oh," he said. "Here we go."

"I think I'm owed an apology for your remark," said Reece, her voice rising an octave. "Don't you think I'm owed an apology, Micah?"

"I'm not involved."

"You apologize right now, Flood Tyner."

Tyner's face lit up. Eagerly lacing his fingers together in supplication, he said, "Would you *accept* an apology?"

Taken aback by the query, Reece thought it over. "No. I don't think so," she said.

"She absolutely would not," said Micah. "I've tried."

"I found the wagon," said Griff. "But it's not exactly accessible."

Appearing between two sprigs of a crooked plum tree grove, he popped in with brambles stuck to his ebony pant legs and stick-tights glued to his hammer tailed coat.

Griff motioned for Reece, Micah, and Tyner to follow him.

Before long, they came to a grassy hillside. The clearing in the woods was less than an acre, and it was surrounded by overgrown stands of elm, shag-bark hickory, hackberry, and pine. A single cow-trail lane led into the glade, and a single trail led out in the opposite direction.

Tyner's red wagon was parked next to a stout old Walnut tree, the ground around it heavily littered with wrinkled husks—dropped walnuts left over from the previous fall. Both of the giant gray Percherons were hobbled nearby, contented and munching on the grass.

"I'm surprised the harvest here was left to rot."

"Maybe the Plummers don't like walnuts," said Griff.

"Shush, you'll be overheard," said Tyner.

If the clean-shaven old coot leaning on the wagon's front wheel heard them, he gave no indication.

The fellow seemed content to carve chunks from a raw turnip with his long iron knife. Lost in thought and enjoying the day, he was balding and nearly as rawboned as Tom Plummer with loose fitting work clothes and mismatched boots.

"He seems friendly enough," said Tyner.

"Everybody here seems friendly at first," said Reece, jerking the Walch Navy out of her waistband. "We almost died finding out otherwise."

Tyner spied the gun he had sold Reece at auction and admired it. "Have you had the chance to fire your new purchase?"

"She has indeed," said Griff, "but perhaps we ought not discuss it right now."

Reece lowered her brow. "Griffin is right. Let's not discuss it."

"Was there a problem?" said Tyner.

"Shush," said Micah.

Taking careful aim, Reece caressed the gun's trigger —gentle as petting a newborn kitten.

The lone, ear-shattering boom sent a flurry of birds from the trees and filled the glade with blue powder smoke.

Between the man's fingers, the turnip vaporized.

He fell backwards against the wagon and didn't move.

Reece called to him through the trees. "The next one goes through your head."

The man held up his hands, and Reece realized he was trembling with fear. "D-don't shoot me," he said. "I ain't doin' nothin' but watchin' these here horses. Don't shoot me."

"You've got nothing to worry about," said Reece. "As long as you do what I tell you."

"I don't like no shootin'."

"Back away from the wagon."

The old man did as he was told and Reece advanced into the clearing, her gun hand not wavering. "What's your name?"

The old man stood at attention, facing the four.

"Jasper Tucks."

"Nice wagon you've got here, Jasper." Reece cocked her head toward the back end. "I can't but help notice it's open. Anybody inside there?"

Tucks was surprised by the question. "No, nobody inside."

Micah waved Tyner back while he and Griff approached the rear end of the wagon along the near side. When they sprang around the open back doors,

Reece saw Griff had his brass gun in one hand, the No. 5 in the other—and both were aimed inside the open van.

"He's right, Miss Reece. It's empty," said Micah.

"More than empty," said Griff. "It's been completely cleaned out."

"Oh, heavens," said Tyner, bustling across the way to his wagon. "Oh, heavens to Betsy."

"Mister Plummer brought this here wagon down to the clearin'," said Jasper. "He says for me to watch it, so I watch it. Make sure the big ol' purty horses don't run off."

Reece kept the Walch pointed at Jasper as she walked to the back of the wagon. Micah hadn't exaggerated in the least. The only thing inside the van was a distinct odor of black powder and gun oil. Every cubic inch of the enclosed wood cargo space was slicked clean.

"You have no idea how much money this vacancy represents," said Tyner. "My life was inside this wagon. Why, it wasn't just my business. It was my home."

Reece rejoined Jasper and picked a chunk of turnip from the ground. "I'm sorry I shot your lunch."

Jasper rubbed the food on his shirt and popped it into his mouth. "Still chews good," he said.

"They've cleaned me out," said Tyner, fuming. "Not only my business inventory, but my personal possessions as well. I had letters, books. Childhood mementos. All gone."

"Serves you right," said Reece.

Tyner wasn't having it. He shot back, "All I did was ask Plummer to park my wagon, and—behind my back —they cleaned me out." Reece thought he would stamp his foot.

"All you did was plan to ambush me, behind my

back," said Reece. "You'll get no sympathy from us, sir."

Jasper spoke up then. "I seen 'em take the guns out, mister. Guns and barrels of powder and everythin'. Mister Plummer unloaded it all beside his sawmill after you and your friends went inside the hotel. Mister Plummer said it was...somethin'."

"What are you trying to say?" said Tyner.

Jasper tapped his chin. "Plummer...he called your cargo something-something...like he deserved havin' it more than you did. Like he earned it somehow."

Tyner complained. "Plummer has been a well-respected stop on the Butterfield Overland for years. There's no reason I should have suspected him of foul play."

"The fox was outfoxed," said Micah. "Happens all the time."

Jasper snapped his fingers.

"I remember what it was Plummer said. *Spoils of war* is what he called it," said Jasper. "He said the content of your wagon was spoils of war."

A BOOM ECHOED ACROSS THE BRANCH VALLEY AT Plummer's hog pen as one last hunk of lead plowed into the turf ten feet behind Lin's boot.

He huddled against the back of the peaked roof shed and took stock of the situation.

The shots were coming slower now as the gathering of men on the high hill lost its initial enthusiasm. Some of the revengers had apparently thought better of their actions when Lin triggered off his twin shots.

Under duress, some of Plummer's ranch hands had opted not to play.

Others had wandered off into the trees, possibly looking for Reece and Tyner.

A small contingency on the hillside were trying to reload. Lin figured they were low on supplies. He hadn't seen anybody with a powder horn around his neck, and a handful of bullets didn't last long.

He shoved his Colt back into its home in the leather holster on his belt.

From where he was positioned, Lin had a good view of the uphill slope. They were a few hundred yards from the sawmill, the green Concord waiting at the summit, still attached to its string of animals.

Brock was curled up behind the next pig shed to Lin's left.

"If you covered me, Brock, I wonder if I could make it up there to the coach?"

"How the hell do you expect me to cover you? I told you—I lost my gun, and yours is empty now."

"I'm thinking about a trick I pulled yesterday with a herd of cows at Wynot's Dairy."

"Wynot's Dairy? I know where that is," said Brock.

"You ought to. Didn't you ride through there last night with Tyner?"

"As a matter of fact," Brock snapped his fingers, "We rode through there last night."

Lin had to remind himself Brock's mind ran about three ticks behind his own.

"The point is," said Lin, "I opened the fence and sent a herd of beef into a slow stampede between me and some other men who were following us."

"Who was following you? Was it the bald man and his smelly wife?"

At the mention of Baldy, Lin perked up. "No, but how do you know about them?"

He had long suspected Baldy wouldn't let the accusation of horse thieving go without retribution.

"These folks got it in for you real bad. They said they've got a score to settle with you all."

After Brock recounted Baldy's speech in the dining room at Mulhaven's station, Lin told him, "It wasn't Baldy who I waylaid with the cows. It was a man named Coombs."

"The German with the wooden arm?" said Brock. "We saw him at Mulhaven, too."

"He won't bother us anymore."

"Pretty smart move with the cows," said Brock. "I don't know if I'd have thought of such a thing."

"I'm thinking we can pull the same trick here," said Lin.

As if on cue, a white bristle-haired sow snuffed at the corner of the fence where it met the shed. The old girl must've weighed an easy 250 pounds, maybe more, and she stood waist high.

Brock looked around. "Ain't no cows here, Ranger."

"This time we do it with pigs," said Lin. He motioned toward the sedentary group of figures on the hillside. "Those hombres are running low on ammo, and they're being careful for now. Once they figure out we haven't fired back, they'll blow in like a cyclone."

"What do you want to do?"

"I want to kick down a portion of this fence and let all these pigs out. Send 'em off in all directions."

"Like a distraction?"

"Exactly like a distraction. The hands won't want to shoot for hitting the pork, and I'll skedaddle up the hill to our wagon."

"They'll see you," said Brock.

"I've got some thoughts about how it could work," said Lin.

While Lin was growing up, his mom supplemented their homestead farming operation by teaching school. Lin had never been much of a reader, but his mom had given him a working knowledge of classic literature, including Homer's *Odyssey*.

Therein was a scene where Odysseus and his men were trapped in a cave with a man-eating cyclops named Polyphemus. After blinding the cyclops by poking his eye out with a sharp stick, the men escape

Polyphemus' cave by hiding under his sheep. They walked out of the cave beneath the four-legged critters.

Lin planned to skip the blinding part and get right on to hiding behind the pigs.

And in the end, it almost worked as well as he hoped.

The problem was pigs aren't sheep. Or stampeding cattle.

Lin reared up, kicked down the rails of the pen, and while some of the pigs simply stood there, moving toward the opening slow as clouds on a windless day, others kicked up their heels and ran.

Taken off-guard, Lin went down on all fours behind three zig-zagging pork butts, only to be left conspicuously in the open when they froze cold, spun, and lumbered off in the opposite direction.

A shout came from the hillside. "There he is! There's one of them now."

And a hail of bullets followed.

At least four or five.

But to Lin, overexposed and unarmed, five was a blizzard of lead.

Right then he would have gone to ground, perforated and expiring, if Tyner's red wagon hadn't come rolling out of the trees. Its heavy steel-rimmed wheels churned up the sod, cutting grooves in the soft grazing ground.

Brock gave out a loud cheer.

Micah sat on the bench seat beside Tyner, flinging a long, braided whip over the heads of two magnificent steeds.

It was the same outfit Lin had seen intervening on their behalf in Syracuse. Different this time was an open square hatch in the center of the painted van, directly underneath Tyner's name, but over top of the *Guns and Service* sign.

The little opening was a gunport, and somebody inside the van was firing a steady blast of powder every few seconds.

Ahead of Lin, Brock made a break for the wagon, but immediately fell over as his ankle gave out under his weight.

Then, even as Lin followed suit, Griff was out the back door, helping Brock up, bringing him to the safety of the van.

Blam! Blam! A pair of well-aimed slugs blew aside a piece of wood trim from the wagon's roof. Lin didn't know if the van's heavy paneling would stop a lead ball, but he didn't like betting Reece's life on it.

Because if Griff was hustling Brock along across the turf, it meant Reece was inside, lobbing shots out the little port with her twelve-shooter.

The wagon came trundling on, rocking on its thoroughbraces, threatening to tip over sideways as Lin approached.

Appearing around the corner of the peaked hog sheds, a burly Irishman with curly red hair wound his way through the hogs, aiming to intercept Lin's path. Just as quick, he met with a bullet from the Walch. The slug hit him in the arm, shredding a hunk of meat from his bicep, toppling him backwards over a skittering boar pig.

"That had to sting," said Lin, now in a flat-out run, paralleling the wagon, opening his hand wide, reaching for a hold on the stair rail.

Three more concussions sounded from the rear of the wagon, and Lin was secure just below the bench seat next to Tyner, hanging on tight, clenching his jaw in response to the rambunctious bouncing of the ride.

He didn't want to bite his tongue.

After all the bullets he'd dodged, what a stupid way to die.

Bite his tongue and get the gangrene.

But stranger things had happened.

And, unfortunately, were about to.

CHAPTER 26

AT THE TOP OF PLUMMER'S HILL, THE SAWMILL'S steam engine was chuffing out a plume of rolling black soot, silky smooth and mesmerizing to watch. The big, hissing boiler had been abandoned when all the action started, and Lin urged Micah to steer the wagon clear of the thing lest it fly apart, unmanned and out of control.

But the steam engine wasn't entirely unmanned.

Alone, standing thirty feet away in a loose mound of cedar-red sawdust, Tom Plummer watched them come.

Beside him, the towering flywheel spun hypnotically, its flapping long leather belt pulled through a series of horizontal tension wheels ending in a vertical rig attached to a jagged iron wheel with razor teeth. Wider than a man's chest the sawblade might cut through anything, given enough steam.

All it would take to get the blade spinning was a solid toss of a long hand-clutch lever near Plummer's right hand.

Tyner's Percherons didn't like the squealing steam

tank and pulled away. The big horses threatened to take them back down the hill toward the posse of men who doggedly refused to give them up.

Lin dropped to the ground, catching the moving earth beneath his heavy boots. "Keep going," he told Micah. "Head out of here up the Overland trail. I'll catch up to you."

The grounds were littered with wood scraps and chaff, and nearby piles of long, well shaved planks, cut straight and true, were a testament to the industrial age.

A horseless wagon loaded with iron wrenches and two spare blades sat behind the boiler, and Lin saw a tall bucket of pork fat grease, and a big, rubber mallet on the tailgate. Intermixed with everything else were Flood Tyner's guns. Pistols of various calibers were stacked next to the mallet. Carbines leaned casually against the wagon's wheel.

At Tom Plummer's side, a waist-high barrel of black powder had been pried open, it's banded circular top propped reckless against the steaming hot boiler.

Another barrel was open and tipped over, a telltale trail of powder showing where it had rolled.

Pants covered knee-high with sawdust, Plummer reached into his pocket and took out a rod of carbon steel and a flint stone.

Lin's heart skipped a beat, but his mouth kept working. "Get to the road, Micah. Get far away!" he urged. Micah cracked the whip, and the Percherons picked up the pace, swerving around a stack of walnut timber, lugging the big red box away from the mill with open back doors.

At the last minute, Reece slid out and jogged toward him, carrying the Walch beside her hip.

Lin waved her away, "Stay back. Reece, stay away."

But she was already there, taking aim at Plummer, though her finger wasn't on the trigger. "We're leaving without you, sweetie," she said. "Why'd you jump down?"

"Plummer needs help," said Lin. "Look at the poor bastard."

Looking like a deflated, flat scarecrow, the man had lost his hat and glasses since Lin saw him sprawled out on the porch. His chaps hugged his legs like security blankets, and the rowels were missing from both spurs.

Tears had carved a map of valleys into his soot-stained face, and Tom Plummer's voice was weak with sorrow. He gazed at the flint stone and rod with unfocused eyes, then struck them together.

A shower of sparks rained down into the black powder.

"Don't do it, Tom," called Lin.

Plummer's answer was a pleading whine.

"Do you know what it's like to be alone, Jarret?" he said. "To be truly alone, with nobody but yourself to cook for, to clean for, to talk to?"

Lin kept his eye on the stick and stone, tried to keep his voice steady. "I do," he said, taking a step forward. "I've been alone ever since my folks died."

"You lyin' piece of skunk bait," said Plummer with a hiss. "You ain't been alone for a good long time."

Again, Plummer sparked steel against rock.

"I ain't gonna argue with you, Tom."

"You got all them friends," said Tom, flinging out his arm. "You got *her*."

Reece swallowed, but kept the iron sites of the Walch glued to Plummer's forehead. "Tell him to drop the fire-making stuff, Lin. Or he'll go just like his wife —two in the brainpan."

"You'd like to do it, too," said Plummer. "You enjoy killing, don't you? You little hussy."

"None of this is worth dying over, Tom."

"It was worth it to Annie."

"Annie was wrong. She was no good, Tom."

"No good?" Plummer's face contorted into a purple rage, and he smashed the flint over and over, creating a fireworks display. "I'll show you what's no good."

"Stand aside, Lin," said Reece. "If the powder goes up, it'll take us and some of Plummer's men as well."

"You got no idea how long I've been alone here. Surrounded by men with their wives and kids. Dogs and cats and stinkin' chickens. But nobody for Tommy. Nobody to cook his supper or scratch his back. Nobody to care for."

"Tom, please," said Lin.

"You got a family now. All them in the wagon."

From the corner of his eye, Lin saw the wagon waiting, saw Griff standing inside, hanging on to a rail next to Brock and Tyner.

"Imagine if you had nobody to die for. Imagine what that's like." Plummer tilted his head sideways. "It's hell, Jarret. That's what it is. It's hell."

A pair of Plummer's men crested the hill. One carried a stout hickory stick. The other clutched a carbine, apparently empty of ammunition. Their puzzled expression traveled from the huffing steam engine to their maniacal boss, over to Lin.

"Back off," said Lin, warning them.

Then he offered his hand to Plummer.

"You were always a good man, Tom. You can be a good man again."

He shook his head and now the tears were coming in steady streams. Lin had a soft heart for a lot of things, but watching a grown man stand bawling like a baby revolted him.

He shook his head and gave up. "Let's get back to the wagon," he said.

Reece lowered her gun and Lin turned his back on Plummer. He looped an insistent arm across her shoulders, urging Reece on to the wagon more quickly than his words conveyed. "I've got no time for temper tantrums."

"There is no good without Annie," said Plummer.

Lin picked up the pace, pushing Reece ahead of him. She waved the wagon on, and Micah cracked the whip, spurring the Percherons into a quick march.

"Damn you," shouted Tom Plummer from his place beside the angry, pressurized steam engine. "Goddamn you both to hell."

When the powder went up, it knocked Lin and Reece off their feet.

When the boiler ruptured, the sky caved in, and Lin saw nothing but red until everything went black.

———

HE WOKE up on the bench seat, rolling through a field of daisies with Reece hovering over his face.

Close enough to brush lips.

Lin kissed her gently and knew he'd gone to heaven.

"Back to work, Ranger. We've got a new team to hitch up."

"You don't sound like an angel," said Lin.

Reece's sweet visage was replaced with a menacing scowl.

"Never met one myself," said Micah, swapping places with Reece, "and I shan't plan to anytime soon."

Lin sat up on the green Concord. Situated between

Micah and Reece, he watched as the Overland trail rolled out ahead of them. Under Micah's sure hand, the coach thundered along beside a small spring-fed stream.

Ahead, two engineered water breaks, mounds of mud and rock reared up and Micah hollered, "Hang on!"

The coach wheels banged hard against the bump, launched into the air, and dropped down with a crash. Lin grabbed at his hat and readjusted his hold on the bench seat.

"Where the hell are we?"

"A couple of miles out of Plummer's. You bumped your head."

"Damned if we're not gonna miss out on fresh horses again," Lin said as the mule struggled to keep up with the three mares in harness.

"Don't be so sure," said Reece. "I don't think we've passed the remuda of mules Plummer mentioned."

"At least we got the Concord back." Lin cranked his neck around. "Where's Tyner's wagon?"

"Directly behind us."

"What happened to Tom Plummer?"

"You don't remember the big boom?" said Micah.

"I remember talking to Tom...then...?"

"The damn fool got what he deserved," said Reece.

They rode for several heartbeats in silence.

"I should've done better," said Lin.

"I'll tell 'em to carve that on your tombstone," said Micah.

Reece pointed to an open pasture full of mules. "Stop here," she said, indicating a graveled pull-in. "It's the Butterfield Overland mules Plummer told us about. Those critters are an answer to our prayers."

Micah pulled hard on the reins, arching the team

into a wide, looping turn and they careened to a halt in the open grass next to the rail-fenced mule pen. The wagon braked with a lurch, Micah slammed back the brake and stared at Lin.

"You gonna be able to function?"

The instant Lin's boots hit the ground he fell back against the coach wheels. "Maybe not," he said as the red gun wagon pulled off the road and parked beside them.

Tyner's wagon was roughly the same size as the Concord, but the van wasn't as sturdy, and it had taken quite a bit of lead. Lin counted at least nine splintered bullet holes.

Tyner climbed down off his wagon like he had back problems.

Rheumatism, thought Lin.

Bad knees. A bad hip.

Micah rubbed his shoulder.

Griff rubbed his forehead and Brock didn't even leave Tyner's wagon.

Every last one of them had some sort of pain somewhere.

They were all in a world of hurt.

Tyner limped over to Lin, but when he spoke, his voice was strong and full of vinegar. "It's no party gettin' old. Makes a man slow on the draw. Slow in the head too. You shouldn't have tried talking to Plummer. Your foolishness might've killed us all."

Lin felt the words strike hard. Tyner's advice dug in deep and would remain there.

Young men traded barbs like shots of whiskey, talked horseshit to each other, and duked it out if need be. Old men weren't a lot different, just slower.

Sometimes the slow pace allowed time for mindfulness creep in.

As Lin stood at the foot of his wagon step, he felt older than he ever had.

"Seven devils trying to kill us," he said under his breath, and Reece heard him.

"You're talking about the dream I had?"

"Seven devils." Lin counted on his fingers. "Baldy, Verna, Dale, Prescott, Seth Coombs, Annie."

"That's only six," said Reece.

Birds sang in the cottonwood trees. The curious Butterfield Overland mules wandered over to nose the fence rail close to the wagon. The leaves rustled in the wind, a calming whisper. Somewhere back in the direction of Plummer's station, a cow lowed, and Lin felt his grip relax on his belt.

He stared at the black column of smoke on the horizon.

Plummer's station was on fire.

Would likely burn for the rest of the day and on into the night.

"They're all gonna be too busy to follow us," said Lin.

But even as he said it, the sound of galloping hooves approached.

Lin reached for his Colt, realized it was empty, then looked to the road.

A lone rider on a fast black stallion careened past. If he noticed the two wagons parked in the pasture, he gave no sign. Instead, he continued pounding up the road until he was out of sight.

"He'll be headed for Springfield," said Lin.

"Reckon whoever the rider is, he'll spread the word about Plummer," said Micah. "About us, too."

"Springfield has a telegraph line back to Jefferson City and St. Louis. Once the local chapter of the Ivory Compass knows what happened..." began Reece.

"Prescott will find out what happened here," said Griff.

"We can't outrun the wire," said Lin, and his head hurt twice as much as before.

CHAPTER 27

THE COPPER-COLORED SUN WAS NEAR THE HORIZON, warming the pale sycamore trees along the Missouri, flaming the evening air with a last temperate charge before giving way to the cold and dark.

It was late in the season for a freeze, but Prescott's bones told him frost would invade overnight. Dressed in a black wool suit coat with matching trousers and thick socks inside his cowhide boots, he turned his snow-frocked visage into the sun and tried to shake off the chill.

It was little wonder his friend from the newspaper office drank his bourbon in such quantities straight from the crystal tumbler.

Bad news and a chilly night went together hand in hand.

They sat at one of seven wrought-iron tables on the boardwalk outside Mendelsohn's Café, in the shadow of the Capitol, the wide muddy Missouri River lapping at the base of the hill. Prescott nodded at a bald man inhabiting a table near to them. "Pleasant evening, Senator," he said.

The legislator nodded with recognition.

Prescott turned back to his coffee, watched the man who sat across from him.

He suspected Blake McCormick only posed as a friend.

McCormick's visage had the same sagging gray pallor of his suit. Though facing the sun, the light didn't appear to touch him.

Prescott sipped brandy and cinnamon-spiced coffee through his beard and stayed quiet.

Never trust a man who dresses like a mortician.

Some said McCormick's family lineage went straight back to Virginia and old Cyrus, the inventor of the mechanical reaper. Blake said nothing to confirm or deny his lineage, but he certainly spread money around the capital of Missouri like an affluent heir apparent.

Heir to the reaper. Prescott figured there was a good joke there.

No matter where it came from, Blake had access to a mountain of wealth and political connections.

And there was death.

Prescott reminded himself any killings linked to McCormick were only unfounded rumors.

There was no denying McCormick took a perverse glee in delivering bad news.

The gray man tapped his finger on the table's surface, reiterating his last point to Prescott as if speaking to a child. It was an annoying habit, the finger and the pedantics.

Everyone in the Compass said so.

"You have to face the facts, old sport," said McCormick. "Seth Coombs is dead, and Plummer's station is in flames. These Hellbenders of yours are more resourceful than you gave them credit for."

Prescott nestled his cup gently in its saucer, doing his best to breathe like the doctor had told him. In through the nose, expanding his stomach, keeping his shoulders level, his inhalations smooth. Out through the mouth, his exhales unfaltering.

It wouldn't do to show weakness. Not here. Not in front of McCormick, and most definitely not in public with the cream of Jefferson City society all around him.

Prescott tried hard to keep the irritation from his voice. "Keep your voice down, won't you?"

His answer was an impish expression of impatience.

Prescott pushed onward. "A Spanish slip of a girl, an itinerant lawman, and a runaway slave. They're most assuredly not *my* Hellbenders."

The gray man wasn't amused at the wordplay, nor was he rebuffed as he once might have been. "They certainly do seem to be your problem. Don't forget, your man Griffin Kale is one of them."

"Kale's being used by the others as a pawn."

"Nevertheless, as of tonight, your payment to the Springfield larder is officially late. Give it another 24 hours, and we'll consider it lost to the wind."

Prescott held his temper and sipped his coffee with a grimace.

They always put too damn much cinnamon in it.

For the past few years, McCormick had been Prescott's trusted ally in the Ivory Compass at Jefferson City. But lately, something in McCormick's attitude had changed. It was subtle, hard to define, maybe nothing more than a tone of voice when they conversed. Perhaps a sour note when Prescott's undertakings were victorious, or a secretive smile when he failed.

Prescott hadn't wanted to doubt the fellow's sincerity, but he did.

McCormick downed his liquor and pressed his lips together, as if he had all the answers to all the problems of the world. "Don't forget, old man, you still have Logan Coombs in Springfield. It's where they are now —in Springfield." McCormick removed his lead-colored pocket watch and pried open the tarnished cover with a long, untrimmed fingernail. "They drove in about a half an hour ago."

"Carrying my money," said Prescott, grinding his teeth.

McCormick agreed. "Carrying *our* money." He signaled a man standing in the shade of the café door for another drink. When his eyes came back to Prescott, they seemed almost lifeless. "Reach out to Logan Coombs. He's a reasonable man. Reasonable and efficient—as you might expect of a German. Explain what happened. Tell him to cut loose on these thieves. Tell him to be as vicious as he likes. Make a lesson out of the Hellbenders' horrific demise."

Prescott wasn't so sure. "You admitted they're better than we gave them credit for. Logan's brother, Seth, was the most capable men I've ever known, and yet they escaped him."

"They killed him."

"It's unfathomable," said Prescott. "It might not be so easy even for Logan. You yourself said they're resourceful."

"Logan Coombs is not without resources himself."

Prescott rubbed his temples. "I can't imagine how they got past Plummer's. Annie O'Fallon Plummer—"

"Is dead," said McCormick, "and those stock shares still aren't in our hands. I shouldn't have to remind you, with only a few months until the election we can't afford to lose a single dime from the war chest. Politics is expensive, especially in the southern part of the state. If the money is lost…"

"It won't be lost, dammit."

McCormick pretended to agree. "I'm sure it won't be."

The café man brought a fresh bottle to the table, tipped a dollop of amber into McCormick's tumbler.

"Leave it, won't you?" said McCormick.

The man bowed and slunk away to his awning.

As if through a fog, Prescott watched McCormick drink. The strain of the verbal scrimmage coupled with the telegram's bad news was a weight on his shoulders. A familiar tingling ran up his left arm, and he worked on his breath even as he sought his way out from under his confusion.

"One thing I don't understand," he told McCormick. "Why am I hearing this from you? The station has been given strict orders not to share my personal messages with anybody. If something comes over the wire for me, a boy is dispatched directly to my office—and my office alone."

McCormick spread his fingers wide on the table's iron top. "Simple," he said as a cool breeze wafted across the river ripe with the stink of upstream sewage. "The message was directed to me from the man I had placed at Plummer's. He rode all afternoon to Springfield to make the communication."

"Your man?"

"You're jealous?" said McCormick. "Surely you didn't think you were the only player with pieces on the board?"

"Not at all." Prescott hadn't come as far as he had through ignorance. Or subtle gamesmanship. He was, and always would be, a brawler.

If McCormick had been mincing around, hoping to avoid a brawl, he'd just said the wrong thing. Prescott would give him a quick comeuppance.

He lifted his tone of voice and was gruff. "I'm

surprised at your lack of loyalty, McCormick. I'm astonished at the lack of trust you've put on display. We expect more from members of the Ivory Compass."

We expect more.

There it was. He'd gone straight at the man with the argument from authority. Prescott's arm was a pincushion, but his breathing came slow and easy now.

He continued his tongue lashing, holding nothing back.

"You've seen fit to remind me of the facts, McCormick. Well, let me remind you who you're talking to. I intend to be the next Governor of this state, and your newspaper tends to support the notion. I'm your senior in years, your senior in society, and your senior in the Ivory Compass. I have the backing—"

"Of men in high places, and so on and so one. Of course," said McCormick. "Such language is cliché and boring as hell."

"I have the finances—"

"From your Colorado venture. Yes, yes, again, nobody will argue your grand net worth. That is, so long as it endures."

Prescott flinched. "Meaning exactly what?"

Instead of nervously tugging at his collar or seething over an inner boil, the newspaper man maintained a gentle demeanor.

Prescott was disappointed McCormick hadn't taken the bait.

If anything, his reply was more confident than before.

"Meaning Clairborne Fox Jackson is just as viable a candidate as you, sir, and his investments are unequivocally more sound. His legacy...more certain."

A past state senator and prominent political figure, Jackson had been appointed Banking Commissioner by the Missouri governor in 1857. He certainly used the connections from his appointment to increase his popular standing. But run for governor?

Prescott's thoughts were a jumble. In sudden fear he jerked back in his chair, looked around the patio at his fellow evening revelers. The senator was engaged with a ham steak, a pair of businessmen at the table behind him, deep in their cups. Fortunately, everybody seemed preoccupied and unaware of his conversation.

But Prescott couldn't help but feel conspicuous. It was like the sky was breaking apart above him. Sooner or later, somebody else would notice the cracks.

"How is Jackson's legacy more certain?" said Prescott. "How are his investments more sound? In what way? What do you know about it? I can't..." He realized he was halfway out of his chair and babbling when spittle flew from his mouth.

The nearby senator was staring at him, as Prescott slowly sat back down.

After the dramatic display, McCormick leaned across the table, addressing Prescott in low familiar tones with his Christian name. "Clairborne Fox Jackson is a name already in the history books. The Jackson Resolutions of a decade past still resonate with a lot of our people."

Prescott knew it was true.

McCormick reiterated the resolutions: "The Federal congress has no right to legislate slavery in the states. The compromise of 1820 is wholly illegitimate. Missouri must always resist Northern encroachment. Missouri must always reject Northern ideas. Missouri must always shun Northern ways."

"N-naturally, I support the same things," Prescott damned himself for stammering.

"You might support the ideas, but it wasn't you who stood up and delivered them under the dome. In 1849, Mister Jackson did." McCormick leaned back and poured himself another drink. "Mister Jackson's legacy is favorable to exploitation by the Ivory Compass. The only thing in your favor is a Colorado fortune. If war comes...when it comes, what will happen to your precious business in the West? How will you handle the operation if communications are severed?"

Prescott kneaded his arm through the sleeve of his coat, worried the inside of his cheek. How to respond to such an affront? What to say to keep himself on top?

McCormick delivered the final blow like a sledge-hammer. "In the trying times ahead, some of us might prefer an administration run by Mister Jackson."

Prescott drained the dregs of his cup, shaking off an uncontrollable trembling.

McCormick poured himself one last shot and raising his glass, offered up a toast.

"On the other hand, friend, you have 24 hours. Perhaps make it count for something?"

———

IN SPRINGFIELD, Missouri, Logan Coombs warmed his fingers by the open hearth of a cookstove. His long, coal-black hair rested in rolling waves on his shoulders, and his heavy mustache filtered the post office smells of ink and paper.

It was midnight, two hours after receiving the wire message from Jefferson City. The simple wooden chair he sat on was unadorned. Plain. Basic. So simple, a child might build one.

A yawning man in a nightshirt appeared behind the tall counter. The postmaster.

Coombs had rousted him from bed.

Now the younger man filled the silence with vapid conversation. "We live in a time of wonders," said the postmaster. "To think—a message from here to the capital city and back again in the same day."

Coombs laced his fingers together, gripping the knuckles in the semblance of prayer until his nails dug into the skin. He leaned closer to the open stove. The heat of the fire felt good. The glow on his hands highlighted a network of scars. He gazed into the soft, pulsating jelly of red-hot oak. "Just answer my questions."

"Of course, Mister Coombs. You know I'm always happy to help you, sir."

"A woman with a green Concord coach. She was supposed to arrive in town today. Have you seen her?"

"I have indeed. Miss Sinclair rolled in around six o'clock, right around the time I was locking up the cashbox. She had a couple tough-looking gentlemen flanking her."

"You spoke to her?"

"Well...yes."

"You hesitate to answer," said Coombs. "Why do you hesitate?"

"It wasn't hesitation...it's just—I wasn't sure what you wanted me to say, sir."

Coombs' voice was little more than a whisper. "I just want the truth. Is it so difficult?"

"No, sir. Not difficult at all."

"Why did they come to your office?"

"They were asking about hotels. Where was the best place to stay? That sort of thing."

"Where did they go."

The postmaster swallowed hard. "To one of the hotels, I imagine."

"The company is spending the night here in Springfield?" Coombs felt his pulse quicken. "They're not moving on?"

"Miss Sinclair indicated they were definitely planning to spend the night."

"What did she say? What did she say—exactly?"

"She...er, that is...she said she was looking forward to a good night's sleep away from the coach. Then this other man with her, this fellow speaking with a British accent, he says something to the effect maybe they ought to just keep heading on down the road. Then Sinclair says, no—they're all exhausted and need a real good rest before moving on. Those were her words straight and true."

"So they are here, in *my* town," said Coombs. "Overnight."

"In your town, sir. Yes, sir."

Coombs brushed at his mustache and unfolded his long, spidery legs. He rose from the chair in one motion and pulled a long woolen blanket from a hook by the door. Without a backwards look, flung it around his shoulders and reached for the latch.

The postmaster had one last query. "May I ask what business you...uh, might have with Mister Jarret, sir?"

At the threshold to the Springfield post office, Coombs didn't turn around, lest the postmaster see his tears of grief.

His tears of rage.

"My business with Mister Jarret...is vengeance," he said.

CHAPTER 28

THE PARKSDALE HOTEL, A FULL MILE FROM THE CITY of Springfield's main street, having only opened the week before, represented the city's southward expansion and current construction boom. In true Victorian fashion, the three-story limestone building looked down on a street not yet paved, through arched windows and high balconies. At ground level, the painted white iron wraparound porch rail with its attendant columns and filigree bespoke of pure Southern elegance. Tulips and wild pansies in cement planters splashed color across the façade, and enticing smells of fresh-baked bread hovered over the board-walk. Along with its unobtrusive locale, Lin had chosen the discreet lodging for its proximity to a new, fully outfitted livery stable. A row of blooming hawthorn trees, their white blossoms casting petals to the wind, grew six feet into the air beside the property line of both establishments. And some grew higher.

Walking out of the kitchen onto the hardwood porch, Lin Jarret greeted the blue morning sky with an upturned face, breathing in a fresh scent of honeysuckle.

The strain of the past several days had been washed out of his bones like the road dirt scrubbed from his carcass in last night's bath. Maybe things were finally going their way.

Springfield was a bustling Ozark town with a score of venues open for business before breakfast. The city air was filled with the work-a-day sounds of hammer and saw, and several new frame structures arched across the horizon. Wagons kicked up road dust, and horse apples littered every boulevard faster than bands of gangly boys could sweep them up. It was an exciting place to be.

"The hotel man said they expect the population to be more than 2,000 people by the end of the year. Even with all the hammering early this morning, I haven't slept so well in a month of Sundays." Lin slapped the breast of his faded blue shirt as he said it.

He wore laundered clothes for the first time in four days, and his cheeks and chin were as clean shaven as was possible for Lin.

Resting her hip on the whitewashed iron rail beside him, Reece Sinclair grabbed his red bandanna and pulled him close. She kissed his cheek and pretended to skewer her mouth on his whiskers. She poked out her bottom lip. "Is this bleeding? I swear, your beard's sharp as a nettle bush and grows back twice as fast."

"One of the things you love about me, Contessa."

"Don't press your luck, Ranger."

She wore a white bloomer suit—loose trousers gathered at the ankles, belt, and vest with emerald and scarlet accents over a free-flowing blouse, and the shirt was open at the neck. Instead of her usual severe braid, her morning hair was an ebony cascade falling over her shoulders, and her jade earrings matched the hue of her eyes.

Lin decided it was good to finally hear a playful lilt coming back into Reece's voice.

Songbirds in the hawthorn trees agreed, adding to the morning's symphony.

Reece had been so dour since their meeting in Syracuse. Her voice, her manner, her demeanor—all business. Even under the stars at Mulhaven's station, and then again at Kelton's abandoned farm, she'd been too serious. Lin was afraid the troubles at Plummer's station and Reece's brush with death at Annie's hand might push her mood over the edge into a permanent state of affairs.

But the sparkle remained in her eyes.

Lin had reason to be hopeful.

Having eluded their pursuers, maybe they could spend the remainder of the trip on more...pleasant pursuits.

With a careless shrug, he tossed an open arm around Reece's shoulders. "We've turned a corner, Contessa. It's all downhill from here."

But she cautioned him. "You're forgetting devil number seven."

"That was only a silly dream."

"You counted six of them yourself," said Reece. "Devil number seven is Logan Coombs."

Lin sighed.

"Yeah, I suppose so." He leaned his forearm against one of the porch poles and surveyed the street.

A pair of rough and tumble men at his ten o'clock position stood watching them from the saloon boardwalk across the way. One of them was bare headed with a thin dusting of hair and a scar down the right side of his face, like a child had painted a thick scarlet line with a brush. The other man was smaller and wore a pork-pie hat with an eye patch.

A third man waited at two o'clock.

Keeping track of Lin as sure as the others, this one was barrel-chested with hair almost as long and dark as Reece. A heavy, black mustache balanced like a hunk of charcoal on his lip. He wore a domed hat and a long, wool blanket, like an Indian. Lin was pretty sure he carried a long gun of some kind under the blanket.

"By the looks of those hombres, Logan Coombs hasn't forgot about us."

"Nice looking blanket," said Reece.

"Kickapoo, I'd guess, by the designs near the fringe. The same fellow who told me about Springfield also told me there's an abandoned village not far from here. Supposed to be near 100 wigwams left to rot. Says they haven't got around to burning them since the Indians left."

"Since the Indians were forced out."

"Anyway, I guess you're right—the sooner we're out of here, the better."

"Where's Micah and Griff?"

"Early risers, both of 'em," said Lin. "I believe they went to see a man about a horse, or rather, a team of mules."

"Mules? Aw, for Pete's sake..." said a voice from behind, and Lin turned to see Ned Brock stumbling across the threshold, not necessarily eager to meet the day.

Immediately on his heels, Flood Tyner answered his awkward query.

"The ups and downs of these mountains, goats might be even better," said Tyner. "Believe me, it's a mighty tough trail from here through Arkansas. Once we get into the Nations things'll smooth out."

"Says you," said Ned Brock, limping out to join

them on the porch. He held both hands to his face, and his balding pate was a wiry snarl of stray hairs.

"I've never seen you without a hat, Brock," said Reece.

Lin knew what she was thinking. The slick hot gunfighter was a lot older than he appeared when duded-up in full regalia. Wearing a sour cream-colored undershirt, loose pants and no shoes, he looked like a busted flat homesteader. Worse, he appeared to be injured.

"What're you wearing around your middle?" said Lin. "Is it some kind of hernia belt?"

Brock pulled up the heavy padded girdle strapped around his midsection and snugged it tight with two silver buckles. "Not a hernia belt," he said. "A back brace."

"And you're not dressing for breakfast?" said Lin.

"You're awful damn chipper this morning."

"After yesterday's trouble, I've got good reason to be—I'm still breathing."

"That makes one of us." Brock snorted. "What's that awful smell?"

"Honeysuckle."

"No wonder I'm all plugged up." He put a finger to one nostril and launched a wad of snot over the porch railing.

"Let's not get too used to not breathing," said Reece. With an inconspicuous motion, she pointed out the hard men across the street to Brock and Tyner.

Brock's lazy face changed in an instant. Now he was the keen-eyed wolf, a predator in every aspect as mean and tough as the men across the street. Lin watched him step off the porch and cross into the middle of the street.

As far as he could tell, Brock was unarmed.

He was quite the spectacle, barefoot, wearing a back brace, staring down three armed men. Lin thought the scene would be quite comical in a play—if it wasn't so serious.

Under Brock's persistent attention, the three bad men decided not to get into the act. First, the big man with the blanket turned his back and walked into the saloon. Then the others followed.

Lin breathed a sigh of relief as Brock mounted the steps to rejoin them.

"You took a mighty big chance there, Ned," said Lin.

"Blanket man is the leader. The other two ain't nothing."

Lin kept his eye on the saloon. Was the man with the blanket Logan Coombs?

Lin bet he was. He didn't look much like his brother, but he seemed snotty enough, what Lin thought of as an air of European arrogance.

"And how did you sleep, Mister Jarret?" said Tyner, interrupting his thoughts.

Lin took his hand off the butt of his holstered Colt.

He hadn't even realized he'd put it there.

"Slept like an innocent calf," he said.

"You sure enough lowed like one too," said Brock.

"You must be mistaking me for one of the other men. Griff or Micah."

"I know whose room I bunked in, and it weren't the British man."

"You snore?" said Reece, teasing Lin with an astonished expression.

"Don't you know?" said Brock.

Lin and Reece turned on him with a disapproving glare.

"Okay, okay. I apologize," said Brock. "You two

wanna play slap and tickle—or not, it ain't none of my affair."

"I don't snore," said Lin.

"Who's ready for breakfast?" said Flood Tyner from inside the hotel. "Miss Sinclair?"

"I don't mind if I do, Mister Tyner."

Lin stood beside Brock, watching Reece disappear into the hotel dining room on Tyner's arm.

"Between you and me, I don't like him too well," said Brock.

"You don't seem to like much of anything today, Mister Brock."

Brock crossed the boards in front of Lin and leaned against a porch pillar. Together, they stared at the boardwalk in front of the saloon.

Lin was startled when Brock's voice cracked with emotion.

"He was only twenty-three years old, you know?" he said. "How's it fair to only live to twenty-three?"

Lin let the words hang in the air without looking.

It didn't suit to look at a man when he was crying.

"You're talking about Curly?"

"The Sodbuster was older. He at least had a life. More or less. Neither one of 'em deserved what they got."

"No, they didn't deserve it," said Lin, but he wasn't sure he believed it.

What he did know was right then and there, Brock believed it. Lin's opinion didn't matter much.

What was done was done.

"I rode with those boys a long spell."

"I s'pose so."

"Got nobody to ride with now."

Lin almost said, "You've got us," but thought better of it and held his tongue.

He'd made peace with Brock. He wasn't sure he wanted to make friends.

"You all still thinking we're gonna split up into two groups?" said Brock.

"Reece thinks so. Personally, I'm against it, but..."

"But she's the boss."

Lin weighed the declaration on an inner scale. "Yeah, I guess she is."

"Even if she don't know if you snore."

"You ain't wearing a gun, Brock. I could paste you in the mouth before you so much as blinked, and you'd have nothing to say about it."

Brock let out a heavy breath of air. Pushing away from the pole, he apologized again. "I ain't so good making polite conversation. Especially with my boys gone so recent."

He put out his hand. "You understand, Jarret?"

Lin hesitated...then shook his hand. "I do, Ned."

Brock snuffed hard and wiped his nose with his fingers. "Tyner's in there with the missy. Where's the others?"

Lin told him. "We'll head out within the hour, take the Concord on down the trail to Dewey's Station. Figure we can make it there by nightfall."

"Who's *we* again? I don't recall drawing straws for the honor of riding with you."

"You, me, and Micah will continue on into Arkansas to Fort Smith. Tyner, Reece, and Griff will take Tyner's wagon on a bit of a shortcut."

"Because?"

"Because they've got their mission, and we've got ours."

"You're not gonna tell me?"

"We'll all meet up again at Fort Smith. I've got

some Butterfield Overland business to discuss with a Mister Wilber, the division man there."

"What if I don't wanna go?"

"Then you can stay here. Buy a horse and ride away. Nobody's with us who doesn't want to be."

Brock scratched the back of his neck and looked at the saloon. Lin could tell he had something on his mind but wasn't sure how to say it.

When they finally came, the words spilled out fast.

"Which one of us you think is quicker on the draw?"

Lin poked out his bottom lip. "I can't say I've thought about it."

"Bull. You're a man makes a living with a gun."

"Not so's you'd notice."

Brock put the tip of his tongue between his teeth. "I think I'll stick around after all. Maybe one time we can put each other to the test. Make a friendly wager on it?"

"Maybe."

"Speaking of guns," said a feminine voice, and the men waited for Reece to join them from inside the hotel. She wore her white napkin like a bib and dabbed at her lips as she moved toward them. From the small of her back, she pulled the big Walch Navy 12-shooter.

"Before I forget," she said, "I wanted Mister Brock to have this."

Brock received the gun with stunned surprise. Cradling it like a precious artifact, he gently fingered the oblong cylinder and caressed the twin triggers.

Then he offered it back. "No, no, you keep it, Miss Sinclair. You won it off Tyner fair and square."

"It's too heavy for me," said Reese. "You'll make better use of it."

Lin smirked. "Take it while you can get it, Brock."

He glanced one last time at the saloon across the street. Logan and his twin skunks stood behind the front window with steins of beer in hand. While Lin watched, Coombs raised his stein to Lin, sending a message.

"Take the gun, Brock," he said. "I reckon we might need the firepower."

CHAPTER 29

REECE DISCOVERED IT WAS A THOUSAND TIMES MORE comfortable to ride on Tyner's down-filled upholstered leather spring bench than the green Concord's pinewood seat. Especially now, with the Walch Navy pistol no longer poking her in the spine.

She sat next to Tyner with the ribbons in hand, driving his red gunsmith wagon past the James River outside of Springfield. As they rounded the last curve past a final fork in the road, Reece waved to Lin Jarret as he and Micah piloted the Hellbenders' express across the Overland trail. The coach disappeared on the other road behind a wide grove of cottonwood trees, and a lump the size of all Missouri formed in Reece's throat.

What if something happened and she never saw them again?

A hurried glance at the road behind showed their trail to be devoid of any followers. Maybe they'd misjudged Prescott's resources. Maybe the rider they had seen leaving Plummer's station had nothing to do with Coombs.

Besides, she told herself, Lin Jarret could take care of himself.

Ned Brock had his reputation as a gunfighter.

Micah LeMay could take care of all three of them.

The trio would be safe enough on the run to Fort Smith.

They just had to be.

Reece shook off her worries and focused her thoughts on pushing forward Tyner's four mules and navigating the road ahead. She, Tyner, and Griff had worries of their own. The leather satchel full of Prescott's stock shares was burning a hole in her calm demeanor.

She wanted the certificates exchanged for real currency as soon as possible, and then she wanted the money delivered safely to Emberville station.

Flood Tyner had a plan to make it happen.

"Dedra's bank in Bad Axe can exchange your certificates for gold. In fact, money changing is her specialty."

"How far to your sister's place?" said Reece.

"Fifteen miles, twenty. Maybe as far as forty. It's hard to know for sure. Bad Axe is a somewhat...mobile village," he said with a sheepish tone. "Let's just keep following the signs."

"What signs?"

Tyner indicated a mulberry tree at trail's edge. A bare spot Reece first assumed was a deer rubbing with an odd, broken branch revealed itself to be a deliberately chopped bare of bark. A sturdy iron-axe head with wooden handle was half-buried into the center of the shaved wood.

"It isn't much to go by, is it?" said Reece.

"It is if you know what you're looking for," said Tyner. "We're on the right trail."

A demotion from the smooth passage of the Butterfield Overland road the crude path they followed mimicked the river, then abruptly looped off to the south to form a series of drunken wheel ruts in an ocean of flowing grass.

Reece steered the mules over a red mound of earth and around a bend in the river to an uphill path. The iron gray beasts handled the ten-percent grade like a stroll through the daffodils—which it literally was—pulling Tyner's wagon along without a break.

Again, Reece queried the old man about Bad Axe. "You said it's a mobile village? I don't understand. How can an entire town be mobile?"

"Bad Axe isn't like any town you've seen before. Where you might expect schools, churches, or parks—Bad Axe has none of those things."

"But there are shops and mercantiles? There's a bank?"

Tyner chuckled. "Indeed. There are a plethora of sales made every day, and like I told you before, my sister owns one of the many banks. Of course, it hardly possesses the brick and iron edifice you might be familiar with."

"No vault?"

"No vault. Dedra's bank is inside a tent."

"A canvas tent?"

"All the banks are tents."

"How many banks there?"

Tyner chuckled. "Depends on the day of the week."

"No churches or schools. Tent banks. Just what kind of den of iniquity are you leading us into?" said Reece.

"Yes, exactly," said Tyner. "It's called Bad Axe because Sodom and Gomorra was already taken."

"Not funny."

"Not meant to be. Bad Axe is a haven for all sorts of interesting and sometimes unsavory characters."

"Like your sister."

"I would never say so to her face."

"You're a regular visitor to this den of iniquity?"

"Visitor, customer...vendor. The community moves around in a variety of conveyances, setting up for a short time in a new location, then abruptly dismantling itself to reappear in a different place on a different day. It's a good place to know about."

"A good place for owlhoots to hide."

"An exceptionally profitable place to deal in firearms."

"Good for buying information?"

"Especially good for buying information. Selling too."

As they crawled up the steep hills and snaked down through treacherous tree-filled valleys, Reece thought about Tyner's last comment. Finally, she said, "I wonder what your sister might know about the Order of the Ivory Compass?"

"It never hurts to ask," said Tyner.

———

"I KNOW Prescott's stock coupons are next to worthless," said Dedra Tyner through a huff of exhaled smoke. She flicked her cigarette outside her cramped canvas tent where it spiraled in a circle of sparks in the main street of Bad Axe before blinking out in the dark. Then she turned back to the satchel Lin and Griff had taken from Seth Coombs in Syracuse. She pulled out a handful of the lavish certificates and tossed them on the ash-littered table in front of her. "Worthless as tits on a bore hog. Ain't fit to clean up my backside."

While Reece, Tyner, and Griff waited, Dedra lit another cigarette.

A drab, shrunken old woman wrapped with a blanket, in the flickering light of sizzling candle wax she seemed like some kind of eldritch spirit cast out of heaven, brimming with evil magic. Every crease in her rocky visage was cast in high relief, every word of her ancient voice the creaking utterance of a backwoods witch.

"I'll give you fifteen dollars apiece for 'em."

"I should say not," said Griff. "Each certificate represents 10 shares. At $10 per share—as printed on the bottom line—it comes to one hundred dollars for each certificate. I believe you'll find one hundred sheets of paper in there, for a grand total of ten-thousand dollars at fair market value."

Dedra's wooden expression was indecipherable.

Outside the tent, in a roped-off pen Reece had seen coming in, one of six thoroughbred horses nickered loudly enough to catch her attention. She queried Tyner with a silent look.

"Dedra is also in the business of loaning out horses. As you might imagine, a fast horse is a valuable commodity in Bad Axe."

"We have some valuable commodities of our own," said Griff. "As I said, ten-thousand dollars at fair market value."

Dedra opened her mouth to speak, closed it, and finally opened it again. She couldn't hide the exasperation she so obviously felt.

"You're making y'r first mistake is using words like *fair market value*. There's *the market* and then there's what's printed here. Those two ain't the same thing, Greenhorn."

Griff's pride was as pinched as Dedra's cigarette. "I'm hardly a greenhorn, ma'am."

"If you think something's worth any different than what somebody else is willin' to give for it, then you're a greenhorn."

Griff rolled his eyes and let his head pivot toward Tyner. "All due respect, Mister Tyner, but let's try somebody else," he said. "There were at least five other financial tents outside advertising their services."

Dedra cackled like the mud hen she resembled. "Better the devil you know, than the one you don't," she said. "You mark my word on it."

Tyner had to agree. "She's right, you know. Nobody else here would likely even make you an offer. Dedra is one of the founders of Bad Axe. She's been here the longest, and she's a consummate professional."

Griff was determined not to give up. "I saw a couple of card games when we came into camp. Maybe I ought to try my luck with them."

Dedra's cigarette bounced on her lip while she talked. "I wouldn't even think of it. Them boys'd skin ya alive and salt your innards for tomorrow's breakfast."

Griff maintained his defiance. "I will not be plucked like a spring chicken."

Again, the horses outside nickered.

Reece couldn't help but feel a smidgen of admiration for Griff. He'd toughed up a lot these last few days.

"I must agree with my sister," said Tyner. "The men of Bad Axe—"

"Are just men," said Reece, "who can die or be bought, just like any other. Last chance, Dedra."

"Sixteen dollars each," said the witch, "solid American currency."

Tyner pulled Reece and Griff back from his sister's table and whispered, "Take her up on the offer, man.

Sixteen-hundred is a tidy sum," he said. "As she says, Dedra will pay us in cash. We can ride out of here tonight under the cloak of darkness, and nobody will even notice. We'll meet the others at Fort Smith within two days."

"Take the money and run, eh?" said Griff.

"You might be sorry if you pass it up?"

"Sixteen-hundred dollars is a far cry from ten-thousand."

"It's a far cry from zero."

Reece pondered the old man's words. He made some valid points. But maybe there was a chance at increasing the final payout...

"At heart, Griffin Kale is a gambler," said Reece, "and from what Lin told me, a decent enough cheat."

"I'm sure I have no idea what you mean," said Griff.

"If there's a game available," said Reece, "we do stand to make a good deal more."

"Take her offer but multiply it at one of the tables outside?" said Griff.

"You'd be taking an awful chance," said Tyner. His tone got hotter, his whispers, louder. "If either one of you gets caught cheating, you'll find out Dedra's not joking about the depredations you'll suffer. I would ask you to remember the name of this place."

"I'm a bit of a gambler myself," said Reece.

"And a cheat?"

"Not a day in my life," said Reece. "But I'm awful good with numbers and remembering."

She could tell by the look on the man's face his opinion was unchanged.

Griff walked back to the bargaining table. "Twenty-five dollars each," he said.

"Sixteen-fifty," said Deedra.

"Twenty-four."

"Sixteen-seventy-five."

The exercise was pointless, and Reece knew it.

"I might as well sell these for kindling to the Kickapoo," said Griff. "I'd get more than seventeen dollars."

"You'll find out," said Dedra. "Prescott's days with the Ivory Compass are numbered." She tapped the side of the bag with a boney finger. "The buzzards tell me his Colorado venture will be gone by mid-summer before he can get himself elected governor."

"Gone? As in bankrupt?" said Griff. "Prescott owns more than his business at Ponder's Peak. What about the railroad."

"One thing tends to affect the other. I predict his name will be swept clean from the frontier. A century from now it will be like he never lived." Dedra raised her index finger and the long, cracked nail glowed in candlelight. "Hear my wisdom, child: you get what you can for those now. Ten weeks from now...ten minutes, they won't be worth chicken scratching."

Her swift hand made a hurried rustle of paper as she swept the certificates back into the leather bag. She locked the clasp and pushed it toward Dedra.

"Twenty dollars each did you say?"

The old lady flashed Reece an amused expression. "I believe I said one-eighteen." Reaching down, she slid a metal lockbox from under her chair. With surprising vigor, she hoisted it to the table, opened it, and counted out $1800 in stacks of paper currency.

When she reached the appropriate amount of money, she opened Coombs' leather satchel, removed the stock certificates and replaced them with the cash.

"Eighteen-hundred dollars," said Dedra, clicking shut the latch.

"We'd best get along then," said Reece. She winked

at Griff, then addressed Tyner with firm conviction. "Show us the way to a card game."

Tyner turned back to his sister. "Have some fast horses, ready for us will? I have a feeling we might need them."

CHAPTER 30

Lin traipsed around the perimeter of a sun-spackled clearing, the soft crunch of last season's beige pin-oak leaves and scattered brush revealing his position to a possum who scurried out from a hollow log. Lin watched the gray and white critter waddle away from the open space in the woods where the Concord sat striped in the last rays of the sun and the long shadows of trees.

Lin had never seen so many trees in his life. Poplar, elm, oak, spruce, mulberry, hickory, hackberry, walnut, cottonwood. He felt no less confined than a few days before, no less hemmed in. But now at least he was used to the squirming tickle at the back of his neck. The crawling sensation of an impending trap.

He didn't think getting used to the feeling was a good thing.

The possum disappeared into the brush. Besides the wide variety of trees, Lin figured during the course of the trip they must've seen just about every kind of Ozarks' wildlife available. The skunk between Syracuse and Mulhaven. The otters near the Osage. The rabbits and squirrels and ground hogs. Micah had sighted most of them before Lin or Reece, and if nothing else it was a comfort to know they would never starve in such an abundant wilderness.

Three miles out of Wicker Station and twenty miles distant from Fort Smith, the Concord needed some minor repair, but Lin was eager to move on.

The fresh team of Wicker mules were restless as Micah worked on the wagon brake, freeing it from a stuck position with a long pry bar. Once they got the brake fixed, they'd eat some grub and maybe catch a quick nap. They'd be back on the road before midnight.

By tomorrow night at this time, if everything went according to plan, he'd be reunited with Reece.

"Why can't I find any damn firewood when I need it?" he said to himself.

Lin's bushcraft had worn thin in the weeks he lived at the south Texas Sinclair Rancho. He'd improved his cowboy skills, even learned to shear sheep and butcher a hog. But his taste for cotton sheets and feather mattresses had also grown strong.

Dropping his hands to his hips, the short hickory handled hatchet he carried banged against his thigh. There was plenty of kindling available, bird's nest tinder and twigs. What he needed were thick, fat chunks of wood to fry some bacon and warm their coffee as the evening air carried in a late frost.

"Find anything?" said Micah, coming around the wagon. He shoved a thumb back over his shoulder. "Brock's got a rope stretched out 'tween a couple walnut trees. We can hang a blanket over against the wind, stake it down to make a wind break." He rubbed the long sleeves of his blue bib shirt. "It's more than a mite chilly."

Lin kicked at the base of a half-rotten hickory log.

At least nine inches in diameter and nearly two feet long, it rolled up from the forest floor, pulling a hunk of wet earth with it. "Other than more kindling, this is all I could find." He showed Micah the small axe. "We sent the bigger gear with Reece and Tyner. If we want to split this log out, this little thing won't do much good. We've got no maul, no iron wedges, nothing."

Micah wore fingerless gloves and held out his hand. "Let me see the hatchet," he said.

Lin shared the tool, then went back to scanning the ground all around.

"I'll probably be crawling with ticks by midnight," he said.

"You sure do complain a lot," said Micah.

"And you talk too much."

He hadn't meant to be rude, but the ride from Springfield to the Fort Smith region had been a monotonous one. He was hungry, and he was tired.

But it wasn't only the long day chewing at his nerves.

"I know," said Micah, "I'm worried about her too."

"Let's just find some wood." Lin bent over and picked up two fallen limbs, each of them measuring more than three feet long, both of them as big around as his wrist. "What about this?" he said.

Micah motioned for him to bring the wood. "Roll the big log over closer to the wagon," he said. "I think we've got all we need."

———

THE THREE MEN gathered in the clearing with the Concord parked on one side, a quilted wind break on the other. Lin sat on his haunches next to Micah while Brock kept his hip propped against the coach's front wagon wheel. Lin had the mules hobbled in a grove of nearby cedars where they gnawed grass and ate the last of a bucket of Springfield livery cracked corn.

Brock watched as Micah used the hatchet to make sparks on a piece of flint and light the nest of shavings he'd made from the tree limbs.

"You've maybe camped out a time or two before," said Brock.

"I've been on my own a while," said Micah.

"Hard to be alone," said Brock.

After a while, Lin glanced up and saw the gunman polishing the Walch Navy 12-shooter with a flannel rag. The .36-caliber gun was partially dismantled, and Brock was meticulous as he tended to it.

With the same care he might confer on an infant child, Brock caressed the iron, cleaning each nook and crevice before fitting the cylinder snug in place. With a deft motion Lin rarely saw, Brock charged each of the six chambers with powder, then added a lead ball, then charged each chamber again before adding a second ball. He finished the cylinder by sealing the chambers with pork fat from a small tin balanced on the Concord rail. When he saw Lin watching him, he grinned. "Lard keeps sparks from jumping down the cylinder."

Next, Brock turned his attention to the percussion caps, whistling as he fit each cap to its own iron nipple. From the way Brock fussed over the weapon, it was clear he adored the Walch. Lin understood why Reece had gifted it to him.

"How the hell does your gun work, anyway?" said Micah.

Brock held it up to the firelight. "Ain't she a beauty?" He was eager to talk about it. After explaining the basic concept of the .36 caliber cap and ball, Brock showed Micah the backside of the cylinder. The Walch had two percussion nipples per chamber. One of them had an oblong flash hole that carried the percussion cap spark to the forward charge first. "When I pull the front trigger, those caps are sparked here," said Brock, pointing to the right-hand hammer. "When I pull the rear trigger, the left-hand hammer goes into play, triggering the back charge."

"Seems overly complicated," said Micah.

"Superior firepower usually is," said Brock.

"Did you tell him how the thing misfired in the woods?" said Micah.

Brock looked at Lin for confirmation. "When did this happen?"

Lin downplayed the comment. "Before we arrived at Plummer's place. Reece was...ah, target shooting."

"Because if one of the front charges happens to misfire," said Brock, "God help the poor devil who triggers the second round with the front ball still in place."

Lin agreed with him, patting his trusty Colt. "Sometimes simple is better."

"Not better," said Brock. "Just simpler." He holstered the Walch and sauntered over to the fire. "Takes a special man to carry a special gun."

"I'll keep it in mind," said Micah.

While Micah continued to feed the flames, Lin climbed up to the wagon's front boot and opened the canopy. He pulled out a wax paper hotel-wrapped package of bacon. In another sack he found biscuits, butter, and molasses. These he carried from storage down to the campsite. He laid his burden on the ground and faced Brock.

"Seems like we gave all the supplies to the other wagon," said Lin.

"You were extremely generous," said Brock, "but it

wasn't my place to say. I mean, I wouldn't want to step on your toes."

"Since when did you get so well-mannered?"

Brock scoffed. "Get to know me, you'll find out."

From his place in the center of the open ground, Micah groused, "If you girls don't stop bickering, I'm liable not to share my fire."

"I'll stop if he will," said Brock, the words dripping long and lean from his laconic mouth.

Lin addressed him directly. "What say you and me go up river and see if there's a spring?"

"Sounds alright."

"How about it, Micah? We'll go fill the canteens? Bring back a few buckets for the animals?"

Micah was busy feeding slivers of hickory bark into the fire. Micah nodded his affirmation. "Don't get lost," he said. "Be back before dark."

Lin picked up the empty corn bucket and pulled another from the rear boot of the coach. Upon arriving beside the nearby creek, they had immediately watered the team, but Lin wanted to make sure they didn't get thirsty on the overnight run. He handed the second pail to Brock.

Together, they rambled off into the thicket.

For the next fifteen minutes, Brock regaled Lin with stories of his ill-fated life. An orphan at nine years-old, he grew up in the wilds of Kentucky close to Boonsborough, where Daniel Boone had ambushed the Shawnee kidnappers of his children. "I always wanted to be Daniel Boone," said Brock.

"Here's your chance," said Lin, sweeping his arm out to indicate the majesty of the wilderness around them.

When they finally found the source of the flowing branch water, Brock waited on the bank while Lin hurried down the slope. "I'll just wait up here and have a smoke," he said.

"Daniel Boone, huh?"

Brock grinned. "Boone was a man who knew his priorities. Just like me. Toss me the makings?"

Lin dug around in his shirt pocket for his tobacco pouch.

He jerked it free, tossed it up toward Brock into the indigo dusk.

Brock fumbled for the pouch, missed the catch.

The tobacco hit the ground.

Two seconds later, Brock collapsed into a mewling heap and Lin spun at the ghastly sound. "Brock? Ned what happened?

Standing tall behind the gunman's squirming body, a tall heavy bastard jerked a cowboy knife free of Brock's back and wiped it on his long, woolen Kickapoo blanket. Keeping the blade in one hand with a pistol in the other, he said, "There's one of you bastards out of the way."

From under his blanket, the man kicked at Brock with dark boots. "Teach you to stare me down in the street."

Lin reached for his Colt but the blanket man already had his gun out. Shoving the barrel in Lin's direction, he said, "I wouldn't do it."

Lin kept his hands still. "Who the hell are you?"

"They call you Lin Jarret?"

"I asked you first."

"I'm Logan Coombs," said the killer. "You got something belongs to me."

It was the long-haired man from the Springfield street.

Devil number seven.

CHAPTER 31

BAD AXE HAD BLOSSOMED IN A VALLEY BETWEEN TWO shallow rivers, a gridwork of canvas tents, box wagons, coaches, and Conestoga lit by kerosene lamps, torches, and the silver moon above. After leaving Dedra's tent, Reece turned right and led the way past the witch's horse pen back along a damp cow trail. Why the trail was damp, with a clear sky above, she didn't want to know. They passed a chorus of drunk men singing a Scottish ballad, snaking between one of the gaming tents and a vegetable stand selling gnarled radishes for ten cents a dozen. "Too high," Reece told the old man behind the table.

The air between the tents smelled like too much humanity, reminding Reece why she didn't live in the city. Talking, laughing, lecturing, cursing, coughing, spitting and sneezing droned through the night like a great swarm of locusts. Horses and mules with riders, tall, small, and in-between forced them to the sides of the road every few yards. It was as if all of Texas were wedged into the courtyard of the Alamo.

Tyner and Griff pressed close behind as they turned onto Bad Axe's main boulevard, a path wide enough for two wagons to meet and pass. Reece noticed Tyner kept both Remington pistols in hand, so as they worked their way north, she pulled her No. 5 revolver.

One side of the wide street was clearly dedicated to carnal pleasure. Some tents were shut up tight, and the gyrating shadows projected from within coupled with shameless moans and the groans made Reece blush. Other tents were open with long tables surrounded by well-dressed men and women. The cream of Bad Axe society. Piano music played while beer pitchers sloshed, and whiskey was poured. Men guffawed over lurid stories, and women followed one another to the privy with giggles.

Rudy's Rowdy Den offered twelve different elixirs to slake a person's thirst, and the Horny Mink was serving fried venison.

At the culinary odors, Reece felt her stomach rumble, but pressed on. Her party was concerned with the other side of the street, the tents specific to cards and roulette wheels, dexterity games and financial challenge.

Lardner's Lair promised "A Wheel That Always Pays", and a barker outside the Tiger's Den claimed players would be rich men come sunrise.

"It's a card game I'm after," said Griff.

"It doesn't matter," said Reece. "Pick any tent."

The sooner they got ensconced inside the better. Ever since leaving Dedra's place, a trio of shadowy men in dark hats had loitered in a lazy fashion behind them.

Buffalo wolves, thought Reece, the expression coming from her childhood on the ranch. These were the most cowardly of predators. The scurrilous stalkers who couldn't be bothered to confront their prey head on, but instead kept to the back of a herd, lingering on the fringes, hoping to pick off a lost calf or helpless old cow.

In Bad Axe, Reece understood buffalo wolves were just part of the scenery. But she was careful, none-theless. These three clearly had their eye on Reece, Griff, and Flood Tyner.

Toward the end of the road, where a grove of cedars cut off forward progress, they came to a black canvas tent fronted by an inviting sign.

"Play Cards Here," Griff read aloud. "Win big jackpot."

"Why not?" said Reece.

Looking over his shoulder at a street filled with shifty strangers, Tyner couldn't be more encouraging if he tried. "Oh, my, yes. Yes, let's do go on inside," he urged.

The buffalo wolves held back, pretending interest in a vendor selling hand-crafted cigars.

Reece lifted the ebony tent flap.

"As long as there's a poker game going on, I shall always feel at home," said Griff.

A quick peek inside the lantern-lit tent, confirmed something different. "What if they aren't playing poker?" said Reece.

"What do you mean no poker?" Griff scoffed. "If there's no poker—which I highly doubt—then I suppose I would have to beat my opponent at some other pasteboard pastime."

He cleared his throat.

"As long as it's not Sheepshead," he said. "Gads, how I hate Sheepshead. But what are the odds they'd be playing it here?"

———

"HERE'S THE ODDS," said the scroungy old duffer sitting on his Mexican saddle inside the ebony tent. The duffer's name was Tuffy. "Shafkopf—that's Sheepshead to you British—is nothing, if not a game of odds."

Reece couldn't decide if the smell of rotten eggs wafted off Tuffy's uncombed beard, his drooping corpse of a hat, or the mangy saddle perched sideways on a worm-eaten sawhorse. "The odds is these," he continued. "It's four-to-one you win. It's four-to-one you lose. Long as you don't cheat, you won't lose too bad, because you'll still be alive. Staying alive is always to be counted a win."

Tuffy pointed out a whitewashed board nailed to a cedar post behind him. The cedar post leaned drunkenly against the north wall of the tent in shadow, but not so obscured from the lamp Reece couldn't read the hand-lettered paint.

You cheat, you die.

Directly across the scuffed green felt of the ancient card table, Griff queried the old dealer with a raised finger. "To be clear, how did you figure those four-to-one odds?"

"We're playin' five handed. Five players. Four against one. Get it?"

Chagrined, Griff lowered his finger slowly and offered Reece a withering glare.

Let's get out of here, he mouthed silently.

Reece ignored him. Batting her eyelashes in Tuffy's direction, she said, "Tell me again which cards are trump. I'm afraid I'm new to all this. With so many rules, you've got me all in a jumble."

"There, there, girlie. You'll catch on to the game as we play."

To Reece's left, a dirt-crusted derelict named Snuff

moved his puffy liver-stained hand under the table. He let it rest on her knee. The lecherous old coot offered a reassuring smile. "It wasn't so long ago I was new to Sheepshead, too."

Between Snuff and Griff, Tyner squirmed with obvious discomfort, working hard to arrange himself on a three-legged children's stool. "It should be easy for you to remember, Miss Sinclair," he said. "The queens hold trump, the King of Diamonds trails behind, and the other three Kings are fail cards."

Reece pretended to fan herself with the hand of six cards Tuffy had dealt. "Queens hold trump. Kings fail." She laughed with staged delight. "The story of my life," she said.

"You don't really gotta know how to play. Just have fun," said Tuffy.

"I'm here to win money, sir," said Reece.

"Hear, hear," said Griff.

"Points are added up at the end of each round. Dollar a point. The picker wins, he or she gets the pot. The picker loses, he puts in what he might've won."

"Which of us is the picker?"

"Whoever picks up the blind," said Tuffy, indicating two upside-down cards in the center of the table. "Would you like those two cards, ma'am?"

Reece glanced at her hand and wrinkled her nose. "I shouldn't think so."

"I'll take 'em," said Snuff, snatching up the blind as fast as she rejected it. The old man added the two cards to his hand, then pulled two cards out and dropped them to the floor. "Them two soldiers is buried," he said with a throaty grunt. Snuff laid down a Jack of Diamonds.

Play continued with Tyner and Griff following

Snuff's trump suit, laying down more diamonds, but nothing as high-ranking as the Jack.

Snuff giggled to himself and took the trick. "There's money in my pockets," he said, "everybody else pay up."

Points were added according to the hands and currency tossed into the center of the table.

Reece jerked her knee away from Snuff's right hand. "Manners," she whispered, and the old man belched.

During the next deal, Tuffy sneezed, and again Snuff was the picker.

"In five-handed Sheepshead, I thought the dealer position shifted around to the left," said Reece. "Shouldn't I be dealing the cards?"

"This is, uh...a variation called Granny's Cross," said Tuffy.

"Well, I should've liked to have known it."

"Granny's Cross," he said again. "Oldest gent...or lady at the table is always the dealer."

Reece raised her eyebrows so Griff would see. He offered the slightest shake of his head.

Like her, he had never heard of such a variant of the game.

And despite her play-acting, Reece had been playing Sheepshead since she was a child.

The two old duffers weren't living up to the spirit of their hand-lettered sign about cheating.

As the next trick got underway, Reece started counting cards.

She'd had a way with numbers her entire life, found herself counting the petals on daisies, the number of birds in a tree, the grasshoppers she saw in a field of clover. It became a habit, something she did without thinking, and her dad would often quiz her about it.

After a picnic excursion, he might ask: "How many horseflies landed on our blanket?"

"Twenty-three," said Reece.

"How many buzzards did we see?"

"Thirteen."

Often, she surprised herself.

She could count the individual gunshots in a barrage of fire. She could count the snowflakes in her horse's mane.

She wondered why Snuff, who had been dealt six cards, carried seven in his mitts.

"Winner, winner, chicken dinner," he cawed, tossing his winning trump, a queen of clubs onto the pile.

"Snuff does it again," said Tuffy with a slow nod. "Who's for another trick? You wanna bow out, just say the word."

While everybody but Snuff paid into the stack of coins and paper money in the center of the table, Reece watched Tuffy shuffle the deck and tidy the edges into an even, square block.

Sheepshead was a unique game using only 32 cards of the standard deck.

He slid the block of cards to Reece. "Cut the cards, ma'am?"

What made the game difficult to newcomers was the unusual point value of the numbers and suits which ran contrary to the assumed rules of other popular games.

Reece separated the deck into two, fanning out the top portion as she feigned a clumsy hand.

Counting.

"I'm so sorry," she said.

"Think nothing of it, sister," said Tuffy. When he pulled the cards back, he engaged in a quick sleight of hand. Adding cards or subtracting them?

The old man's deal was lightning fast. As per the rules, he dealt three cards to each of the players for a total of fifteen. Then he separated two cards from the pile and laid them upside down in the center of the table to create the blind. Finally, he pitched another fifteen.

Or was it seventeen?

Griff fanned his hand of six, as did Tyner.

But Tuffy held eight cards, and Snuff had nine. And Reece thought there were a few extra cards in Tuffy's lap.

There was more than one deck of cards in play. Worse, the old boogers weren't trying overly hard to hide it.

As the trick commenced around the table, Snuff didn't seem to lose any cards from his hand. When he laid down the queen of diamonds, Reece saw her chance.

Over-confident, the old man had made his mistake.

Reece held a queen of diamonds in her hand, too.

She tossed it down on the table next to Snuff's offering. Almost immediately, all the color drained from his face. To Tuffy's credit, he simply let out a loud sigh and reached casually under the table for a shotgun.

But Reece was too quick for him.

Nodding at Griff, she brought out the Number Five revolver from the small of her back. "What's the sign say, Mister Tuffy? You cheat, you die?" Reece made a clucking sound with her tongue to shame him. "Looks like you've checked one of those things off your list today. Shall we go for the second?"

Tuffy dropped the shotgun to the dirt floor with a clatter, and as Snuff went for his gun, he found Tyner's Remington jabbing his ribs.

"Gol-darnit," said Snuff. "I was just startin' to have fun."

"You got careless, Snuff," said Tuffy.

"Me? You're the dealer. What the hell, Tuff?"

"You all sort it out between each other later." Reece kept her gun leveled at Tuffy. Then she addressed Griff. "I suggest you stash our winnings in your leather satchel?"

While Griff swept up the pot, Reece talked to Tuffy. "I'm sure you boys will keep quiet as we walk out of here with our winnings, won't you?"

"I won't say a word," said Tuffy. "You caught us fair and square ma'am. Long as you don't kill us, I count it as a win. After all if I'm still alive—"

"It's a win—yes, I remember." Reece addressed Tyner, "They'll start hollering the second we make the street. Those three wolves are out there waiting."

"Dedra will have the horses ready for our quick escape," said Tyner.

Griff finished stuffing the satchel full and heaved shut the clasp. "What about your wagon?"

"I'll pick it up next time I'm in town," he said. "Our main objective now is simply to stay alive."

Reece nodded her understanding. "Staying alive is always a win," she said.

CHAPTER 32

COOMBS AND HIS TWO MEN STRUNG LIN JARRET UP less than 100 yards from Ned Brock's crumpled body. The thin-haired man with the scar tied one end of a heavy piece of hemp around Lin's bound wrists, tossed the rope over an oak bough, then jerked his feet two feet off the ground. Coombs' man with the eye-patch and purple hat tied the loose end of the rope around a tree stump.

Dangling from the enormous oak tree bough, Lin was helpless as Coombs set to work on him, pummeling his face, his kidneys, his ribs. Each blow was delivered with maximum force and efficiency. Designed to make pain without causing too much damage, it was clear the beating would continue for some time.

Scar-face had built a fire not far away, and the flame was a spotlight for Coombs' mad vengeance play, lighting the woods, sending up a shower of sparks and rich, oaky smoke.

Coombs, finally out of breath, reared back and drove his fist like a steam-driven piston into Lin's guts, once, twice, three times. Then he shucked his long blanket to reveal a linen Sunday shirt and paisley decorated vest. He handed over the wool to the thin-haired man who draped it with care over a nearby tulip tree.

"We're only just getting started," he said.

He was a like a doctor, thought Lin between the blows, performing precision surgery. Picking select spots on Lin's body to inflict the most agony without ending him too soon.

The end result was preordained, but Coombs obviously wanted the ordeal to last a long time.

"You're going to die tonight, Lin Jarret. Or maybe tomorrow. How does it feel to know there's nothing you can do about it?" Coombs' German accent was clipped, not as heavy as his brother's. He wiped a stream of drool from his chin and spun around into a kick, slamming the heel of his boot into Lin's ribcage.

Lin sucked air, let the pain roll up and over him. He was close to blacking out as Coombs' words came through a scarlet-gray haze. "Nein, nein," he said. "You don't sleep yet."

A sudden dash of freezing cold water jerked Lin awake. The one-eyed man grasped a half-empty water bucket with both hands. He shoved it forward, spilling another helping of winter across Lin's face.

"Enough, Crow," said Coombs, waving back the bucket. "Enough for now." Satisfied with his initial progress, he stepped back into a relaxing posture and removed a fat package of pressed tobacco from his pants pocket. Lin watched as Coombs used his knife to slice a thick corner off the wad. He lifted the brown serving to his mouth, shifted the wad into his cheek, then returned the blade to a sheath on his belt.

Lin watched Coombs work the tobacco with his jaws. Watched him swallow the thick, black juice.

Blood trickled down Lin's cheeks and chin like a

leaky valve, dribbling onto his sweat-drenched shirt. His chest was on fire, his kidneys bruised. He wouldn't feel like riding the wagon seat for a while.

Wouldn't feel like doing much of anything.

Salty sweat burned his eyes and stung the abrasions of his face. The rope around his wrists was more than chafing. It was starting to tear into his skin. Lin remembered the way he'd felt at Baldy's place when he and Griff had been noosed and set up high. Helpless... but nothing like this.

At least then he had his wits about him. Now everything swirled around in a fog of pain.

At least then he'd known Micah was out there. He'd known Micah had his back.

Now where the hell was Micah? Had they captured him too?

Had they killed him?

Coombs addressed Lin around the hunk of chewing tobacco. "*Freund Jarret*. Let's start at the beginning."

Coombs inhaled smoke and let it out slow, through his nose. "Before you killed him, you stole my brother's property. My property." He stroked his mustache and pinched his nose, pausing to emphasize the words. "Yes, *my* property. Financial gain rightfully owed to the Compass. To *me*."

Lin worked hard to answer, his sandpaper tongue too big for his mouth. Finally, he said, "You people are...crazy as...tom cats in springtime."

"You violated the trust of the organization." Coombs made a dismissive gesture. "You have no right to judge us. After the offense you've perpetrated you have no right to anything."

"Get screwed."

One-eyed Crow glanced at Coombs, and Coombs nodded. The small man slapped the tin pail across Lin's head. The impact set bells ringing inside Lin's skull, and he wobbled at the edge of the abyss.

"Let's start again," said Coombs. "Where are the stock certificates?"

Through the cacophony of anguish he felt, Lin tried to stay focused. How had Coombs managed to follow them to the clearing without him, Micah, or Brock noticing? How had he got the jump on them?

Either the German was a good tracker, or the three Hellbenders had gotten sloppy.

Probably both.

Lin tried to take the measure of Crow, Coombs' little soldier. The man's hair was dark and cropped short. An Indian? Maybe he would know how to track them without being seen.

It didn't matter. They were here now.

Lin tried to turn his head back toward the clearing where the Concord was parked. In the dark night, and with Coombs' fire crackling away nearby, he couldn't see if Micah's fire still burned or not.

Lin had to assume they'd already searched the stagecoach. Maybe done away with Micah sure as Ned Brock?

His wrists screamed as he fought against the hard knots, shaking the tree branch above, his shoulders ripping from the sockets. Gazing into Coombs' ruddy arrogance, the fire light glowing in the evil countenance, Lin suddenly faced the truth. He was going to die here, alone, without ever seeing Reece Sinclair again.

The realization gave him a last boost of energy.

If only he could buy some time.

"The certificates aren't here," said Lin. "You already know it."

Coombs confirmed Lin's speculation. "We have searched your wagon."

"Killing me won't get your money back. Cut me loose. Let's talk. We can make a deal."

"Here is my 'deal' for you. You do the talking or I beat you again. And again. And every hour of every day until you tell me where my money is." Coombs crossed his arms with satisfaction. "What do you think?"

Lin blinked rapidly, clearing the cobwebs from head. Finally, he was able to spit. "I don't like your deal," he said.

"I'm not surprised." Coombs pitched forward, landing a jarring blow to Lin's face. Abruptly, he brought his knuckles to his mouth. Crow handed him a towel for his hands.

In the firelight, Coombs' hands showed a delicate tracery of scars, and he bruised his knuckles plenty while abusing Lin. The German wasn't as tough as he wanted Lin to believe.

Cold comfort thought the Ranger.

"I'll give you some time to come to your senses," said Coombs. "Then we'll resume our conversation." He told Crow to give Lin some water. "Not too much. We wouldn't want him too comfortable."

As Coombs walked away toward the adjacent fire, Lin felt everything inside himself fall.

Discouraged, but not defeated, he thought to himself. Wasn't it what Reece had once said?

But what the bloody hell difference?

"You want water?" said Crow, approaching slow. This time he held up a canteen instead of a pail, and Lin nodded. Carefully, almost tenderly, Crow trickled water into Lin's mouth.

"Tell him what he wants," said Crow. "He'll kill you if you don't."

"He'll kill me if I do. We killed his brother."

Crow's face was tight and indecipherable. Finally, he backed up and seemed to be taking stock of Jarret's injuries. Gritting his teeth together, he scratched the back of his head, tipping up his cap. "You won't last much longer," he said with a final sigh. "You want a smoke?"

Crow held the makings of a cigarette in his hands.

Lin had tossed his pouch of leaves to Brock just before Coombs came onto the scene.

He admitted to Crow a smoke sounded good.

"Odd how a body reacts," said Crow. "All of you what's broken and bruised...but still craving a smoke." He smiled at Lin as he rolled the tobacco up inside a paper. "What'll you trade me for it?"

"I've...got nothing to trade."

"Bullshit. You could tell me where the money is."

"And then you'd tell your boss."

"No, no," said Crow. "You misunderstand. You tell me, I'll cut you down. We'll run out of here together."

Lin closed his eyes. He didn't have an answer, and right about then he was beyond caring. "Keep it then, you son of a bitch."

But Crow was keen to continue the ruse and he quickly stepped forward, jamming the cigarette into Lin's mouth. "I don't owe that Kraut bastard a damn thing," he said. "You and me would make a good team. Even beat up like this, I'll bet you could take him. The bastard is big, but he's soft."

Crow patted his pockets and showed Lin a toothy grin. "Sorry, no lucifers."

"You dirty, rotten—"

"Hush. We've only got a few seconds. Tell me where the money is."

Lin tried not to gag on the vile man's stinking breath, tried not to grimace at the pain he felt.

Tried not to smile when he looked beyond Crow's shoulder. But he couldn't hide the expression.

"What's so damn funny?" said Crow. "What—?"

The little man spun around as two things happened at the same time. First, Lin felt the taut rope above him go slack and his reflexes took over. In the space of a half-second, every muscle inside his body tightened up and he fell, slamming into the ground with a bone-jarring impact.

Simultaneously, the air in front of him erupted into a flurry of sparks and orange fire. Two deafening bursts sent a pair of lead balls tearing through Crow's upper chest, knocking him flat to earth beside Lin where he lay twitching under a cloud of blue smoke.

Two seconds had passed since Lin caught his first glimpse of Ned Brock over Crow's shoulder and he crab-walked backwards across the forest floor on his butt, bootheels kicking. His wrists were still bound in front of him, but adrenaline numbed his body's pain.

Then Micah was at his side with the knife he'd used to cut the rope, hoisting Lin to his feet as Brock spun toward the campfire.

"You okay, friend?"

"I'm...yeah, I'm...good."

Coombs appeared with Scarface, but the unsure pistols in their hands did little good against Brock's unbridled fury. Standing tall like a stone monolith against the charge, a bloodstain marring the back of his shirt, Brock gripped the Walch Navy at arm's length, spewing forth chunks of flaming death.

Bam, bam, bam, bam!

A quartet of screaming slugs pounded into Scarface,

slamming him to ground as Coombs screamed in defiance.

How could Brock still be alive? Lin had seen Coombs stab him, had seen the German remove the knife from his back.

The back brace!

The damned back brace Brock wore had saved his life. It had to be!

It's what protected him from the worst of the blade's intrusion.

"Nein!" bellowed Coombs, as Brock engaged the left-handed hammer and tapped the second trigger to unload the final six shots. The trick pistol might've malfunctioned before, but now Lin watched it operating smooth and slick in the hands of a master gunner.

Brock grouped the half-dozen lead balls into a tight circle on Coombs' heaving chest.

With his dying breath, Coombs shifted his eyes to Lin.

Astonished.

He couldn't believe he'd lost.

Lin shrugged, sharing one last moment of disbelief.

He couldn't believe they'd won.

CHAPTER 33

THE HORSE REECE RODE THROUGH THE BLACK
forested night was a mousey-dun gelding with powder-
charged hooves and dark rum coursing through his
veins. Pounding ahead of Tyner's black mare and Griff's
flaxy stallion, the grulla had more explosive energy than
any horse Reece had sat atop since leaving Texas.

She decided to call him Meg.

More than three miles out of Bad Axe and the
buffalo wolves were still on their tail, three nameless
shadows barely visible in the anemic prairie moonlight.
She didn't dare slow down.

Instead, she urged Meg forward with her heels, sure
of only one thing—she was unsure where to go.

The next time she glanced over her shoulder, Tyner
and Griff were gone with only a thin scarf of dust
topping a hill trail to the right. Instinctively, she'd
taken the lead, but of course Flood Tyner knew the
geography better than she did.

Spinning Meg around and pointing him in the
direction of her friends, Reece wondered why she
hadn't put a lead ball into each of those two old card
cheats when she had a chance, rather than let them

alert the town posse. The three enforcers seemed relentless. One could only imagine what Tuff and Snuff had told them.

Lin Jarret always did say her kind heart would get her killed.

Leaping over the crest of the steep grade, the grulla came down into a sure-footed gallop and Reece saw she hadn't lost much time. In an open field ahead, Tyner led the way toward the southern horizon and a range of steep hills blotting out the stars.

By now, they were in Arkansas, they had to be, thought Reece. It did her heart good to be one state closer to Texas even as a burst of flame showed in the corner of her eye and a distant pistol crack told her the posse was still in pursuit.

She hoped Tyner had a plan of escape.

Of course it made sense to let the old man take the lead. He was the one who led them to Bad Axe in the first place, and he was the one who would know the best trails out. The mobile village apparently covered a specific region. Though they never remained in the same place too long, they didn't necessarily stray too far afield either.

Up ahead, Tyner seemed to have a purpose as he picked up a visible cow trail with Griff close behind.

Reece pushed her horse to close the gap between them.

Behind her, somebody snapped off another gunshot, but this time it barely registered on her ears. Far too distant to worry about.

For now.

Did they have a chance to lose the Bad Axe security boys?

Reece had no idea.

All she could do was sink her fingers into Meg's

mane and hunker in over his withers. "Let's ride," she said, digging in her heels.

———

DAWN CAME TOO EARLY for Lin, and too cold. His eyes snapped open, but nothing else moved. He felt like a side of beef hanging in a December barn, every inch of him frozen stiff, every pain and contusion setting up permanent shop.

He forced himself to roll over on his sleeping blanket, cracked open an eye.

Even his eyelashes hurt.

It took every ounce of willpower he had to hoist himself to one elbow. His reward was to rest for a few minutes. Maybe an hour.

As always, Micah had a fire going, and he whistled to himself as a pot of coffee bubbled and boiled. The aroma of cooked, black grounds seeped into Lin's awareness. The coffee smell slipping between his joints like oil, soothing the pain, easing his movement.

He flexed his right leg—an experiment in agony.

Then moved his left. Sheer misery, and he winced against the pain.

But he lived, and the coffee smelled so damn good... he pushed himself to his feet, surely like one of the labors of Hercules.

Micah looked up, then inexplicably went sideways with the campfire.

"Hang on there, Ranger," said Ned Brock, catching Lin in mid-fall. "You've had a hell of a time." Brock helped straighten out the earth, and Lin realized then how clammy he felt. How much his clothes were soaked through with sweat. His teeth chattered as he let Brock lower him onto a log next to the fire.

"I thought you were killed," he told Brock.

"Too ornery to kill. All three of us."

Lin accepted the non-answer as all the explanation he needed for now. Rather than look back, he focused on the future. Half a minute or so was all he could muster.

"The coffee sure smells g-good," said Lin.

Brock removed the pot from the fire by its wooden handle and poured each of them a thick dollop in tin cups. "I found a jar of sorghum in the coach," he said. "Want some mixed in?"

"I do," he said, with growing anticipation. It sounded like paradise.

"Whiskey?" said Brock.

"I'll take both—sorghum and whiskey."

"What d'you call such a concoction?" said Micah. "Irish coffee?"

"St. Louis Catholic coffee," said Brock. He held up the crock of sorghum. "Home grown."

While Brock doctored his coffee, Lin queried Micah. "Where are we anyway? This doesn't look like the same clearing from last night? What happened to Coombs?"

"You need to catch up. You're thinking back to two nights ago," said Micah. "We've covered quite a bit of ground since last time you were awake."

Brock handed over the coffee. Lin clamped his hands around the hot tin cup, raising it to his lips to let the steam curl around. His aching face felt thick and misshapen, and the warmth was a soothing balm. "How long was I out?"

"Like Micah says, since the night before last," said Brock. "We're in Arkansas now, not too far from Fort Smith."

"No more devils," Lin said. He tried the coffee, let a

small sip trickle across his tongue, down his parched throat.

"No," said Brock. "No more devils."

Before Lin could empty his cup, Micah served up a breakfast of campfire basics—beans and hardtack with canned peaches. Never had staple food been so delicious. Lin asked for seconds and had a third drink from the coffee pot.

Once he was well fed and dressed, Lin almost felt whole again. As long as he sat still.

Micah invited him to the bench seat beside him, and it took more time than usual to mount the steps and get himself situated.

Brock opted to ride on the roof of the wagon. "Damned if I'm ever gonna be cooped up inside this crate like a city songbird," he said.

The day was dry and chilly, but the sun shone down bright.

As they set out through a pleasant wooded valley, Micah explained how, two nights before, he'd heard Coombs and his men coming through the trees. He told Lin he had managed to hide while the bad men ransacked the coach and snuffed out his campfire.

"Naturally, they didn't find the money since Reece and Tyner took it with them."

"Did they take anything else?"

"Apparently the satchel was all they cared about."

Once Coombs had lit his own fire, Micah had crept to the place where Lin was strung-up via the spring-fed branch. Staying out of sight in the grass, Micah found Brock bleeding on the bank. Once he ascertained Brock's stab wound was serious, but not life-threatening, he revived the gunnie. Together, they then made plans to rescue Lin.

"I had guessed the back brace saved Brock from Coombs' knife?" said Lin.

"You guessed right," said Micah. "The night we rescued you, he fussed like a baby when I stitched him up," said Micah. "But he'll be fine. You, too."

A few hours after lunch, they crossed the Arkansas River on a flat raft that scraped bottom on the sandy mud flats of the shallow concourse. Lin wanted to tip the old river guide who ferried them across a few gold coins, but Brock held him back. Instead, he presented the amiable coot with a long black Indian blanket. "My family's treasured this a good long time. Cold as it gets out here on the water, you look like you could use it."

The river guide shook all three of their hands in appreciation.

On the Fort Smith side of the water, Lin asked, "Along with the Kickapoo blanket, what else did you graverobbers steal off Coombs and his boys?"

Brock confessed. "Everything weren't nailed down."

"You're better off not knowing," said Micah.

If Springfield was merely busy, Fort Smith was a frenetic circus. Every carriage on the brick-lined streets seemed to travel at locomotive speed with a preordained sense of purpose, and men walked at a martial pace in determined clumps of twos or threes. Lin admired two merchants not much older than him, but certainly more flush dressed in their long black coats and felt top hats. From the bench seat of the coach he gave them a nod, and they returned the greeting with white gloved salutes.

The cow trails gave way to gravel roadbeds, the gravel to brick-paved streets lined with decorative trees and wildflowers. A church steeple rose about the highest branches, and the air smelled of horse flop and spring-blossoming orchards.

When the forest green Jarret-Sinclair Concord pulled up to the boardwalk in front of the Butterfield Overland office in Fort Smith it was just about supper time.

On top of the coach, Brock stood up with a hand cupping his side. The gunslinger hadn't complained once during the trip across the Arkansas hills, but Lin knew his injury pained him. For his part, Lin had likewise kept his gripes to himself.

Like Brock, it was how he'd been taught to behave.

Lin noticed Brock wasn't wearing his holster.

"Where's your twelve-shooter?"

"Gun belt's too heavy. For the time being, hurts too much to wear the damn thing."

Lin felt the weight of his Colt next to his hip. He understood Brock's point of view, but he was glad to carry the burden. The iron gave him a sense of security.

An unassuming man with thick spectacles met them on the dusty boardwalk.

"Ted Wilber," he said, introducing himself to Lin. "I'm postmaster here at Fort Smith and superintendent of the Butterfield Overland's 7th Division mail route across Indian Territory."

Lin shook the man's hand, introducing him to Micah LeMay and Ned Brock. "I'm mighty pleased to be here, Mister Wilber."

"You sure do look awful run down, Mister Jarret. Awful run down."

Lin managed to ward off the curiosity of the postmaster with a string of tall tales.

"We almost tipped the cart over back Van Buren way," said Lin, lying through his teeth. "Of course, that was only after we warded off the bear attack."

"You fought a bear?"

"With these two hands." Lin showed him his clenched fists. "I have to tell you, Mister Wilber, it's a hell of a trek from middle-Missouri."

"We're improving the line all the time, sir. All the time."

"I've got some business I'd like to discuss with you, Wilber. But first..." Lin put his arm around Wilber's shoulder. "Do you expect you might set the three of us up for some grub?"

"You'll be staying in town?"

"Just long enough for supper. We're meeting up later on with a friend."

"I see." Wilber nodded. "How about steak and potatoes? Bread pudding, milk and coffee—all the trimmings?"

"Now you're talking."

"The Ramrod hotel is just across the street. I'll make sure you get the best possible service."

"I'm obliged to you, Wilber. Aren't we obliged to him, gentlemen?"

Brock and Micah both agreed they were obliged to the diminutive bureaucrat.

"I'll just go ahead and make the arrangements," said Wilber. "The livery stable is back up the road to your left, one block there. You probably saw it when you rode in. Hotel and restaurant are here. Down at the far end of the street, to your right, you'll find a congregational church—if you'd like to join us for worship tonight after supper? As a man who fights...bears, you look like someone who could benefit from prayer."

"I'll take it into consideration," said Lin.

"Prayers of thanks, or prayers of petition?" said Micah.

"Then we'll address this...ah, business you mentioned?"

"Yes, we will."

Lin watched Wilber cross the street toward the Ramrod.

"Right now, I'd pray for a fat mattress and a feather pillow," he said.

The hotel wasn't as big or ostentatious as the new Parksdale where they stayed the night in Springfield, but its white-washed siding gleamed in the sun. Its black shutters were open and each of five visible windows featured a colorful flower planter hanging from its sill.

Wilber pushed open the entrance with its big brass handle. Once he stepped through and out of sight, Lin almost sank to his knees with exhaustion.

Micah propped him back up. "You took a beating would kill most men. Rest yourself."

"I'll rest myself when the family's back together."

"Family?"

Lin didn't miss a beat. "Yeah...family."

Lin felt dizzy drunk, but his voice was sober. "Reece isn't here yet," he said. "If she were here, she'd have left word with Wilber."

"I'm sure she's fine," said Micah. "You'll be fine too, as long as we keep the rest of this trip peaceful."

"I like your plan," said Lin, looking out across the Fort Smith main street. The town square was richly populated, with folks of all ages making their way along the boardwalks. "Let's go on across to the hotel. There's nothing to be gained standing around over here chewing on our problems."

Micah agreed, gripping Lin's arm in support. "Let me give you a hand."

"I especially like you promising to keep things peaceful," said Lin.

They almost made it.

CHAPTER 34

HALFWAY ACROSS THE STREET A FAMILIAR VOICE FROM the alley beside the hotel sounded out, stopping them in their tracks.

"My, my, my. If it isn't our old friend, the Ranger," said Baldy, strolling out of the shadows into the street with a tall horse in tow. He wore butternut trousers and a checkered shirt with a red silk tie. Maybe Wilber had invited him to church, too.

"I guess he didn't expect to see us again," said Verna, also leading a horse, this one a roan gelding. Her dress was equally fancy, blue with lavender lace trim.

"I guess it's time to even the score," said Dale.

In contrast to his companions, Dale's untucked flannel shirt, dirty trousers, and sorry boots were contemptable. He couldn't have looked more haggard had he covered most of the vast distance from String-town to Fort Smith on foot.

Dale gripped his old Maynard .28 caliber pistol. He waved it around so Lin would be sure to see it.

"Bad fortune has finally caught up with you, Jarret," said Baldy. "Or maybe call it justice."

Lin licked his dry, chapped lips. After all they'd been through...to face these three idiots again.

He wanted to laugh, but his jaw hurt too much to smile.

"Listen, Baldy—" he began, but never finished the sentence as four thrashing hooves and a wall of hurtling horse flesh came between them.

Reece Sinclair thundered through on a foam-flecked Grulla, blood flowing down her arms.

There wasn't time to think.

Lin only had time to react.

As Reece breezed past, she tipped and fell from the saddle. Lin backpedaled and caught her in both arms as the grulla continued on, half-crazed and mad with exhaustion.

"Reece! God sakes, what happened?" Dropping to one knee, cradling her head gently, Lin brushed away strands of dark hair from her sweat-drenched profile. She was wearing the same form-flattering outfit he'd left her with in Springfield, but the tattered fabric was ripped and stained with road dust and blood.

Her eyelids fluttered open. "Ranger?" she said. "Oh, thank heavens." Even as she wrapped her arms around him, another peel of pounding hooves tore the evening asunder. Low-slung in his saddle and dressed in gray, a rawboned rider on a wild-eyed roan careened toward them from the direction of the livery stable.

The rider lowered a big iron in his right hand, pointed it directly at Reece and Lin.

Without hesitation and faster than the gunman could respond, Lin drew his Colt and triggered a charge into the center of the gray chest, ripping him from the back of his horse. The rider hit the ground with bone-crunching fury, rolled over, and breathed his last. The roan streaked past, following the grulla. Both slowed to a trot and shied away from Micah as he ran to capture them.

"Dead as box of rocks," said Brock. "Holy Jesus, you're fast, Ranger."

Lin ignored the compliment, carrying Reece to the hotel's front porch where he perched on the wide steps. Brock sat down next to them.

"Make sure she's okay," said Lin.

"I just...need to catch my breath," said Reece, lifting herself into a sitting position. The blood on her arm was glistening wet and bright red, but Lin couldn't see a wound.

"Get her inside," he said. "Get her checked out."

Ted Wilber appeared on the hotel porch. "What's all the ruckus out here?"

"Stay out of it, Wilber," said Lin as another pair of horses, blond and black barreled around the livery stable at the end of the street. Lin recognized Flood Tyner and Griff, leaning into the manes, hanging on hell bent for leather.

Almost immediately, a third horse appeared with its gray rider, a twin to Reece's nemesis, this one popping off shot after shot.

Lin leapt into the street with his gun held high.

Griff and Tyner soared past like eagles on the wing, one to Lin's left, one to the right, leaving the enemy horse crashing in on top of him. A hail of lead whistled past Lin's ears, chin, and shoulders, but with deadly precision, he pressed the Colt's trigger.

The blast lifted the man from his saddle and hurled him to ground with a back-breaking somersault.

For a beat, nobody moved, and the gunfire continued ringing through Lin's ears.

The last horse slowed its crazed run to an easy trot,

and once again, Micah caught up and lead him away from the street.

When no more riders appeared, Lin holstered his gun and went to where Brock and Reece remained on the hotel steps.

"I told you to get inside," he said.

"And I told you I just needed to catch my breath," said Reece, still breathing hard. "I'm okay."

Lin indicated her bloody arm. "You don't look okay."

"Bullet grazed the back of my arm. Hurts like hell, but nothing serious."

"Who were those men?"

Lin watched as a crowd gathered around the two cadavers in the street.

Ted Wilber rejoined them with a glass of water from inside the hotel. He handed it to Reece.

"Bad Axe security," said Reece, swallowing some of the water. "We thought we'd left them behind last night. Thought we'd lost them. Then this morning after we broke camp they showed up on at the river. They chased us the last few miles into town."

"They must've had some reason to chase you."

Reece assented to the fact. "We won some money at cards. Griff's got the satchel."

"Some...or a lot?"

"Enough to make them chase us," said Reece.

Lin looked down the street, to where Micah, Griff, and Tyner were shaking hands and getting reacquainted. Then he swiveled his head back up toward the livery. "Were there only two of them?"

"Three to start with. Tyner shot one of them crossing the Arkansas."

"Three more devils than in your dream," said Lin.

"Who's keeping count?" said Reece. Coming from

her, with such a straight face, the comment made him laugh.

Helping her to her feet, he said, "Let's get you cleaned up." Then he cupped a hand around his mouth and called to the others, "Can't you fellas hear the dinner bell when it rings?"

Micah waved and clapped Griff on the back.

"I gotta say, Jarret," said Brock, "You're a heck of a lot faster than I thought."

"Thanks, Ned."

Reece took Lin's arm and they turned toward the hotel entrance.

"Mister Jarret?" said Wilber. "These folks were asking about you?"

Baldy, Verna, and Dale stood fanned out between him, Wilber, and the hotel entrance.

Waiting.

"Ain't you forgetting something, Jarret?" said Baldy, an irritated look on his face.

"Surely he ain't forgot about us," said Verna.

"He's scared," said Dale.

Reece broke away from Lin's embrace and had her old No. 5 pointed level before Dale finished his words. Lin too had the Colt drawn at the ready.

Brock let out a loud whistle. "Now there's a wrinkle," said Brock. "I do believe the Missy is faster'n you, Jarret."

"Had you but asked, I would've told you," said Lin.

"Whoa, whoa, whoa," said Baldy, putting up both hands. He complained to Wilber. "Are you going to let these ruffians point weapons at us, sir? Is there no law in Fort Smith?"

"There certainly is law in Fort Smith," said Lin. "I know the town marshal personally. In the meantime,

Mister Wilber here is a different kind of law, but an officer just the same."

Lin got Brock's attention and cocked his head at the Stringtown trio. "Get their weapons."

"Weapons?" said Verna, "What—"

Brock wrinkled his nose as he pulled Verna's arm from behind her back to retrieve a little single shot revolver.

"Still takin' them milk baths, Verna?" said Lin.

Brock confiscated two more shooting irons—Dale's Maynard and a revolver from Baldy. He held on to the pistols and carried them back to stand beside Lin.

"What's this about me being the law?" said Wilber.

"There's a Butterfield Overland man named Price up in Syracuse. He's cozied up with these three horse thieves to smuggle animals away from the stagecoach line."

Wilber's expression showed sudden understanding. "Oh, yes—I did get a message from him a few days ago. He confessed to the entire sordid tale."

"I'll wager the horses these folks brought in with them have BO brands," said Lin.

"So what if they do?" said Baldy. "You ain't the only ones who can make a deal with the Overland express."

"True enough, but I doubt Price has fingered any of us in his missive to Wilber here. In fact, if Wilber says he's got the whole sordid tale...well, then I'd hate to be in your shoes."

Lin strolled over to Wilber and put the Colt firmly into his palm, pointing it toward Baldy, Verna, and Dale. "You take those three to the marshal's office. Return this to me after they're locked up."

He winked, then turned to Reece and Brock. Micah, Griff, and Tyner waited on the steps.

"This is an insult, Jarret," whined Baldy.

"We won't forget you," said Verna.

Resolute with his new-found power, Wilber waved the Colt's barrel through the air. "You three get going," he said, herding them off the hotel porch and into the street.

"You'll pay for this, Jarret," said Baldy by way of a parting shot.

"Believe me, Baldy, I already have." Lin gave him a high-handed wave.

The Hellbenders watched as Wilber led his charges off to the hoosegow.

"Let's get something to eat," said Lin.

"I don't know about the rest of you, but I'm famished," said Reece.

"Famished?" said Lin. "You mean hungry."

"She's been traveling with Griff too long," said Micah.

"So what if she has," said Griff.

"Yes, so what if I have?" said Reece.

Lin took her arm and led her into the hotel dining room without saying a word.

"You're not bothering to answer my question, are you?" said Reece.

"Nope," said Lin with a grin. "I'm not even gonna bother."

———————

At Emberville in Texas, life was hard for Sylvia Martin. The station never had more than two people on staff, her and another woman named Mabel.

Sometimes there were others—visitors who stayed underground, out of sight in the tunnels. Emberville was a one-room affair, but its trap door led down and away through the woods.

For two women alone, maintaining the place was grueling in the best of times. And now they were running short on provisions.

Across the Red River and two miles off the main-traveled road, south into a deep woods glade, Sylvia hung the last of her washboard-scrubbed laundry, trying to remember the words to a hymn her grandmom taught her when she was young.

Too tired to remember the chorus, too hungry to care, she let her arms drop to her hips where she adjusted her gunny sack dress and plodded back toward the log cabin. Once again, there would be no breakfast.

Her body was discouraged, but her mind drifted toward hope, and try as she might, she couldn't stop it.

When Micah LeMay escaped from the north Texas plantation where both of them had been kept, she thought she'd never see him again. After she followed suit, breaking her chains and running, she landed at Emberville where she helped ferry other folks away from their jailers to freedom in Mexico. When Micah showed up at her door with a white couple on a green Concord, she was joyous...then suspicious.

She confided in him anyway, showing him the dwindling larder, confessing the lack of funds needed to buy provisions.

The lack of funds needed to bribe certain authorities to look the other direction as they passed by on the Butterfield Overland spur.

Micah promised to help, and all her prayers seemed to be answered.

But weeks later...so many weeks later...he had yet to return.

On the doorstep, she clutched the wooden latch, facing another day, wondering if she would ever see him again.

At the sound of an approaching team of horses, her heart sent her an extra kick and she burned off the energy ducking inside, bolting shut the door.

"Mabel," she called. "Somebody's coming!" No response. The other woman must be out back in the garden.

Sylvia peered out the window at the lumbering quartet of animals coming around the bend. Good looking animals. She had always loved horses. Always admired the sleek, powerful muscles, the long, stoic faces.

These four pulled a stagecoach, slowing as they drew near the cabin.

Travelers, thought Sylvia, leaving the door locked while she went to light the wood stove. She wasn't scheduled to receive travelers this evening, but then—the majority of the travelers she received were never scheduled. Once she had the wood smoldering, she turned from the stove and approached the door.

She jumped at the heavy-handed knock, almost afraid to pull the bolt.

Swallowing hard, marshaling all her courage, she opened the door.

Micah LeMay stood at the threshold holding a leather satchel. His smile outshined the morning sun.

Sylvia felt her lower eye lids start to burn.

"Wonder if we could impose on you for some breakfast?" said Micah. "We don't have much, but we'd be willing to pay for it?"

Swatting away the tears running down her cheeks, Sylvia said, "H-how much you got?"

"Only about twenty-thousand," said Micah. "Give or take."

"Dollars?"

"Dollars," said Micah. "And oh, before I forget," he

pulled a long-chained locket out of his pocket, "this is something else for you. The others wanted you to have it."

Behind him, the white couple Sylvia had seen before waved from their place on the Concord coach bench, and three more men waved from inside the carriage.

Sylvia held the delicate brass brooch and unclasped it. Ink drawings of a heart and a butterfly.

"What is this?"

Micah was slow to answer. He seemed to be searching for the right words. Finally, he said,

"It's sort of a reminder. Anytime you're lonely, anytime you feel like giving up...you take a look at those drawings and remember something."

"Remember what?"

"Remember you're never alone."

*A LOOK AT BOOK THREE: A
KILLING AT RIMROCK*

BY RICHARD PROSCH

**THEY ARE OUT FOR JUSTICE, AND THE FIRE
AND BRIMSTONE AREN'T FAR BEHIND.**

When Ranger Lin Jarret and Reece Sinclair ride in, Lambert's
Ferry across the Red River was a disputed oasis fueled by
illegal alcohol and on the brink of a powder-smoke war.

It's 1860, and Lambert and the Indian police were done with
bootleggers, vowing to kill the next man freighting liquor
across the Red—a man who just happened to be Lin Jarret's
best friend.

Navigating a shifting Texas landscape of loyalty and deceit,
Jarret and Reece are out for justice as the Hellbenders bring
fire and brimstone down on the feared Order of the Ivory
Compass, uncovering a heinous plot to blow the Lone Star
state sky high.

COMING SOON

FRAMED IN THE NORTH-FACING WINDOW OF HIS office the Capitol dome taunted Hart Prescott with a reflection of moonlight. All he could feel was darkness closing in.

The weak flicker of his cut-glass lamp threw ghastly shadows to the walls and the Persian rug design under his feet, once so lush and wonderfully ornate, now seemed a writing patterned abyss.

When the door opened behind him, Prescott clutched his arm but didn't turn around.

He waited for the dark to overtake him.

They sent the same magpie messenger as before. He recognized the smell of the boy's hair tonic. He recognized the stammered greeting.

"Spit it out," said Prescott.

"Message from Springfield, sir."

"Read it."

The magpie cleared his throat. "L-logan Coombs killed. Hellbenders gone."

"Gone." The word was flat on his tongue, bitter, like crumbling dry tea leaves. "Gone," he said again. Beneath him, the floor seemed to shift, and the open maw of the rug threatened to suck him down in a never-ending spiral.

"There's a second message, sir."

Agony drew a hot poker from Prescott's groin through the paunch of his torso into his vein-lined neck. It jerked him around with a spasm, tossing him across the room in a white-hot rage. Even as he gathered the magpie's collar in his closed fist, pain coursed through Prescott's body.

Half-crazed, eyeballs straining to break free of their sockets, he demanded, "What do you mean, *gone?*"

The magpie wasn't more than twelve years old. His pudgy face squeezed into a lump of terror with lines of tears forming at each slit of his eye. His oiled hair was a smooth shellack of black tar and he wore a gray corduroy suit. He dropped the first slip of paper to the floor. "P-please, sir. You're hurting me."

Prescott put all his weight into a single shove, slamming the kid against the door frame with a satisfying crack. The magpie wilted but stayed standing. He held out another piece of paper and tried one last time to make himself heard. "The second message..."

"Get out," said Prescott. "Get out before I tear your head off."

The boy's horrific expression was so pleasing, Prescott couldn't stop the laugh gurgling up from his gut.

"B-but...sir..."

Prescott spoke again, this time through a series of uncontrollable spasms. "Get out!"

The boy turned, ran, left the door open. He footsteps echoed down the hall and the paper fluttered in the air behind him like some ghostly moth.

Then a blood-spewing cough gripped Prescott by the guts. Doubled him over. Again, and again.

The magpie's paper messages landed on the rug, stared up at him with grim defiance.

Hellbenders gone.

Blindly, Prescott kicked at the words, scattering the news to the wind. He reeled back into the dark office, staggering, off-balance, reaching for a wall to steady himself. He grasped nothing but air, then felt himself falling.

He swung his left arm out to the side.

When he hit, there was a shattering of plate glass.

At first, Prescott thought his suit coat was melting. Everything felt warm and wet, and the oozing sensation coursed over his bare forearm and elbow. Only after he opened his eyes did he see the broken shard of glass half-buried in his wrist, the blood flowing like the mighty river below his office building. Only when he opened his eyes did his see Matthias Byrne O'Fallon's accusing glare leave the wall and tip toward him in final judgement.

In blind rage, Prescott had smashed the old man's portrait, and now the Compass was coming for him.

"It wasn't my fault," he told O'Fallon. "What could I do?"

The heavy framed visage plummeted forward, the dark, skeletal eyes, the gray beard, the tightly drawn lips that seemed to move in the lamplight.

Never trust a man who dresses like a mortician.

"It was your fault," O'Fallon seemed to say. "The failure is on you—Hart Prescott, builder of railroads, master of plantations, lord over a thousand acres of sorghum and corn."

"The next governor of Missouri," he whispered.

"No," said O'Fallon's portrait. "Not anymore."

The floor came up to meet him with a thud, and Prescott felt something snap in the back of his neck.

There was no pain then, only a gurgling sound from somewhere south of his bushy white beard.

He had always assumed he would die in bed, surrounded by family, surrounded by fame. The newspapermen would be there. The wires would sing his dirge across the United States. He would be remembered forever.

There were no more words from O'Fallon, only the weight of the canvas and broken frame pinning his face to the rug. Directly before him, in full focus and flickering in the lamplight, the magpie's second message sat balance on edge.

As if a phantom were holding it upright so Prescott could read it.

He knew then he'd die alone.

His company bought out, merged with others.

He would be forgotten.

A shattering wave of loneliness crashed through him, breaking him into a million pieces, washing through everything he was and everything he knew.

He slipped into the abyss, unseeing eyes glued to the paper balanced on the rug in front of him.

New gold vein discovered. Prescott Ponders Peak company stock triples in value.

Rejoice.

ABOUT THE AUTHOR

Richard Prosch's western crime fiction captures the fleeting history and lonely frontier stories of his youth where characters aren't always what they seem, and the wind burned landscapes are filled with swift, deadly danger.

His work has appeared in *True West*, *Roundup*, and *Saddlebag Dispatches* magazines and online at Boys' Life. He won the Spur Award from Western Writers of America for short fiction, and his Jo Harper stories have received nominations for the Peacemaker award from Western Fictioneers.

Richard lives in Missouri with his wife and son, Gina, and Wyatt, assorted cats, and a Great Pyrenees named Moose.